The Mars Virus

The Mars Virus

by
Mark R. Sneller

Published by Fresh Air Press

Visit Mark's website at
marksneller.com

This edition was prepared for publication by
Ghost River Images
5350 East Fourth Street
Tucson, Arizona 85711
www.ghostriverimages.com

ISBN 978-1-7330238-9-4

Library of Congress Control Number: 2020921623

Printed in the United States of America
November, 2020

Other books Mark R. Sneller:

A Breath of Fresh Air

Greener Cleaner Indoor Air–a Guide to Healthier Living

Dying to Read

Toxic Exposure

The City Beneath the Earth

In Progress books:

The Fight at the Poker Game and Other Stories

The Magical Powers of Lazlo Pearce

Dedication

To my grandparents who raised me from the age of three.

To my grandmother from Odessa, Russia, who permitted me to allocate my growing collection of paperbacks to a little cupboard in a little hallway in our small home, and who fed and cared for me. She endured me well, especially while I wrote and read to her my first one-page stories.

To my grandfather who grew up on a farm in Lithuania and who worked his small dime store in a poor section of Los Angeles. He overcame holdups and worked six days a week and ordered me to stop playing baseball in the streets and help him in the store.

My greatest regret? I never asked them about their own stories.

Author's Note:

This novel was originally intended to be a basic science fiction novel in which the good guys win with the original working title The Mold from Mars. Instead, it morphed into a dark story in which the planet becomes contaminated by a virus and into story that begged to be described in some detail.

I have endeavored to maintain accuracy regarding elements that describe the cities and places mentioned. Admittedly, poetic license was exercised to embellish scenes and settings. All characters are fictionalized and are not drawn from known persons, other than to sprinkle some of my own personality characteristics and personal preferences throughout the novel.

In terms of current scientific knowledge, I have done my best to provide explanations of genetics, geological events, and ecosystem interactions, while confessing to becoming pedantic at times in my effort to provide this information to the reader. I possess a certain amount of guilt about not including so many issues that revolve around changing climatic conditions in order to create a readable story. As the saying goes: Sometimes one has to suspend disbelief for the sake of the story.

Ultimately, it does not take an alien invader to change an ecosystem in a closed environment such as planet Earth; it only takes a significant change to a single variable to alter that environment, from within or without. In this novel, the change is more rapid and profound than might normally be expected. This is because a new variable is introduced: The Mars Virus.

Finally, this story is meant to entertain and not to serve as an extended lecture for an ecology class. I hope the reader feels the same way and enjoys reading it as much as I enjoyed writing it.

ACKNOWLEDGMENTS

The author would like to thank my friends Ron Richardson, Gil Drubin and Bill Downey for their sufferings through the various episodes of this adventure. It was they who looked at the very first completed short story version of this novel and told me, almost in a single voice, "You can't end it there."

I would like to extend my thanks to Jessica Dufour, M.S., teacher of biological sciences at Yavapai College in Prescott, Arizona, for her input in the areas of biology, genetics, and ecology which helped to add substance to the story. This thanks also extends to her husband, James, a geologist, who greatly assisted me with many technical aspects of this endeavor.

My appreciation is extended to Robin Peel, my editor in chief, who helped me learn new elements of the English language and who was instrumental in bringing this book to completion.

Preface

Before the Yellowstone volcano exploded, the radical climate changes ravaging Earth led to an increase in the level of all major bodies of water. This put more pressure on the tectonic plates that lay on the floor of the oceans. One of these was the Pacific Tectonic Plate, which ran side-by-side with the North American Plate. The latter covered most of North America, Greenland, Cuba, the Bahamas, extreme northeastern Asia, and parts of Iceland and the Azores. It extended eastward to the Mid-Atlantic Ridge and westward to eastern Siberia.

Locally, the two plates met at the vertical San Andreas Fault with fracture lines spreading outward somewhat parallel and perpendicular to one another. One of the most sensitive of these fracture lines in California was off the San Andreas. Called the Ventura Fault, it ran through the heart of the city of Ventura with a population of a little over 100,000. When the fault slipped offshore from the excess of ocean pressure, a quake registering 8.1 in intensity occurred which leveled the cities of Ventura and Santa Barbara. The seismic waves caused a ripple-effect throughout the numerous other faults in the region causing a chain reaction. Because the Ventura Fault opened to the Pacific Ocean, a tsunami occurred as water rushed in to fill the void when the block dropped and ocean water flooded the same two cities. More southerly, it eroded the low cliffs protecting Santa Monica and took out the pier.

Over a period of weeks, vibrations from the Ventura quake caused movement in the San Andreas, which began to unzip from the bottom up. The water of the Gulf of California merged with the Salton Sea, 432 miles northward. A second earthquake followed that now ripped Los Angeles. Registered at 7.8, it equaled in intensity that of the San Francisco Quake of 1906, which was not spared at all in this series of events. Nor was the upper end of the plate that bordered Alaska. Thousands of fires broke out wherever gas lines were ruptured. Explosions occurred throughout the affected regions as fuel sources ignite, even as water mains burst.

At the time these events occurred, undersea volcanoes in the Pacific and other oceans became either active, or more active than they had been. These included Mount Tambora and the ring of volcanoes in the Sea of Sumatra, again due to changing pressure differentials on the Indian/Australian and Eurasian tectonic plates. New volcanoes were now created at the meeting place of dozens of major and minor plate-junctures around the world as plates began to separate or subduct one another.

Virtually all of the 1500 offshore oil rigs that were clustered in 30 different locations around the world were disrupted. This resulted in uncountable millions of gallons of crude oil spilling onto the surfaces of the oceans and seas. Land-based oil and gas wells fared no better, with close to two million of them in the United States alone.

In western Wyoming, over the course of the next year, the normal 15 inches of rainfall had more than doubled to 35 inches, all within a six-month period as clouds of volcanic ash and fumes blanketed the planet and the temperature rose. The water weight caused numerous ground fractures in the area to open. This resulted in a flow of water through the cracks into the Yellowstone area causing a phreato-magmatic eruption from pressure in a magma chamber. Steam pressure increased within the two chambers of magma that comprised the caldera, adding to the internal pressure caused by the already high-fluxing molten rock; thus triggering the eruption of the long-awaited super-volcano. Some 240 cubic miles of molten lava blew into a fireball thousands of feet in height and released pent-up pressures through numerous vents surrounding the caldera. Ash, gases and sulfurous acids were shot to four times that altitude and soon traveled as far south as Mexico and as far east as Chicago, a thousand miles in either direction, even while ten million tons of carbon dioxide entered the upper atmosphere to be carried around the world.

PART ONE

1
November — The Beginning

It was three weeks before the official start of winter, and the brightness of the orange-mauve clouds began to fade into gray over the farmland of Lincoln, Nebraska, as though one were looking at orange islands surround by blue seas. The day had been breezy. Airborne dust from the barren fields caused the sun to appear enlarged while the lingering waning wind made the remaining aspen leaves flutter like butterfly wings.

The grains and most of the forty or more fruits and vegetables grown in the state had been harvested. The temperature dropped rapidly as the foursome concluded dinner. They began taking their plates and leftovers back indoors from Jason's backyard where the range grass had been replaced with a lawn of versatile Zoysia grass.

Once the outside table had been cleared and the dishwasher started, the couples took their seats in

Jason's house. Don and June sat in the recliners and Jason and Linda sat opposite them on the leather sofa. June brushed back a lock of red hair that had fallen over one eye and she came out with a total non-sequitur. "Jason, I have an idea to further your reputation."

The three waited for her to deliver one of her noteworthy off-the-wall statements. Jason laughed, "I'm open to suggestions, as long as it's legal."

June continued, "How about if you invent a germ nobody ever heard of before. You own your own research company, right? So you can mess around if you want. Have some fun in life."

"I don't have to invent anything," Jason replied, in his self-assured manner. "There are plenty of unknowns to find. And my lab is my fun."

"I'll testify to that," Linda laughed, giving a quick wink to June and Don. In her British accent, Linda ignored Jason, speaking as though he wasn't there. "I have a better idea, June. He makes one up and sells it to the press."

"Good idea," June replied, happily. "I mean, the man can be a stick in the mud sometimes. I vote he makes a discovery that is a fun for everyone." Her version of moral depravity was eating half-a-box of chocolates washed down with red wine and complaining about having a headache the next day.

June added, "Don will back you. Won't you dear? Jason can say you brought him, let me think, your rock from outer space and he found some new germ in it," she concluded, excitedly, seemingly astounded at her own brilliant idea.

Don looked askance at her and retorted, "Well, let's not get too carried away, sweetheart." Don protected his rock as though it were his child. He had spent too many cold lonely hours in the Antarctic looking for it and its brethren to give it up easily for passive displays of affection.

Linda suggested, "Making believe, what would you call it, Jace?"

Jason thought for a brief moment and stated slowly and dryly, in as deep a voice as he could muster, "The Mars Virus."

They all laughed. June caroled, "Okay, got it. Neither of you want to sully your reputations. But really, Donald, you guys should give your rock another look-see. What's the worst that could happen?"

Jason Randolph had never married. Any relationships he'd developed eventually dissolved because of the man's dedication to his scientific work. His hazel eyes matched his naturally wavy hair that he neatly parted on the left side and swept back the remainder that showed no sign of loss. His eyes were somewhat remarkable in that they were wide set with fine lines at their outsides from a life of smiling and laughter rather than from age, with a face that was square cut. He wore a light mustache that could have given him the appearance of a riverboat gambler in another century.

Jason considered himself a true outdoorsman. His hands were strong enough to field-dress a deer, quarter it, and carry the portions back to his pickup, or carry a smaller animal back to his truck once it had been cleaned. The same hands also manipulated sensitive laboratory equipment.

Linda Beaufort, one of Jason's employees, sat next to him. She had joined him a dozen years after obtaining her doctorate. She had been shopping for a smaller research facility away from a larger over-populated lab setting. She responded to an advertisement in a biochemistry journal that read:

Cancer Researchers Wanted. Small start-up laboratory in small community, good pay and benefits, excellent equipment. Send CV to Dr. Jason Randolph (Pls. see contact information below).

Don and June Jennings were Jason's best friends. A prematurely gray-haired geologist, Don's hair was almost Einsteinian in its tendency to flair and needed constant attention to keep it within acceptable limits. He stood three inches shorter than Jason's six-foot height and presented a stockier stature.

Don claimed a full professorship at the University of Nebraska in Omaha or UNO, a position Jason had never coveted. Ten years older than his friend, Don was in his mid-fifties whose Irish family name was Jennens. The green-eyed geologist's father had spent considerable time in Germany as a diplomat. There, he met and married Inga Schoënfeld, a teacher. The couple moved to the States to begin a family.

They spoke to the children in both English and German at home.

Nationally respected as a geologist, Don exemplified the precision and exactitude of his mother's German heritage. He worked his way through school hired on as a weatherman at a small local television station.

Combining a PhD in geology and his basic understanding of weather and climate, Don obtained a journeyman's job with NASA. Years later, he found himself serving as a consultant to NASA on their Viking Deep Space Probes when it photographed the surface of Jupiter's moons. Subsequently, he served on the Mars Lander project. His real claim to fame, though, came from a simple fact. He was one of the first persons to recover a rock in Antarctica that experts believed had come from Mars millions of years before. It had been dubbed the Jennings Meteorite.

Don's wife, June, a short be-freckled red-head, tended to her home greenhouse when she wasn't drawing medical diagrams under contract by doctors and book publishers. She held a Master's Degree in Ornithology from Cornell University in New York. Both she and her husband were avid bird watchers.

At this point in the conversation, Don got somewhat piqued, not because of June's flagrant idea that Jason should try to discover something new—he was long accustomed to dealing with his wife's wild ideas—but because of her pursuit of this particular one. He declared, "Look at it for what? NASA and everybody else beat to hell out of the rock I gave them twenty years ago and nobody found a thing."

"Everybody looked at your meteorites, but not Jason the Great," June persisted.

Don looked at Jason, who rolled his eyes as if to say, "Here she goes again."

"I saw that, Jason," June groaned. "You guys are supposed to be adventurers. You're hunters in your own way. You made your names on your whims and instincts. All I'm saying is, let Jason take a look at your meteorite. No big deal. How long will it take you, Jason, an hour?"

"It'll take more than an hour, but I'll do it just to make you happy," Jason sighed, becoming irritated. Sometimes the woman would grab onto some whimsical idea and wouldn't let it go. She was brilliant in her own way, although, sometimes, the price to pay for brilliance can be an occasional foray into the realm of public ostracism.

"It won't be any elaborate series of tests. I'll tell you that right now. And only if Don is willing to bring over his rock," Jason concluded, feeling confident his friend was say no to the deal.

To Jason's surprise, Don scratched his head with both hands, flaring his hair. "Fine. I'll bring it over for a few minutes. You take a sample and she leaves us alone."

June smiled at Linda as a victory won.

2

A few miles from Jason's home, in Don's house, in a Plexiglas box, lay Don's meteorite. Somewhat oval, it measured about eight inches in total length by five inches across. It tapered down to two inches, with half of its larger end blackened by atmospheric heat, or perhaps, from the original blast that had created it.

Don thought it might have originated from the largest volcano in the solar system, Olympus Mons on Mars, when it erupted millions of years in the past. Ejecta could have easily escaped the red planet because the volcano stands 14 miles in height, over twice as tall as Mount Everest. According to theory, given the force of the eruption, the low gravitational pull of the planet might not be sufficient to keep the ejected particles, gases, and rocks from traveling into outer space.

Don's rock weighed 4.37 pounds. Red and pitted to varying extents, the edges of the pit craters were smoothed by searing heat, in sharp contrast to a charred glassine finish on one side, which, apparently, had suffered the worst heat. Don explained about how he found it in the Antarctic near the Lewis Cliff, which had shed thousands of its own stones, as they were called, over time. He used various devices to locate those he believed to be qualified as having come from space.

In addition to having the proper chemical signatures, the stone he found was not porous or layered like many earth rocks that form due to gravity, and it possessed a thin fusion crust on one face due to its fall through the atmosphere. While Don held to the volcanic eruption theory for its origin, other experts believed that many millions of years before, a large meteor struck Mars with such force that megatons of Martian soil and rock were hurled up beyond the planet's limited gravity into outer space, eventually making its way into Earth's gravitational pull. In both theories, the meteorite Don found once belonged to a larger piece that probably fragmented during its descent through Earth's atmosphere. Some scientists postulated that one fragment possessed indications of bacterial habitation.

There was nothing new about any of this except for Jason's entrance into the picture. Although he didn't really give a damn, Jason did consider the concept of trying to grow something previously unknown. In order to conduct a simplistic experiment to comply with June's suggestion, three things would be required: an original growth formula; proof of no contamination by bacteria or other microorganisms; and proof of its extraterrestrial origin. This last one would bring the project to an abrupt conclusion. No problem. End of story.

Don used his inside information their advantage. He made the necessary contacts to find out what had been used for nutrient sources by other labs in their quest for alien life, not only for the meteorite he had loaned to NASA for study, but also for investigations of other meteorites. Once he obtained the information, he passed it along to Jason.

The pure researcher in Jason noted the broad scope of the investigations and wanted to do something other agencies hadn't done. Nothing complicated. What life form could survive a multiple-warhead nuclear blast from a volcano and spend millions of years in outer space while exposed to all that radiation?

While he maintained a limited teaching position at the university and had access to its research facilities, Jason decided to use his own laboratory in order to avoid distractions. There need be no inquiring professors or students, no hellos or goodbyes. His inquisitive mind led him to spend a modest amount of his evening time reading about Mars. He found that the atmosphere of Earth is comprised of 79 percent nitrogen and 19 percent oxygen with .04 percent carbon dioxide. He pulled out one of his old astronomy books and found the atmosphere on Mars is comprised of three percent nitrogen and 0.1 percent oxygen with carbon dioxide at some 95 percent –- the latter almost 2500 times greater than Earth' percentage.

To him, trying to recover a life form from those conditions was impossible. It was like trying to recover a sea creature living in total blackness at over 36,000 feet deep at the bottom of the Marianas Trench. At that depth it would be subjected to eight tons per square inch of pressure compared with a mere 15 pounds of pressure on the surface. Once you recovered your specimen, you place it in a freshwater goldfish tank, feed it algae flakes, and ask it to survive.

Jason had cut most of his ties to the local branch of the university a few years before he founded Randolph Cancer Research. Born into money, Jason never flouted his wealth. He hid his riches by living what he considered to be a middle-class lifestyle, which might be somewhat above what others might consider to be middle-class. His reputation in the community came from his regular appearances on local television when he told about progress being made in the various fields of cancer research.

The Randolph family were true bluebloods. A chart on the wall of Jason's personal lab depicted his complete lineage back to the Godspeed, the first ship arriving from England to establish a colony in the new country in 1607, some 20 years before the Mayflower landing. Unlike the commoners aboard the Mayflower, those aboard the Godspeed belonged to the aristocracy. To this day, they refuse to hobnob with descendants from the Mayflower who had rooted themselves in Philadelphia.

Randolph's ancestors founded the Virginia Company. Four centuries later Randolph's father became a businessman and sole owner of the largest solar panel company in the country. Raised in a conservative area of Virginia in the presence of abundant money, Jason attended operas and concerts with both parents at an early age, while learning the ways of outdoor life with his father. His excellence in science and mathematics brought him to Berkeley where he earned two PhDs in both biochemistry and clinical genetics and a Master's in a new subject called Molecular Ecology. He considered himself a perfectionist, not a narcissist, who tended to blame himself for whatever went wrong in his life, yet became annoyed at the inability of others to conform to his standards. Jason had no bent toward politics. He wanted to teach. He also didn't want to spend a lot of time at it.

At the age of twenty-four Jason interviewed for an adjunct professorial position at the University of Nebraska located in Lincoln, otherwise known as UNL. The ad claimed they were looking for someone who could teach both chemistry and ecology. To his great delight he soon discovered all they were looking for was someone to teach basic ecology to freshmen and sophomores.

Totally overqualified, he signed on. He could have gone anywhere in the country where he could find ample fishing and hunting, yet found what he wanted in Lincoln, a city with a strong pride in the Czech community. Indeed, the Czech capital of the USA was only 40 miles up the road in Wilber. He had grown fond of the people, thanks to one of his graduate professors who was a Czech and had once attended the University of Nebraska. Everything considered, he followed where the flowing stream led.

He had found a home in Lincoln. He was distant from the intellectualism of his wealthy Virginia life; away from the every-man-for-himself competition and drive of academic work. Jason found himself a place where he could see the big Midwestern sky at night that stunned easterners with its broad scope and meteor showers. It also offered him a chance to feel small, something that appealed to his sense of introversion.

How many times had he walked away from noteworthy people who had a crowd of listeners around them to find solace in his aloneness? Now he could have it all—accomplish something useful through his research, yet remain relatively obscure at the same time.

Once established, he taught a single course in freshman ecology the first year. The trial period ended. He then morphed into teaching both basic ecology and human genetics. This afforded him the opportunity to gain the respect of serious scientists in the department and was promoted to Assistant Professor. He soon met Don Jennings at a faculty luncheon and the two became friends.

Jason didn't wait long to start his company and, with his own money, built it into a well-respected research facility. When Don brought him the meteorite, Jason scraped off some of its surface dust under sterile conditions using the hood in the lab. The hood, a large Plexiglas box, had a clear face with gloves set beneath the visual area. Jason didn't need to go to this extreme for a sample of dust. He did it because it out of habit. He also did not condone sloppy work, especially for one who sought perfection in research.

He decided to use a simple liquid culture with no agar plates. Why put in extra work? However one looked at it, what they had was a laughable fly-by-night effort that would accomplish nothing except to get June off their backs. He felt foolish and manipulated. It was beneath him. He was a happy-go-lucky guy who took his cancer research seriously. There was no challenge here. This was beyond the ridiculous when he could have been putting his time into serious work in order to prevent suffering. Hadn't he been featured in Forbes and Business World as an upstart company to keep an eye on? Didn't he receive a million plus each year in grant money with only four employees? He was the one who had already made breakthroughs by developing a new technique for screening combinations of cancer-fighting drugs that would take hours or minutes rather than weeks or months to process. "Dot your i's," a professor had once told him. Be ingenious, industrious, and insurmountable, not inconsequential or indolent.

Jason argued with himself. "Take a little time and be kind to June. Do her stupid little experiment. What will it hurt? She won't ask you again after this. Be true to your principles, whatever they have to do with this nonsense?"

After labeling four flasks A, B, C, and D, he seeded them with meteorite dust. Each contained a different liquid formulation of his design. He placed the flasks into a rubberized clamp that gripped each flask by its neck and rocked it back and forth at room temperature, figuring he'd dump the lot of them after the weekend. Ensuring the clamps on the rocker were secure, he went about other more important duties.

This was on a Thursday. On Friday, after work, he exited the rear door of the institute and casually strolled the concrete pathway to his home. It was time to get out of Dodge. He punched a button on his key fob to open the garage door, pulled out his Subaru SUV, and walked to the side of the house where he kept an old red Ford 150 pickup, which he then drove into the garage. He pulled it next to a small boat with an Evinrude 40 horsepower 2-stroke motor. Situated on the other side of the pickup was a refrigerator, floor freezer, tackle box, a large and small ice chest, and a gun safe. A few days still remained in the deer season and it was his intent to take advantage of the time left to bring home fresh meat.

He entered the house to change and returned to the garage several minutes later, having decided against hauling the boat. The day had been breezy, the water would be choppy. As it was, fish would be catchable, if the silt wasn't too bad. He knew of a small protected area with good cover that should be fine, as long as he didn't have too much company; opposite his father's approach to fishing, which included a lot of friends. To Jason, the less the merrier worked fine.

Picking up the large ice chest he placed it in the back of the pickup, then lifted the freezer door and pulled out two 10-pound bags of ice which he threw into the ice chest. He added several bottles of water, some basic sandwich-making material, granola bars and a fifth of Jack Daniels.

Jason punched codes into the outside of the four-foot tall gun-safe and waited a moment for the heavy door to unlock. He decided against the Beretta .380 and pulled out a S&W .45 semi-auto handgun in a holster, a 12-round magazine with cartridges, a Winchester 12-gauge pump action shotgun and two boxes of shells. He thought for a moment and also removed a .22 long rifle with scope in case he wanted to add geese to the menu; geese that might settle in the wet grass. This would add variety to any fish he might catch before the weather turned.

Finally, he grabbed a small tent, a zipper bag, his fishing tackle box, two poles, and a headset for music. Securing thee items, he backed out the vehicle and moved the SUV into the unoccupied space.

He had quickly transformed himself from a khaki-slacked dress-shirted scientist into a camo-wearing outdoorsman with a .45 on his hip. He headed out to an area only a few miles distant where deer hunting was permitted.

Linda declined the invitation to spend a cold windy weekend sleeping in a tent. Instead, she opted to stay home in front of a crackling fireplace reading Chaucer. Given the proper weather, she did enjoy spending time outdoors with Jason learning new skills; however, facing the time necessary to return herself to a respectable appearance afterward didn't excite her. She required her own space on occasion and this was the perfect time for her to say no to his invitation.

3

Jason found himself in a place where he wanted to be—alone. He didn't consider himself a person who needed attention or companionship. If attention came with success, so be it. If companionship was easy to come by, he would accept it. If he could be alone, he preferred it.

He liked these people of the Midwest—hard-working religious folk with solid values and patriots to the core. That, and their provincialism. No, it wasn't the small town of Gopher Prairie, Minnesota, population of 3000, described in Sinclair Lewis' Main Street, but to Jason it smacked of frontier. These folk were different from the people of the eastern intellectual social circles to which his parents belonged, and worlds apart from the free-wheeling Californians he had encountered while attending Berkeley.

His father had been born in Richmond, once the seat of the Confederacy; his mother in Charlottesville, 70 miles to the northwest. Both cities were closely tied in many ways. They were moderate-sized communities at less than 50,000 to 175,000 population, respectively, at the time of his birth. Although his father found success in the business realm, his parents were still Jeffersonian in their thinking. They were pro-agrarian, self-sufficient, anti-government, and supported low taxes. Thus, Jason had been infused with their thinking. In short, start your own business and support farmers.

There was one problem with that thinking. If there were little to no taxes, there would be no money to put into public education and teachers would go on strike because of their low wages, which tended to even things out. He had long since resolved that if the day ever came, he would put money into education, but it would be under his direction. Weighing all the options, Jason had found the best of all worlds in Lincoln.

He did his best to make discoveries in keeping with his philosophy—some might call it his default setting: You can accomplish anything you lock your mind onto doing. If there is an obstruction, you either go through it, around it, or find a way to eliminate it. If you want something badly enough, there will not be the smallest doubt that your goal will be reached, given common sense reasoning, of course.

His education had been intense despite government directives that forced educators to teach mind-numbing soul-destroying revised versions of history in classes where no knowledge was required to take or complete them. To him, these courses had no social, creative, or educational value whatsoever.

Not long after moving to Lincoln, he purchased a 2600-square-foot three-bedroom two-bath home on five acres of land. The home was situated on flat, expensive land just northeast of the 270 acre Holmes Lake at the heavily trafficked intersection of Van Dorn Street and Normal Blvd. With fishing pole in hand, he could walk to the lake in ten minutes. A large copse of cottonwood and hackberry trees filtered much of the noise of city life.

Jason found one problem with the home. He could not see the horizon or incoming weather on any side except to the east where his grassy yard replaced the trees. The home had no immediate shelter from the rain, sleet, hail, wind, ice, snow, or tornadoes, except for a small cluster of trees which were native to the area immediately north of his home. Those would provide a slight windbreak for storms blowing down from Montana or the Dakotas, but not much more.

Typically, the home possessed a strong pitch to its composite roof with the wide driveway. The front entrance and garage faced to the south. He bought furniture and moved in, fencing the back yard with chain link. He hired a bimonthly service to keep the range grass short. Next, he contacted the Nebraska Game and Parks Commission for literature on types of fish and game and their habitats within the state and did the same for Iowa, in case he wanted to drive a few miles eastward for fishing and hunting.

It took four years to construct the institute just west of his home that he named Randolph Cancer Research or RCR. Now he could enter his property from the west or from the south.

Before Jason could write grant proposals, he would need to purchase and install equipment and obtain necessary licenses and certifications. He then submitted numerous applications for specific cancer-related projects. The National Cancer Institute approved him for two of them and he began the hiring process.

Jason pulled the parka's headpiece tighter and wound in another trout. Maybe June was right. Maybe he did need a little more excitement in this life; something different. His thoughts brought him back to the outskirts of Richmond, Virginia, his birthplace, a city founded in 1737, where his father took him into the wilds from his young years while his mother made arrangements for social events. Winters there were still cold, the leaves still fell, but the company they kept was different from the company he kept at this point in his life. For them, business and politics ruled their lives. Science ruled his.

After a weekend on his own, Jason felt refreshed and in great spirits. He carefully packed portions of a goose in the large ice chest. He packed the fish in the small chest. No deer had been sighted.

Within twenty minutes, he turned east onto his property from Van Dorn into the paved parking lot in front of the building lit by a single spotlight. A large rough-bristled mat of coir lay outside the building's overhang at the double-paned glass entrance doors. The rolling shutter was down. He got out of the truck and checked his watch. It read 6:55 p.m. The sun had set almost two hours earlier.

When Jason hit the remote on his key fob, the rolling shutter engaged, triggering the interior front office lights. He entered, intending to check for messages on his private phone. The overhead neons lit up the floor made of synthetic tiles, each square depicting brown and red pottery pieces typical of the Lakota and Cheyenne Indian Art of the region. The floor gleamed. The husband and wife cleaning crew had done their work.

Behind the reception desk hung business licenses, building permits, diplomas, and awards. A lone phone sat atop the desk. A trio of three-drawer filing cabinets stood to the right of the desk.

Jason had employed a part-time secretary for the few years of operation for purposes of organization and phone calls. When she left, he never rehired. Most of the phone calls coming in these days were trash, so he kept the phone on mute and checked the answering machine each morning and each evening. Serious callers got used to it. Very serious callers had his cell number or that of his private line in his office/lab.

The institute was also called the laboratory, in general, and contained four individual labs within it. Jason claimed the first one as his own, immediately past the office. Three more labs followed this one, identical in structure, each with specialized equipment. All four laboratories followed Biosafety Level 3 or BSL-3 protocols, each maintained in scrupulously clean conditions. Because bio-hazardous materials were not used that might threaten respiratory health, there was no reason to go to the expense of creating a BSL-4 lab with separate HEPA filtration and mega-containment conditions. Space-suited workers were nowhere to be found.

A break room followed the fourth lab, which contained a fridge, microwave, and single-serve coffee maker, followed by separate bathrooms for men and women, and a small conference room. A door located at the east end of the long east-west hallway led downstairs to the animal facility. Beyond the stairwell, an eight-seat conference room welcomed staff and visitors. A rear exit door opened onto a concrete pathway that led to Jason's house only 50 fifty yards to the east.

Passing through the front office, Jason took a half-dozen steps to the first lab and flipped on the light switch. From the doorway, he glanced to the far right toward the four cultures some 20 feet distance at the end of the north side counter.

The cultures gently rocked on the shaker, clear as ever. No growth. He mused. Gee, what a surprise. I'll toss them in the morning. How pleasant it will be to pour them down the drain. Why couldn't he have just said no to June and be done with it? No, not good ole Mister Nice Guy.

Jason took a quick look at the caller ID on the private phone line and saw the name of Bill Wainwright listed. "Great, the President of the University," he muttered, then remembered to turn on his cell phone. He habitually maintained the cell in the Off position while out in the elements. From experience, a call or a notification always occurred at the most inopportune time.

He didn't have many connections with the university anymore other than the single course he now taught, similar to when he started with them; or used some of their advanced research equipment; or attend departmental meetings. Sometimes, when requested, he would serve as a committee member for a graduate student. He the moment, he was at a loss as to why Wainwright might call. He'd known Bill for years and the man had always been supportive. He returned the call. "Jason, thanks for getting back to me," Wainwright replied, genially.

As if Jason had a choice. "I went fishing."

"Invite me along next time," Wainwright suggested, now with a slight edge in his voice. He added, "Perchance, have you seen the papers or turned on TV?"

"No, I just got in. Why, what's up?"

"Some woman claims to have seen a strange creature behind her home. She swears it came from your lab." Wainwright sounded a little stressed. This puzzled Jason. The man was not prone to pulling practical jokes.

"Sorry, Bill, that one got loose," Jason retorted, waiting for the punchline.

Wainwright said evenly, "You on top of this?"

"On top of what, Bill?"

"Whatever is going on over there, keep us out of it, if you can, all right?"

If Wainwright wanted to talk in circles, so could Jason. "I guess it depends on what is going on in my lab. As far as I know, all research is under control. My people are here five to seven days a week, sometimes nights. So yes, we have our research under control. Not to worry." Jason suddenly realized the words came out almost glibly.

"Keep me in the loop." Wainwright signed off.

Keep them out of what? Jason wondered. That call was one more reason why he should have cut ties with the university long ago. But no, he had to teach one course a semester, so they figured they owned his life. Right now, priority one was to get home and clean his weapons and ice chests full of fish and game. To heck with Wainwright.

Jason turned off the lights at the lab entry, preparing to leave for the evening, when he noticed a slight reddish glow coming from the area reserved for the little Mars' project. He turned on the lights and the glow disappeared. He turned off the lights and it reappeared. Now two hours past sunset, no background light filtered in from the hall windows, although the rolling shutters were up. Hello, what's this? With eyes locked on the glow, he slowly walked over to the area. The luminescence came from one of four flasks of liquid he had prepared. He stopped the shaker and pulled the glowing 500-ml Erlenmeyer flask from the shaker, a size universally used in labs around the world. Similar to the others, this flask held a cotton plug filled half-way to the top with one of his basic formulas.

He set the glowing flask on the counter. He walked back to the doorway and turned on the lights again. As if to define the moment, the heaters in the building cycled on and a rush of warm air suffused the room.

Slowly, Jason examined the sample marked with the letter A, while the others marked with B, C, and D failed to glow. Holding it up, he saw that the liquid shone with a slight murkiness in the brightness of its own reddish light. There appeared to be a little effervescence. Had he not known better, he would have sworn he was looking at a couple hundred milliliters of the imitation strawberry soda he liked to drink as a child, less the murkiness. He took out a microscope slide, set it on the marble counter, and lit a Bunsen burner. He deftly removed the cotton plug from the flask. With his right hand he pulled out a sterile six-inch long sterile Pasteur pipette, flamed the mouth of the flask, stuck the pipette into the solution and withdrew a tiny drop of liquid. He flamed the mouth of the flask again, replaced the cotton plug, set down the flask and added a tiny drop of the liquid from the pipette onto the slide. Placing the pipette into a solution of chromic acid to sterilize it, he then covered the drop on the slide with a coverslip he obtained from a very small flip-top box.

Jason set the magnification of his microscope at 400X and focused in, not having any expectations, knowing that expectations of results may lead to their false interpretation. At first he saw only countless micro-bubbles. That made sense. The acid he had added to this batch caused the formation of carbonic acid and carbon dioxide from the carbonates he had included in the crude formulation.

He increased magnification to 850X to see needle-like forms stacking on top of one another. They appeared to be bonding side-to-side forming something. As he watched, more tendrils appeared to be joining the others while the main structure grew on its own accord forming structures resembling crystals.

The micro-fibrils were reminiscent of asbestos fibers, but dark and ominous looking like railroad ties with rounded ends. However, asbestos contains silicon and Jason had not added silicon to the medium. On the other hand, asbestos does produce crystals. Like asbestos, what he saw was incredibly thin, but what he saw had a width-to-length ratio of 1:5 compared to a ratio of 1:20 or longer for asbestos. Straining his eyes he increased the magnification to 1200X, playing with the fine focus. He thought, What an odd little insert into my day. What got into this solution? Red yeasts don't glow and luminescent bacteria aren't red like this.

Jason prepared a second sample. He saw the same dark and ominous fibers. He didn't know if they were pigmented black or if light wasn't able to pass through them. A half-hour later he determined the other three cultures did not have either the fibers or the bubbles.

Jason didn't know a lot about crystals, but a geologist would. He called Don, who laughed hard and long. Don must have put his hand over the receiver because Jason could hear him tell June what Jason reported in a muted tone and heard her laugh in turn.

Jason felt like a fool, as if he had missed the most

obvious. How can a person be so smart and be so stupid at the same time he would wonder about others on occasion. Now he wondered the same about himself.

"Jason, what's the matter? Not enough publicity for you? You have to try pulling one over on your old buddy? Getting even with June, are you?"

"Don, they're crystals. You know about crystals. You can laugh after you look at this." What publicity?

Jason expected Don to arrive within a half-an-hour. The weather was turning and ice would soon be forming on the roads.

Jason knew what to do and what not to do. He made no decision at all. Returning the culture to its original place with the others, he turned on the rocker again. He grabbed his lab coat off a coat rack, put it on, and flopped down in his desk chair to wait, pondering the problem and thinking about the load of ice-packed food in the bed of the truck, and about Linda.

The pair were an item, but only after-hours. Tall and stately, she could be delicate and tough, philosophical and coldly objective. She claimed to have a fair amount of Scandinavian blood in her, which may have contributed to her height. Always meticulous in her dress, her short well-styled layered blond hair balanced her pale face perfectly. This, in turn, was accented by a small un-British-like nose that supported tasteful not-too-bold black rim glasses. Similar to Jason, she had been born into money. The couple found themselves in an easy-going relationship. Each had learned to adjust to, if not tolerate, the other's personal habits.

RCR needed to bring in a half-million a year to turn a profit, which it did consistently. At present, the institute was severely understaffed. Employees consisted of himself and Linda, Dustin Jones from Seattle, and Tomás Angel Rubio, a virologist originally from Mexico City. Prepared to leapfrog to the next level and hire another four to six scientists—his original intent when he'd had RCR constructed—Jason decided to walk before he ran. Perhaps the time had come to pick up the pace.

Everyone on Jason's formidable staff possessed one PhD at a minimum, except for Rick McIntyre, former Afghanistan veteran Drill Sergeant who had served two tours. Although he did like his wine on occasion, the man was gold. Rick took good care of their research animals and he followed orders to the letter. You do not mess with Rick or his territory.

As Jason sat waiting for Don, he became somewhat annoyed at this temporary nonsensical intrusion orchestrated by a glowing flask of liquid. He recalled the conversation with Wainwright and thought he knew what must have happened. The cleaning crew consisted of a husband and wife team. The wife's brother was a reporter at a local television station. She must have seen the curious glow and told her brother about it and he passed on the bit of information to the news anchor. Don and Wainwright probably saw the news program and called him out for wanting publicity. The problem lay in that the crew came in on Friday evenings, which meant the flask must have begun to glow only a day after Jason had inoculated it with the tiniest amount of dust. It didn't make sense. Nothing grows that fast.

At the sound of the door buzzer Jason felt a sense of relief. This would soon be over. He got up and walked to the door of his lab as Don and June were entering into the front office. They wore jackets with earmuffs over their hats. A cold blast of wind blew snow inward and Don quickly closed the door, ensuring that it clicked shut on its latch behind them. Don held two books under one arm.

Jason held a finger to his lips, as though a great secret were unfolding and he did not want to break the spell. He motioned them to the first lab. Holding up a hand to halt them, he switched off the lights. A subtle gentle reddish glow appeared in the darkness at the far end of the room. Remaining silent, he let the glow speak for itself as the couple stopped and stared. "Oh, boy," June muttered.

Jason flicked the switch up to turn the lights back on. The trio walked to the four flasks on the rocker staring at the first one as though it would disappear, if they looked elsewhere. He explained the situation again. From his narrowed eyes it appeared to Jason that Don wasn't totally convinced as to his motives.

At Jason's direction, the others put on lab coats, seemingly to play along with his game. He prepared another slide for viewing and motioned for Don to have a look.

Don knew microscopes, although his were generally low-power stereoscopes for the viewing of rocks and gems. Like Jason, he also worked with an electron microscope. Unlike Jason, he had worked with x-ray crystallography equipment.

"Well, I'll be dipped," Don stared through the eyepieces. After several moments he stood up and June took his place.

"Tell me about crystals, Don," Jason requested, and pulled two more chairs forward. The men took a seat and June swiveled around to face them.

Having known his friend for a number of years and after reconsidering his doubts, Don believed the man to be deadly serious. "By definition they're repeating patterns of ions or atoms or molecules in three dimensions." He opened one of the books he'd brought to display several pages of crystalline structures. "Some chemicals or substances can form more than one crystalline pattern, depending on environmental conditions. Atmospheric pressure is one of those conditions. Water is one common example where H_2O takes on different configurations with changes in pressure.

"Crystals come in many different shapes such as cuboidal, hexagonal, and rhombohedral, and they each have different properties. For example, some will carry electric charges or will polarize light. Table salt layered inside a plastic water bottle placed over an antenna can sync WiFi signals to enhance the power of your modem, or so I've read. We've also created crystals in outer space from chemicals such as insulin. To complicate matters, we think silicon crystals are made during formation of a new star. In fact, crystals are nothing new in outer space. This may be far-fetched, but these things could have been born in space itself," Don concluded, with a grin that Jason could not read behind.

June shrugged. "Like baking a pie. Add some dirt, a heavy dose of radiation, bake for a few million years, place it in the oven on high, freeze it for a few million more and put it on ice for eons. Ready for consumption."

"Like the hot dog that bites back. You eat it or it eats you," added Don, smiling, showing teeth. Nobody laughed. Don scratched his head beneath severely tousled hair. "It could be we have a contaminant; forcing, say, sodium or magnesium to bind with potassium in some bizarre arrangement of atoms. I assume you have those ingredients in the mix?"

Jason gave a single nod.

"Why is this solution different than the other three?" Don asked.

"This one has distilled water, trace elements, potassium, magnesium, a little baking soda, some nitrates, sulfur and phosphate. I added a little acid to it just for grins. Sample B has the same ingredients without the acid and Samples C and D have a lot of amino acids. I'm thinking the acid caused the sodium bicarbonate in the baking soda to give us the carbon dioxide fizz."

Don contributed, "Aside from the acidity, those

are the basic ingredients necessary for life and are also the constituents of Martian soil. We established that by information sent back by the Lander. We also found them in our spectrographic analysis of airborne dust, especially during dust storms. We've also found amino acids in meteorites. There is a large school that believes life on earth originated from these flying objects. We can't discount it."

"It might be nice to know the origin of these fibers other than to think they might have come from Mars. The important thing is whether it represents life outside Earth," Jason uttered.

"How would you define life?" asked June. "It can't be merely self-replication?"

Jason thought about giving a flippant answer, such as, life begins when the dog runs away and the kids leave home, but thought better of it. "With a genetic code, life is supposed to grow, reproduce itself, and put up with a certain amount of abuse. Viruses are not alive. Though a good percentage of them have DNA, they cannot self-reproduce. They enter a living cell and force the cell's DNA to make more virus particles. They're assembled piece- by-piece to be released in great numbers to infect more cells."

"Which suggests what we have here might be living?" June added, with her head canted slightly to emphasize the question, her voice raising slightly at the end.

Jason tried to keep down his excitement. "That's scary and fascinating at the same time. If it's not a crystal, it sure does look like a filamentous virus except that this is a good hundred times larger than any we know of. It's definitely larger than viruses that cause a cold or influenza and a lot of other diseases. This is territory for Tomás, my virologist."

Scratching the back of his head, Jason continued, "Other than the size, a second problem is this: Viruses don't make more of themselves inside a container of liquid without living cells to infect. This includes latent viruses like herpes that hide inside tissues until their release is triggered by sunlight or other factors."

June proclaimed darkly, "There's nothing exciting about the thought of this microbe going up my nose or entering my bloodstream."

"Can you imagine these little creatures flying around in the Mars' atmosphere during their planet-wide dust storms?" Don hypothesized.

Jason shivered at the thought of suited space men covered with these particles. As if speaking in defense of the unknown particles, he declared, "As we can see, these things have very specific requirements for their nutrition."

June's medical laboratory training came to the fore. "Sorry, won't wash with me. Crystals grow, too, and they're not alive. We don't have a clue as to what its requirements really are. If I had to guess, though, I'd say it appears to be happy."

Don did not see the slightest trace of mirth in his friend's eyes and finally took him seriously. "We established one thing: Your ingredients contain the basic stew for life to form. However, the formation we're looking at is troublesome. The strands are stacking like two-by-fours next to each other longitudinally. The luminescence has me totally stumped. We'll need to look for some internal structures, such as a nucleus."

Jason considered: Why didn't I take the samples from under the hood and not out in the laboratory where they could become airborne? In my excitement, I violated the basic tenets of microbiology and of the hunter: care and caution. Presume the gun is always loaded. Hopefully, they're not airborne. Even if they were, their number would be so low as to be inconsequential.

Jason's voices began to argue. Maybe you made a great discovery. That's the way things happen. I'll bet more discoveries are made by accident than are found on purpose. Either dump it or follow up on it. No, it is forbidden to dump a possible discovery.

The couple stood and put on their cold-weather clothing. Don turned to Jason. "I'll do more research on crystals. What we have here is possibly Nobel Prize winning material and he who reports it first or steals it first usually wins. So let's keep our mouths shut."

June agreed, "First, you guys have to make certain this is undiscovered. Can you imagine making a big announcement and it turns out to be a simple contaminant?"

Jason leaned back in his chair, trying to hold the flow of adrenaline in check. "I'm going to make up a batch of this growth medium tomorrow so these things can be transferred. I don't want this one to be dropped or contaminated and not be able to reproduce it again. I'm also going to try to get a high-speed camera from the athletic department so we can take a closer look at how it reproduces. We can hook it up to a screen." Then he told them about the call from Wainwright and their conversation. "What were you saying to me on the phone when you mentioned publicity?"

"Don't you watch the news?" June asked, smiling.

"You know I don't have a TV," Jason parried.

Don said, "Some news anchor guy late Friday evening reported an unknown glowing substance here in the lab that had never been there before and wondered if it might be radioactive material you were dealing with. Your ties to the university were mentioned. The next night the story got amplified after a bunch of people called in, and since nobody could reach you, the story got warped. You know how the media likes to sell their product."

Jason told them his thoughts about the cleaning lady and her brother, which made the entire matter completely understandable. After all, wasn't he their local spokesperson for cancer and the one person the local press relied on for updates in the field? They were all family. Okay, got it. No big deal.

He'd call the reporter in the morning. He would join forces with them and laughingly explain his team had some luminescent bacteria they had under investigation. They wanted to try and find a new line of non-toxic chemicals to reduce cancer's rate of spread. He had been planning to tell them about it at their next interview, anyway.

To Jason, on a superficial level, the whole issue of media involvement was funny when he thought about it. Not so funny in the bright light of reality. A culture had been inoculated only three days before with 10 milligrams or one one-hundredth of a gram, nearly one part in 50,000 of an ounce of dust. By the next evening, it had reproduced at such an incredible rate that it emitted light. That was when the cleaning lady must have seen it. These were not glowing bacteria recovered from some swamp down south or from the ocean floor, but glowing self-reproducing virus-like particles harbored in a rock from outer space—in fact, in all likelihood ,were still in that rock.

Jason checked the phone in the front office and saw numerous calls had been logged, many of them repeat calls from radio and television stations. Before he left the office for the short drive home, he called Linda to tell her the latest news. She picked up on his enthusiasm, eager to see his little discovery. She offered to return the phone calls for him in the morning.

Jason pulled out of the parking lot and drove down the immediate south side of the institute building to his house, pulling up to the garage. He opened it, backed out the SUV, and drove the pickup inside. Heavy flakes of wet snow fell, so sparse at first one might be tempted to count them. He unloaded the

Ford 150, methodically put everything back in its proper place and took the game and weapons into the kitchen. He switched cars once again, closed the garage door and entered the house, where he took on the necessary cleaning chores.

By the time Jason flopped into bed near midnight, fatigue had set in, but he felt good spirits, fired with enthusiasm with research challenges ahead of him, perhaps with great and wondrous discoveries as part of his destiny.

4

In a half-sleep, Jason's laboratory called to him. She, who persisted in seductively whispering his name to come to her for another round of excitement; she who beckoned to have another look at the breasts made of glass, aluminum and copper wires. The same breasts that sang lilting songs about thin-layer chromatography, scintillation counters and tissue cultures housed in glass Petri dishes; of gas chromatographs; of genetic sequencers and atomic absorption spectrophotometers. After all, true scientists only know what they can n measure and Jason was that scientist personified. That's where he belongs, with a woman who might be petulant, if not laborious at times, but one who never refused him. He was all for improvisation and saving money when it became necessary, but in the world of high-stakes competition for research dollars, efficiency and state of the art equipment paved the way for great discoveries—that, and more importantly, a good sense of intuition.

His single-story home held four-bedrooms. Constructed of brick, it was situated in the central portion of the city with a good slope to its shingle roof. Aside from the master suite, he used one bedroom for office purposes which included a small desk with a microscope. Another room served for purpose of exercise with bike, treadmill, and universal weight machine. No television allowed. A fourth served as a guest bedroom. An open floor plan included a half-wall between the kitchen and great room with a picture-windowed view of the grassy yard and trees on the east side of the property.

No mountains of significance were visible here or in other parts of the state, similar to the flat lands west of the Mississippi which reached into Canada and south into New Mexico. A total of over a million square miles, the flat grasslands of America attracted visitors from around the world with plenty of room to spare. The land supplied corn and other vegetables, fruits, wheat, beef and pork, coal and minerals; enough food to serve tens of millions, and did.

A six-foot leather sofa stood against one wall in the living room, just long enough to accommodate a sleeping man. Behind it hung a wood-framed picture of Ludwig Von Beethoven with the complete miniaturized score of his 5th Symphony framed next to it.

Opposite the sofa, on the window side of the room, stood two Lazy Boy recliners, also of leather, with a moderately-sized coffee table between them on brown Berber carpeting. On the far wall between the sofa and chairs hung a large mirror to further enhance the size of the area. A love seat was situated beneath the mirror near the corner fireplace.

No papers or stray bills lay on the counters, no chargers for electronics or dishes in the sink ever self-reproduced to increase in number. Only one device stood atop one counter nearest the fridge, a single cup coffee-maker with multiple coffee selections available in the cabinet above. The same cabinet held a coffee pot and filters for use when guests might arrive.

Before walking to work the next morning, Jason remembered to pick up a camera from the athletic department. Once back in the lab, he hooked it up to a microscope he had carried into the conference room. He called in Linda, Dustin, and Tomás, to explain what he had discovered and what they needed to do. He had prepared several slide samples of the virus for show and tell, insisting there would be no leaks, no press, nothing about any of this, simply because it might be an unusual crystal. He had hired his employees for their excellence and their burning desire to better themselves. And their secrecy.

The four watched the high speed images projected onto a drop-down screen, seeing a single fibril create a length-wise shadow image of itself in slow motion. The shadow image filled in and two fibrils were present side-by-side, each creating another shadow image to create four stacked fibrils. The reproductive process had been captured on film; a treasure which might be shown for a hundred years.

"If it were true binary fission," Dustin murmured, "I'd expect division to occur in half across the width. Each side would separate and grow. It's all wrong."

Tomás, the virologist commented, "My sentiments exactly. It's too big to be a virus. I do remember reading something about a recent discovery from the ocean where a new virus was found to be ten times larger than any other with only six percent of the genetic code of anything else. With this thing, if it is a virus, we can check out the code and compare it with what we know. If that's what it is, we can expect the outer capsid to be made of amino acids and protein, like most other viruses. There might be a membrane there, too. Right now, I don't know what to call it."

"No life I ever heard of reproduces by making a shell of itself and then fills in the shell," Linda contributed. "I can't even imagine how that would work."

The electric window shades were drawn, but the sound of howling wind penetrated the building, infusing as sense of sadness into Jason. From the time he had left his home and came to work, enough blowing snow had fallen to turn the greenery of the scene into a near barren landscape, whitening as it became bleaker.

Nobody believed the contaminant theory. Jason related to the others his early morning phone call from Don, who had spent the better part of the night deep-searching the literature online, but could not identify the crystal. In all probability, they were viewing a life form foreign to all of them in the shape of a virus.

Two weeks after first discovering the virus, nine people associated with the lab came down with a number of similar symptoms: slight cough, occasional sneezing, slight headache, overall joint aches and soreness in the shoulders and thighs. Those reporting the symptoms included the four researchers along with Don, June, and Rick, the animal attendant. The husband and wife cleaning crew also reported similar problems.

Jason considered sending a sample of the virus back to Berkeley or even the Centers for Disease Control and Prevention (CDC), for analysis and decided to wait for a while before showing his hand. He had no interest in feeling stupid after somebody discovered they had a certain species of bacteria that occasionally grew on rotting meat, or whatever. He wasn't an egoist but a self-critical scientist who revered good work, one who considered himself to be old-school-diligent because he had been trained under those types of people.

Thinking of the heavy workload ahead of his them all and the additional people he wanted to hire, Jason decided everyone should take a 10-day vacation beginning after work two weeks from Friday. Once they returned, work would begin in earnest, followed by a short 3-day New Year's weekend. Anxious to escape Randolph Prison, everyone graciously consented, understanding that if they became too involved in this new project, they could be locked in. Jason didn't need to explain one of his rules: Either take a break first, or regret later that you didn't.

Some two weeks later, most of the staff left the city on that Friday evening or the next morning. Dustin flew to his home in Seattle, Linda traveled to London, and Tomás and his family flew down to

Mexico City. Jason returned to visit his parents in Richmond to spend outdoor time with his father and catching up on social dinners with family friends. Don, June, and Rick remained behind on a staycation.

At 9:00 a.m. on the first workday of their return, all members of RCR, including Don and June, still retained their symptoms, now acknowledged by local health department as something that was going around. Authorities explained that symptoms of a cold typically do not last beyond a week, but new strains of virus can cause different effects. The researchers at RCR had no reason to believe these reports related to their work in any way.

In order to regain some momentum, Jason asked June to assist him as sole keeper of the front office and research-note-consolidator. She agreed and Jason turned the team toward working on the new virus. Funding for another cancer project was imminent, as well.

For the next three months Dustin and Tomás concentrated on completing research on government cancer research grants, while Jason and Linda spent a large portion of their time working on the new virus, as they called it. Despite their efforts to extract its DNA or to identify the composition of its capsid—its outer protective shell—they were unsuccessful in either project. Thus, there could be no comparisons made with any of the tens of thousands of genetic codes that had been defined and obtained from virtually all classes of organisms on earth.

March of Year 1

Four months about a news report from a local television newscast he had seen the evening before. A veterinarian was being interviewed while he stood in front of a table covered with a blanket. He had a slight cough as did the reporter, symptoms of the cold raging through their own city, in Omaha, and even in Council Bluffs, Iowa, across the Missouri River. On the blanket lay six deformed American Cocker Spaniels. In each of the dogs the left eye was lower than the right, the left ear was lower than the right, and the shoulders were somewhat hunched. As a lover of dogs and as a scientist, the vet thought it very curious; perhaps a mutation caused by a genetic abnormality in the parents. During the broadcast itself, other persons called the station to report the same occurrence with their own dog and cat litters. Those in the room listening to Tomás' tale gave no thought that the occurrences might be related to them.

At the morning session, Linda mentioned the good news that their new-found virus would not grow in whole blood obtained from their refrigerated blood stock. It saved them from being accused of harboring a potentially infective alien life form in case they got blindsided again by another news flash. More importantly, it would protect them when Jason made the announcement of their discovery of life beyond Earth. When he would do that seemed to be a mystery, even to himself.

The Lancaster County Health Department is based in Lincoln. As part of the Nebraska Department of Human and Health Services, it maintains watch over health issues in the city and the overall health conditions of the state, including food safety and water quality. There is a dental division and a vital statistics section, plus a Communicable Diseases Division that deals with everything from colds and influenza to Ebola, HIV, and West Nile Virus. There is no division for diseases attributed to extraterrestrial sources.

April of Year 1

Jason wanted to get to the electron microscope situated in the biology department at the local university campus. To do so, he would first have to embed samples in resin and slice sections thin enough with a microtome so electrons could pass through them or be deflected, similar to an x-ray.

When Don could take time from his university duties in Omaha or UNO, an hour's drive away from the geology department, he spent time with Jason learning to make thin sections of the virus imbedded in the resin.

Once completed, the men took the sections with them to UNL and logged into the electron microscope facility, occasionally photographing sections as they appeared on the screen in the darkened room. After two hours of viewing, a longitudinal section appeared which had been cut perfectly, similar to slicing a short, dark toothpick down the middle from end-to-end with an ultra-sharp razor.

"What's that running down the middle?" Jason asked, leaning forward to get a closer look at the view screen.

"Don't know. Increase the magnification," Don requested.

Jason turned the magnification dial and the men leaned closer, now only inches from the screen. "Could be DNA with knobby structures," he conjectured.

"I agree. I'm going over to x-ray. Can you ask Linda to join me?" Don declared, ejecting the sample.

Jason wanted to play it straight when he called the office, but his emotions got the best of him. "June, it's me."

"Find anything?" she asked.

"Nah, another dull day. Could you ask Linda to go meet Don over in x-ray, please?"

"Sure. Where are you? Are you still with the electron microscope?" June inquired.

"We're finished with it."

"Where's Don?"

Jason took a deep breath, trying to say it exactly right. "He's taking care of something else. Oh, by the way, before I forget, tell everybody we think we might have found DNA. This thing could be alive."

Damn if the little woman didn't have a loud scream. Jason heard her yelling his exact words loud enough for the others to hear her two labs down.

He smiled as put away his phone, already running through a Nobel Prize acceptance speech in his mind.

The moment Jason walked in the next morning the office line rang. He saw June pick up the receiver, listen for a moment and motion him over. She pushed the HOLD button. "It's Brooks," she whispered, just as Don arrived after an all-nighter in x-ray with Linda

"The department chair? Great," he muttered, keeping the swear words under wraps.

Jason took the receiver from her and pushed the HOLD button again. "George, nice to hear from you."

"Don't give me sweet talk, Jason," Brooks growled. "We had a departmental meeting yesterday afternoon, the one you accidentally on purpose forgot to attend. Guess what one topic of conversation might have been?"

Jason held a hand over his eyes and hung his head.Hazarding a guess, he replied, "I'm thinking my name came up."

"Jason, I'm happy for you and your lab and I wish you well. However, as long as we pay you, I expect you to attend meetings. I've always been adamant about the importance of meetings. You couldn't come up with a credible excuse?"

"George, we're on the verge of something here . . ."

"Either come up with a good excuse next time

or don't show up at all, if you get my drift," Brooks concluded.

"Okay, okay, I hear you. I got wrapped up in a project and honestly forgot about it."

"All right. Stay in touch," Brooks concluded with a final harsh note. The phone line went dead. Jason set down the receiver and the phone instantly rang again. June picked up, spoke a few words, hung up, and it rang once more.

Don pulled out a pen from his pocket, checked to make sure the point wasn't out and put the end of it into his ear to scratch an itch. He knew it was one of Jason's hot buttons and he didn't care. His ear itched. He spoke while he scratched. "I got a call a couple of nights ago, too. A reporter needed a science news story and wanted an update on our glow-bug findings."

"What did you tell him?" Jason asked, reaching up and pulling Don's hand back from his ear.

Don put the pen away and stuck his little finger in his ear. This also got pulled back. "I said we might be on the verge of announcing something, but it's too early to talk about it. So the guy wrote that we made a breakthrough in fighting cancer at UNL"

Jason's mood took a reverse swing. He chuckled, "So the jerk turned it into fake news and got the university pulled into a story that had nothing to do with them. I guess, dealing with the press is all right. Let them put their spin on it. I'm kicking myself for not cutting ties with the school a long time ago. I don't need them. Undoubtedly, the feeling is mutual."

"The phone's going to be ringing all day. Can I resign now?" June queried.

Don suggested, enthusiastically, "Jason, don't you think it's time to tell the world we found life? I mean, the reporter's story is accurate to a degree in terms of making a great discovery. It may not be better than a cure, but it sure will change our way of thinking about life and the universe. Hell, man, go for it."

"No, not yet. For what reason? I'm not going to get pressured into announcing cold fusion when good scientists in past years may or may not have reported a new source of energy too early and got blasted for it." Jason replied, angrily. To his way of thinking, there would no way he would tell anyone outside the lab until it was time to do so. First, it could be a false declaration which would make further grant money more difficult to obtain. Second, if he sent samples to other labs, even the Centers for Disease Control or CDC and they found it was nothing, he couldn't withstand the embarrassment. Admittedly, he knew that his concerns about being found in error in terms of his research to be a personality flaw. Most importantly, once he made the announcement, conspiracy theorists would connect him with the cold season or anything else going around, including beings escaping from his lab. His mind began to imagine the worst scenarios. The press would be all over the place, and quite likely, all their careers would be finished because, according to them, he and his people had let loose the virus.

Before Don could reply, Jason added, "And don't tell me it's the right thing to do."

"Where's the scientist in you? Are you that selfish?" Don suddenly turned on his friend, with a trace of bitterness in his voice.

Jason retorted, defensively, "The scientist in me is alive and well. So is survival. Thank you for asking."

June sat at her desk, stone-faced, watching the argument. She loved each of these men in their separate ways and felt pain at their exchange of words. In her heart, she knew her husband to be right.

Jason also knew Don spoke the doctrine of good science. They had been close friends since the first week Jason started teaching at UNL after they were introduced in the teacher's lounge, more than four years before he had started building the institute.

Don implored, "Jason, we just now found out the virus has DNA—Linda and I. Now is the time to send it out for others to confirm our findings. All you have to do is to make a couple of phone calls. You'll still get the credit, if that's what concerns you."

Jason could make appropriate calls, send out samples and summary statements, while continuing to work on the project. Under other circumstances, the collaboration with other labs would springboard the project to another level. With that done, no problems would arise. Glory would be there for the taking. Alternatively, if the virus were kept solely in their possession without anyone else knowing about it, he most definitely would be in trouble, if that were ever discovered. Was it now or never? He didn't want glory. He made the decision to learn more about their discovery before he chose a direction to follow. How long could it take to crack the code?

Jason proclaimed, "I don't want credit. Would you give up your child for someone else to raise? June, turn off the ringer and check for messages every couple of hours. If we get cornered, we'll say it's another dead end."

Coughing, Jason softened. "Come on, Don, you know me. There is no way in hell I am going to announce that we found life. If I give something to the world, I want it to be wrapped in roses. I want it to mean something from the get-go, not just turn loose some raw data about an unknown? I want us to understand much more about what we found and give the world something solid."

"You'll be heavily criticized if you wait," said Don. "You will appear absolutely selfish."

Jason wasn't certain he believed what he had told Don. It sounded cheap and superficial. He had exposed his fear of failure to his friends. His sense of perfection had gotten the best of him. In fact, he was confused. His success came from a natural intelligence and advice his father had provided over the years: "If you want to be financially successful, watch out for gambling (as differentiated from taking calculated risks), bad investments, bad women, and bad friends." "Learn your language skills and your numbers." "Dedicate yourself and be focused." "Hard work over time equals success." "Establish your principles and stick by them." "Try not to be angry at yourself." "Be your own best friend, not your own worst enemy."

By the time his father had finished with his occasional lecture, it sounded as though he were reading some monk's writings from ages past. Socrates might have written those words about children being unruly, unkempt, and inattentive in school. All that advice came with a price. Jason was antisocial unless he working with people in his lab. He detested public speaking. He would be hard-pressed to think of a worse torture than to stand in front of a crowd to make the announcement that they had found life elsewhere. He had stage fright as if it were a form of claustrophobia, gripping him by the throat at the moment.

Because all discoveries needed to be safeguarded, Jason resolved to hire a security company to patrol the building after dark. Did he need to remind anybody to seal the lips to seal the ship? No, they understood the stakes.

Jason abruptly abandoned his recollections. "We'll discuss it during the morning meeting," he announced, exiting the front office and leaving Don and June to stare at each other. Don put a finger to his head and turned it around and around while June nodded in agreement.

An hour later, a very tired Linda passed around the photographs she and Don had taken earlier that morning. She said, "Yep, our friend's got double-stranded DNA, like your herpes virus; possibly single-stranded in some areas, if you can believe that. It goes from one to the other. It's a freaking virus from hell. As such, there are a lot of ways it can bind with other DNA. A typical virus only needs one way. This one covers the bases while it's also contorting onto itself. Nothing we see there should work."

In a rare moment of cursing, Dustin proclaimed, "And we can't get inside of it the damn freaking thing to find out."

"Ergo, no DNA analysis," inserted a frustrated virologist.

"Linda brought up a good point," Jason admitted. "Does it bind to other DNA? I'm open to suggestions as to how we might proceed from here."

Nobody could come up with a suggestion.

8 May of Year 1

One of Jason's chemistry teachers from his high school days once gave the class an experiment in observation. He had placed a candle on the counter and lit it. Then he asked the class to describe this phenomenon without mentioning the words candle, holder, wick, and flame. At the finish of the exercise, the teacher handed out a sheet of paper to each student. The paper had a total of 43 valid observations. "If you are to be scientific detectives, you must observe and get the most out of each observation," the teacher summarized.

Jason remembered each of the 43 observations and, at the time, added a couple of his own to the list. The teacher politely smiled and complimented him, expecting no less from his top student. The teacher confessed that he purposely left those two off the list to see if anyone would notice.

Something rankled at the back of Jason's mind about the pictures Don and Linda had shown him. As he lay in bed preparing to sleep, he thought about the candles, the x-ray photographs, and bioluminescent feature of their virus. He recalled a sloppy student who was researching a fungal toxin that had fluoresced with a black light. Scanning the lab together, they found glowing splotches of toxin in various locations.

That memory woke him at 1:00 a.m. from a restless three-hour sleep. To him, tossing and turning in bed awaiting the morning made no sense when his active mind demanded coffee and activity. His baby was crying for help. He dressed without showering and took the time to brew a pot of strong caffeinated coffee and filled a large Thermos with the brew. Opening the front door, he prepared to walk the short three minute hike to the lab when a blast of unusually cold May air hit him. Turning back momentarily, he grabbed one of his warm jackets and a hat from the hall closet, then closed the door behind him.

A motion-sensing spotlight at the rear of the institute guided him up the path to the rear of the building. He unlocked the security door, feeling somewhat apprehensive. The auto-lights turned on as he walked the long hallway to enter Lab Number 1, his own. Flicking on the light switch, he deposited his coffee on the counter and reached into one of the lower cabinets for a portable battery-powered UV light. Without expectations, he turned it on and began scanning the counter surfaces.

Instantly, it all went wrong. Completely stunned, his heart missed a beat and his breathe caught. No, anything but this. In his terror he felt a cold draft followed by a hot flush at the sight of a coating of pink-to-red glow covering virtually everything the light touched. If he had possessed a stronger light, he feared the ceiling would also be pinkish.

Robotically, Jason set aside the ultraviolet lamp. From beneath another cabinet, he recovered a small air sampler. He operated the device for five minutes then pulled apart the cassette collector and held up a glass coverslip. Turning off the lights, he shined a black light on the coverslip. To his great dismay, it glowed red. He placed the coverslip on a microscope slide sticky side down, slid it underneath one of the higher magnification lenses and looked through the twin eyepieces to see the virus particles were present in all their black glory. The bastards are airborne, he thought.

Emotionally supercharged, he then sampled various surfaces using fresh cassettes as miniature vacuum cleaners, sweeping them across the countertops and sides of the cabinets and even the glassware. The particles were everywhere. The little Martians owned the building. Jason flopped down in disbelief. The cold sweats returned.

Another thought hit him. With single minded purpose, he got up and loaded a fresh cassette onto the hose, started the pump and ran the cassette over the skin of his arms and face for a total of ten seconds. Thirty seconds later he reluctantly looked at the sample, knowing what he would find and confirmed his suspicion. He was covered with the foreign particles. "What the fuck. They're everywhere!" he muttered out loud.

Jason found himself in an unusual situation, confused and at a total loss of what to do. He checked the clock on the wall. It read 2:15. He had to tell somebody. Linda awakened quickly when he explained the circumstances and she arrived within a half-hour. He showed her all four labs. The surfaces faintly glowed the air rife with little fibers.

"Can we clean it up?" she asked, stunned at the news.

Jason shook his head slowly. "With what? Bleach, degreaser, acetone?" They pulled out everything from under the sinks and tried one after another. The glow diminished somewhat with bleach.

"You better run surface tests again," Linda said, assertively, "Maybe we were removing the glow and not the fibers."

"Good idea," he said, and retested. She was right. The particles still remained on the surfaces. At that point he reluctantly told her about the skin tests results.

"Dear Lord," Linda muttered, fear striking her heart, "Jace, if it's on us and in the air, then it's probably inside of us, too."

Jason had considered the respiratory aspect, but didn't want to broach the topic until Linda's mention of it. He was unaccustomed to the sinking feeling of woe that started in his brain and quickly ran down through his guts giving him the worst kind of feeling one gets. The feeling that occurs when, suddenly distracted, a person accidentally cuts off a hand with a table saw; or worse, steps on a land mine and can't step off; or finding out they have a month to live. It was the terrible feeling of there being absolutely no way to go. What was done was done.

"You checked the labs and they're all bad, so let's check the hallway and the front office," Linda suggested, a tremor in her voice. She turned out the lights to the building from the central control panel in the hallway outside Jason's lab. Hunched over, he shined the light on the floor where sets of luminescent footprints were amply displayed, despite the cleaning crew's regular efforts to maintain spotless floors. Following him, Linda saw footprints leading outdoors to her car.

Once they reached her BMW, he shined the black light inside it. Portions of the interior emanated with their soft red light. The steering wheel and the floor were the worst areas. It was impossible to miss. Her conclusion matched his: fibers were on the hands, bottoms of the shoes, bare skin, and clothing.

"We're going to my house," she declared, tossing

the light onto the passenger seat.

"All right. Let's lock up," he stated, scared witless. "Give me a ride back to my house so I can get my car."

From their perspective, surgical room HEPA filtration wouldn't have helped. Even at 99.97 percent efficiency down to 0.3 microns wouldn't do a thing, even if the room was critically contained in a Class 4 facility, which is not what they had.

Jason's confidence had evaporated. He did not feel comfortable with himself. This was a new place for him outside his boundaries, a portion of his life out of control with absolutely no clue as to how to proceed. Chalk it up to pressure. It's darkest before the dawn, isn't it? No panic permitted. All problems have a solution. You just have to find it.

This is what he always told his students the first day of class and added that certain solutions may be a challenge to their intellect, counter-intuitive, and perhaps not to their liking. But what do you do when there is no solution to be found? You can't put your hand back on.

Jason followed Linda's car to her two-bedroom town home, a 15-minute drive east in the direction of Don and June's residence. He pulled next to her in the drive. Linda grabbed the light and hurried to her front door, not waiting for him. She left the lights off in the house and slowly scanned around her. She found faint glows where shoes had tread. She found the same to be true of her bedding, in the bathroom, on her cosmetics, and clothing in her closet.

She cried, "Jace, how did it get loose?" Tears began to form.

"I don't know, baby, maybe it follows its own rules," Jason answered, skirting the question.

NASA and everybody else who had access to it dug into the meteorite and nothing happened. Therefore, it got loose when I opened the flask. But I flamed the opening as per absolutely accepted procedure.

Jason's vague statement about the virus following its own rules did nothing to reassure her. "I know that much," she snapped. "I also know my fucking house has been invaded by an alien, and it probably invaded you and me and everybody else in the lab. Maybe it's cancer-causing."

Jason visualized headlines in the sky. They weren't the fun type Don had made up reading only months before. Jason viewed the headlines to denote a class of stories he referred to as 3-D: demean, debase, and destroy.

"If you want to be objective, it's not the whole house, baby," he retorted, cutely. "The only glowing parts are portions of the floor, the TV remote, the sofas, kitchen counters, bedding and your clothes. The ceilings aren't bad and, hey, look, the toilet seat in the hall bath appears to be affected only slightly."

Instantly, after having said those joyless words, he wondered if Linda's gun was under lock and key. Then he remembered she kept her .38 Police Special snub-nose revolver in her purse. It was hammerless to prevent it from snagging on anything when she pulled it out. She preferred to keep the next chamber in rotation empty. If she accidentally pulled the trigger while removing the weapon, it would click on an empty chamber, but the second through the fifth rounds of hollow-points would work just fine. He ought to know. He'd bought it for her and taught her how to use it.

"Stand still," he demanded. He shined the UV light over her, then over himself. Portions of their clothing glowed and so did parts of their naked skin; what could be seen of it with their clothes on. Turning on the room lights he directed, "Take off your clothes," and followed suit, leading her over to the clothes washer set back in a nook in the hallway. Its dryer mate stood next to it, watching, waiting for its turn to power up.

Each threw their clothes into the machine. Jason tossed in an excessive amount of bleach powder and detergent and switched on the machine, not concerned about the temperature setting, considering it to be irrelevant.

"You're going to wash that into the sewer system?" she asked, almost accusatory.

Jason shook his head sadly, "Do you really think it matters at this point? It's everywhere in the lab. It's on us, in the air, and in us. Our homes are contaminated. Our footprints glow and so does everything we touch. With everybody coming and going, we open the doors to the building how many times a day? And OSHA says that an industrial setting must supply a lot of fresh air to employees which means stale air must be exhausted—you know, the same air with the virus in it. Do you really think it matters?" he repeated, completely frustrated and frightened enough to the point of nausea.

Linda's head swung downward and her shoulders slumped in a momentary posture of defeat. In her parlance, he was spot on. Where was the end point? It didn't take a scientist to see a careening vehicle out of control.

Scanning every inch of their naked bodies with the black light, the red blotches became clearly apparently in some areas and randomly located elsewhere. Both surmised that those were the areas normally touched or scratched. If the fibers were toxic to any extent, the entire team could be in serious trouble. Even a bite from a rattlesnake, brown recluse, or black widow could be treated with anti-venin. Not so here. If toxicity were present, it would likely be associated with the chemical causing the glow. Maybe that part was all right. There was no skin irritation, no hives or rashes.

"Let's get into the shower," he directed, coughing, to which Linda conjectured, "I took a shower this morning, so this must have either been on me from before and it didn't wash off, or it accumulated today after the shower."

"One or the other," he responded. Or both, he thought.

They gave themselves and each other a good scrubbing until their skin was pink from rubbing and the glow had diminished significantly, probably because the outer layer of skin cells had been removed. Jason knew better than to try and assuage Linda's feelings. She might want to pin her grief on him. Both of them felt self-revulsion, insecurity, desperation, and a need to survive. There weren't a lot of positives to build on.

"Why don't you get dressed," he suggested. "When the clothes are finished, throw them in the dryer. Right now, I'll borrow one of your robes and go home. Neither of us is going to sleep much tonight. After I change and think, we'll meet at our diner for breakfast at 8:00."

Linda told him, adamantly, "Oh, no. I'm going with you. I'll throw the clothes in the dryer later."

Jason reluctantly nodded in understanding. She needed company. He wanted to be alone. He acceded to her wishes. "As soon as I get to the office, we'll have everyone start cleanup. What we really need to do is to flood the place with fresh air."

She answered, "If we did that we would be accused of malice aforethought while we let loose the creature from outer space."

"Yes, my dear, and that might be a proper accusation. Guess what. It's already out there. We'll do it anyway."

After a quiet breakfast, each submerged in their own thoughts, the couple returned to the building. Once inside, Jason walked over to the system control located on the wall in the hallway and turned off the heaters. He adjusted the settings to bring in more fresh air and to exhaust as much stale air as possible.

Still in May, five months after Jason had cultured the meteorite dust the previous November, the mainstream news featured the spread of a new strain of cold virus and the abnormal birth of animals. All of these events were occurring on a more regular basis among other household pets, including guinea pigs, gerbils, ferrets, snakes, lizards, chickens, parakeets, canaries, parrots, and tropical fish. The occurrences were concentrated in the cities the researchers had visited during their vacations. The curious coincidences did not escape the attention of Jason's team. They began to suspect that the impossible was happening.

To Jason, there was no going back, no way to reset, to return to default and start over. He had committed them all to do what? To find out why they were all sick? To find out why everything they touched glowed? To find out why the outer shell of this space virus is not made of protein like any other normal virus on the planet? Most importantly, as a remote possibility, were they connected in any way with what was happening with the abnormal births? If so, were abnormal human births next on the list?

For three weeks, all work remained in limbo. The four labs within RCR, the office, break room, bathrooms, everything, was bleached and the building was continually flooded with fresh air to keep it from smelling like an over-chlorinated indoor swimming pool. From a scientific standpoint, it was the definition of putting lipstick on a pig. From a common sense perspective, one might argue they were promoting reckless endangerment of the public at large. There were no alternatives.

Jason felt terrible about getting in deeper. It went against every principle he believed in. He felt himself the coward, a purveyor of dishonesty which infected all those around him. He should have farmed out the virus as Don had suggested. Never having been forced to question his own character before, his sense of security or his own morality, he had betrayed himself, painted himself into a corner and it ate at him like a deep and spreading cancer; one for which there may not be a cure.

Somewhere in this jumble of events, Jason considered making Don an offer to join him full time, not in the capacity of a geologist—this was a genetics facility—but as a trusted friend who could help in data assessment and be of value using advanced microscopy. Jason desperately needed help and Don seemed to be the perfect logical choice. June was already onboard and Don was at the institute so many hours each week he might as well be hired. If Don quit the university, it would also save him those back and forth hour-long trips to Omaha. He'd think about it a little more before making an offer.

The time had come for animal studies to find out if this virus was the cause of the cough or the abnormal births. In his best scientific manner, he was going to prove that it didn't have anything to do with either of them. Both were long shots and Jason felt confident a series of coincidental events was taking place. Hell, man, didn't numerous reports point to a single mistake in Wuhan, China, that set loose Covid-19? Coincidences aside, in all likelihood, this current epidemic might be another Chinese virus, one of many the world had endured over the past century. While they were at it, they might also take a look at their own DNA with the electron microscope, just to show the harmlessness of his little glow fibers.

Animal studies would require the purchase of 100 six-week-old mice weighing about 40 grams each, all of the same sex. They would also require enough labeled cages to segregate the animals, 10 mice in each. One 10-mouse group would serve as the controls and would receive natural mouse food pellets containing contain fruits, vegetables, vitamins and minerals. The other groups would fed the same food with differing concentrations of the virus added to it.

Jason had to plan carefully for separate generational studies. A female mouse can produce a lot of babies in a year, so one small litter of about half-dozen pups would be fine. For their research, they would use one male and one female per cage in a separate investigation.

Normally, the study of offspring is not included in initial experiments. A month later, he decided to have two control groups for observation and separately cage them in his personal lab. One would have ten mice, all the same sex. The second cage would house a single male and female. Both groups would be fed natural untreated mouse food.

Over the next two weeks of observation, none of the original mice appeared to show any obvious change after eating the virus-laden food, although their wheel-running appeared to be faster. This was difficult to measure, as rate-of-wheel-revolution tests is not a normal part of a research plan. Should they choose to measure their rate of rotation, wheel-o-meters were available for purchase,

After extracting samples of DNA from saliva and skin cells of the mice, the researchers found there were two-to-three times as many base pairs as normal in every sample. Their DNA physically much larger than it should be, including the untreated controls.

The mice still appeared healthy, and encouraging observation, until the first litters were born in late June after the 20-day gestation period and the researchers' hearts sank. Offspring were found to have deformations in their legs and faces. Every mouse born downstairs was affected, including those born to the untreated controls. Their weight remained within normal parameters. The implications were horrific. The deformities matched those reported from Omaha and the other cities they had visited while on vacation. Was it all due to their virus, or had their mice contracted what the other animals outside the lab had contracted? That must be the case, Jason believed. Linda carefully picked up one of the babies and declared, "Their faces aren't symmetrical. The mouth, nose and ears aren't quite centered, the upper legs slightly thicker. Are the shoulders rounded more?"

They obtained one type of standard puzzle-learning aptitude test to challenge the original parents of the newborn mice. A variety of tests were utilized, such as progressively difficult mazes that encouraged mice to obtain food at the other end, or learning to press a sequence of levers to obtain a reward. Not only were the mice faster to learn on the first try than the reported norm in all the tests, but much faster on the second; more so on the third—well beyond expectations. Their short-term memory had been enhanced. As the baby mice matured over the next three weeks, their scores were compared with those of their parents and were superior to them in all regards.

The sight of the malformed pups was frightening, especially because the offspring belonging to the untreated controls looked and reacted similarly to the others. Although they had not eaten food laced with the fibers, they were just as smart. Thus, the food had not caused the malformations. There weren't too many other possibilities.

At home, Jason began to consolidate the copious notes from the ongoing animal experiments when his cell phone rang. Linda called to say she had forgotten her phone at the lab. While there she took a quick look at the mice in his lab. "That's nice. And how are the little dears," he inquired, fearing the worst.

Linda had a pleading note to her voice. "Honey,

please come down here. They've got a new litter."

The only thing better than working out of one's home is having their business situated within walking distance. Five minutes later the couple stared. The cage with ten of the same sex mice appeared to be somewhat shorter limbed and hunched, matching the control parents downstairs, while the new litter in the cage with the single male and single female possessed the same symptoms along with deformed faces.

"The food is clean," he stammered. "How. . ."

"Admit it, Jace. It's the building, not the food."

"We cleaned the building," he complained.

"Check it again," she demanded. This time she gave an order.

Jason pulled out the black light and turned off the room lights. The pink-red glow had returned to cover every surface, this time more than before. The glow was redder and on more surfaces. He turned off the black light and the two stood there in the dark, like horses facing each other with their heads touching.

She put her arm in his and held his hand while she threw another hardball at him. "There's something else, Jace. Honey, I'm pregnant."

Jason froze in place for an instant and smiled as widely as he could, forgetting about the mice. He wrapped his arms around her and said, "That is simply fantastic, babe. I'm overjoyed and I know our parents will be, too."

His mind raced. It didn't matter whether the baby was planned or not. At the least his parents would get off his back about continuing the Randolph lineage. Whether a boy or a girl, he would name the baby Chris or Kris, as the case may be. He had always been enamored with the stories about the first settlers in America. To him, the name was exciting, after his childhood hero, Christopher Newport, a British adventurer—a government-sanctioned pirate and privateer. He captained the Discovery, one of the three ships that came to Virginia along with the Godspeed and the Susan Constant. Newport had returned to England and came back to Virginia in 1610 on the New Venture after having been shipwrecked, and helped found the new colony.

Jason was about to tell her about the name he had long thought about when she pulled away and said, "I don't want it, Jace."

He shook his head not understanding.

"I don't want a mutant baby," she declared.

He stammered. "What are you going to do? What are we going to do? How do you know it will be a mu....abnormal? We don't know. I mean, it's too early to tell. It will be another five months before we even know the sex so you can't..." He was rambling and couldn't stop himself.

Linda interrupted. "What I can't do is have a deformed baby looking like those mice, Jace." she began to cry. "I'm going to take care of things. Don't worry," she said, despondently.

He turned on the lights again and paced, trying to evade the topic of losing a baby. "Let me think. The virus particles are probably entering through the lungs because the lungs are rich in carbon dioxide, the primary gas on Mars. That's why every one of the untreated controls is also affected. We know it's in the air. That's one common denominator. We exhale more than 100 times the amount of carbon dioxide than we inhale which would serve as an attractant for the creature. Hell, we. . . I did it all. Don't you understand? I let it go."

Linda followed his lead, trying to get her mind off her own problems. "That's why you got the bubbles in your original flask of liquid culture. When you acidified the solution, the carbonates provided carbon dioxide. The carbon dioxide triggered its release when you pulled the stopper."

Jason spoke as though he were an actor in a cheap melodrama. "Yes, that damnable single act took only an instant to bring to life some microbial thing that had been dormant for maybe tens of millions of years."

Another terrible fear ran through him. He flushed. He needed to grab Linda and run away as fast and as far as they could from the pursuing monster, not in their dreams, but in real life. His mind spun off into the worst possible scenarios straight out of Edgar Allan Poe. There could be no good end to this.

"Wait a minute." An appealing thought came to him. "We may be out of the woods. Maybe it is the food. We must have been shipped a bad batch," he theorized, almost convincing himself, ranting. "It wouldn't be the first time."

"Did you change suppliers?" she asked, doubt

clear in her voice, weak with fear.

"No, but it wouldn't make any difference. They all have to get their raw materials from somewhere," he replied truthfully. "Mouse food is made with different grains and grasses for good nutrition, including wheat, barley, oats and hazelnut. Some suppliers also add soy and GMO corn. All you need is for one of the grains to sit in a damp storage area to have been contaminated with fungal toxin or a pesticide or both and you've got your mutations. That would explain it all."

"Except for the fluorescence everywhere and the abnormal births in a half-dozen cities we know of so far," she added, dryly.

Jason stopped his theorizing and went back to her. "How long?" he asked, stroking her cheek.

"Pretty close to a month," she confessed, through her tears.

"We'll talk," was all he could offer.

"I don't want to talk about it. I've pretty much made up my mind," she declared stoically. "I'm going home to sleep. Tomorrow morning I'll work with Don in x-ray again and see if I can find out more, just to be sure."

Jason needed a break. Dustin had been after Jason to play one-on-one basketball with him during lunch across the street at the park so the next day Jason took him up on his offer. An hour later he returned thoroughly defeated. His opponent knew how to play. His defense was impenetrable and he revealed he had played ball in high school. A fleeting idea came to Jason during the game. He gave chase trying to grab onto it, but the idea outran his efforts.

1 June of Year 1

Jason had a bad night. He tossed and turned, paced, read, drank water, peed, and took aspirin. He did everything except what he needed to do. In the early morning hours he lapsed into a half-sleep when an idea about the virus formed and dissipated; base-pairs within genes interchanged like partners in a do-si-do square dance. There were images of a parade of animals with distorted faces and of a virus that locked onto its secrets tighter than weapons in a gun vault.

Finally, after the longest night of his life, he showered, still reeling from the dream. He really needed to take the morning off and shoot at things. At the moment, he'd settle for tin cans. His back yard had enough space for short range shooting fun, but the city might have other ideas about gunfire within the city limits. With no real appetite, he settled for hot coffee and a warm English muffin spread with peanut butter to hold him until lunch.

The dream faded, the sense of loneliness remained. The idea he'd had while playing basketball returned. The more he thought about it the more he liked it. He needed to talk to somebody trustworthy who wasn't local, a person who didn't have a stake in the game. Asking a lot of questions in his department at the university would not be wise. People get together during cocktail hour and trade gossip.

The one name that came to mind was that of Jeffrey Shenero, a full professor at the University of Oklahoma in Norman. The man had a national reputation for busting up a couple of terrorist plots. If he remembered right, terrorists had added aflatoxin, the deadly poison made by molds, to the ink of newspapers to infect readers who touched the ink. Shenero also caught the gang trying to use the same toxin to poison the air in a big arena in Phoenix. He saved thousands of lives.

Googling Shenero's name, Jason pulled up a picture on his phone. Yep, that was him with a shaved head and a scar in the forehead. What else? He read on. The mold toxin/antibiotic expert was universally described as being impulsive but brilliant. Reportedly, he had acquired the scar from a stalactite that had gouged him during a caving escapade in Palau while looking for psilocybin-infused mushrooms. Another story about him told he had been sued by a wacko lady because he didn't find mold in her house when she claimed there was—she could feel it. And the lady's son had sore knees from the mold, and her husband...well, that was another story. You don't easily forget a character like Jeff Shenero, unless you want to.

Jason contemplated about what he would tell Shenero and what he shouldn't tell him. Why call at all? He was calling because his team had discovered an unidentified contaminant. They wanted to grow up a large amount of it to see if it produced any byproducts that would be effective against certain cancer cells. Yes, Shenero would identify with that because that was what the man did. He would not tell him anything about its genetics because they didn't know a damn thing about them except to say its DNA may be binding with human and animal DNA. He wasn't going to go there. Aside from the one class in microbiology way back when, he would have to confess to his own ignorance in the field, an easy confession to make. It was another subdivision of a subdivision. You can't be an expert in everything.

After breakfast, Jason waved a quick hello to June and headed straight to his lab where he made the call to Shenero's department at the University of Oklahoma. He discovered the man also had a research institute similar to his own. He tried the university number first. The departmental secretary took the call, and explained, "Sir, Doctor Shenero has irregular business hours. You might want to call him at his research facility. Would you like that number?"

"Yes, please." The number the secretary gave him matched the one he had gotten from the Internet. He went online and saw seats were still available for the next United Airlines flight down to Oklahoma City. Then he called Jeffrey Shenero.

A woman answered. "Shenero Institute for Medical Research." She possessed a slight Spanish accent and, coughing, transferred the call. The hour was 8:35 a.m., the same time as in Norman.

"Shenero here," came a response. He, too, had a slight cough, almost a clearing of the throat.

"Doctor Shenero, this is Jason Randolph. I'm with Randolph Cancer Research in Lincoln, Nebraska. I wonder if you have a few minutes to talk."

"Of course," Shenero offered. "How can I help you, and, by the way, you can call me Jeff."

Jason noted the man's sense of humility despite having been awarded the Medal of Freedom by the President in a big ceremony—that and many more awards. In appreciation, the government had also given him acres of land and had built his research center to Shenero's specifications in the heart of the multi-acre tract of land they gave him. Then he thought about commuter flights from Lincoln or Omaha traveling to Norman—flights that must have brought along people with the disease months before, like spokes radiating from a wheel with Lincoln at the hub.

"Jeff, I'd like to personally consult with you. I need some guidance regarding how to grow a microbial life form in a large amount."

"Certainly. We do that quite frequently," Shenero replied, carefully. "I know you have people up there who do the same thing. Save yourself a trip."

That caught Jason short. "I can tell you about it when and if you consent to meet with me. I don't see this as a topic for discussion over the phone," he stated.

"Of course. I'm always ready to meet with a real scientist as opposed to a real charlatan. Goodness knows, there are plenty of those around. When do you suggest we meet?" Shenero asked.

Jason pushed it and said, "Today at 12:30?" He heard some rustling of papers on the other end of the line.

"Can you make it at 1:00?" returned the mold expert.

"I'll GPS your facility and see you at 1:00. Thank you."

"See you then, Jason." Shenero hung up.

Jason reflected about the conversation for a moment. Shenero was cordial with reservations, sharp with suspicions. Why shouldn't he have suspicions? Large fermenters is what the terrorists had used to grow their poison.

Once he landed in Oklahoma City, he could rent a car, drive to the college town in 30 minutes, and return to Lincoln by that evening. Having presented a paper there a few years before, he could vividly visualize the community with its population of less than half that of Lincoln.

Jason caught the 10:00 a.m. flight and arrived at Will Rogers International Airport in Oklahoma City at 10:50 a.m. Straight shot. A little over 400 miles in less time that it would take him to drive from his home to the farther reaches of Omaha. One briefcase. No baggage. Return flight open. No doubt he would be on the radar as a person of interest with no baggage and an open return ticket.

He flew first class, his normal habit. The flight was easy, no thunderstorms or heat waves to bounce the plane, no drunks. During the flight he contemplated. If he had everything to lose, what strategy might he present to a man who had nothing to lose? Play it conservative and innocent.

Their personalities were almost polar opposites in many ways. While both men boasted independence and could take care of themselves, Jason tended toward self-deprecation as a defense mechanism, withdrawing under pressure. Shenero seemingly headed toward conflict; he possessed self-confidence to an extreme level, possibly with a touch of narcissism; but not so much that he wouldn't take suggestions and consider options. While Jason could readily forgive, Shenero would carry a grudge. No, it's best to be honest with this man. Like many virtues, honesty does have its limitations. If patience can have a time limit, does honesty mean one has to reveal one's motives?

Jason deplaned and followed the signs to the car rentals where he obtained a black Chevy Malibu. Arriving in Norman by noon, he had enough time to stop at a diner on Campus Corner north of the university where he had eaten on a previous visit. He ordered a BLT sandwich and a glass of orange juice. At 12:40 he left the diner and let the GPS guide him to Shenero's building.

Although the building was larger than his own, its appearance suggested a similar mindset. Jason's had been built with his own money and Shenero's with government money, but apparently under the scientist's guidance. Both buildings possessed a brick face with iron, roll-down shutters. In terms of naming their business, both scientists had named themselves as the first word in the title. Shenero's business was situated in a forested area, but Jason had built his in the city proper, albeit across from a large lake. Apparently, Shenero employed a lot of people. The parking lot held a dozen cars with another half-dozen open slots. His own held half that number. Most of the cars in the lot appeared to be fairly new.

A tall, leggy and attractive Hispanic woman with long black ringlets greeted Jason. She wore a blue shift accented with a Navaho Concho belt studded with turquoise. She introduced herself as Carmen, Dr. Shenero's office manager. On the wall behind her hung a Doctor of Medicine degree in her name from the Univesidad de Guadalajara, Mexico. Checking her appointment book, she made a quick call. Impressed by the quality of Shenero's staff at this point in the game, he followed Carmen to a private office, whereupon she departed.

The large office measured twelve-by-twelve with a sofa long enough for napping, a desk, small white fridge, computer monitor, three office chairs, copier, and printer. A window opened to the west to reveal trees and sky, similar to the view Jason enjoyed from his living room. Jeffrey Shenero saw him and held up a hand to both halt his visitor and waive hello as he closed out whatever he had on the monitor screen.

Jason observed a very fit looking man nearly his height, well-muscled, somewhat odd in appearance, with a shaved head and the deep scar over his left eye, as the on-line photo had depicted. While Shenero wore a gray pullover under a lab coat, Jason wore a dark blue pullover. Both men wore khaki slacks.

The scientist stood from his desk to shake hands and Jason took a seat at the motion of the microbiologist. Above the desk were a number of technical books. Wedged between the massive tomes was a hard cover book titled Arrowsmith by Sinclair Lewis, the same novel he had read over and over, along with the Microbe Hunters by Paul de Kruif. Those two books had inspired him to follow his beloved career path as a pure researcher when he could have easily become a medical doctor.

"I like a punctual man," stated the microbiologist.

"Jeff, I'll get to the point," Jason offered. He related the story about the discovery of the virus, how they did it on a whim. He left out any suggestion that the virus might have anything to do with colds or mutant animals. He also left out any suggestion the armored virus might be turned into products, a flagrant idea that had come to him in his half-sleep triggered by a concept he'd had during the basketball game. He needed to go on the offensive.

The product aspect had nothing to do with money. It was an effort to make things better; no, to make them right. He desperately needed to find out more about what made this thing tick. It would be nice to find a cure for his mice. If that worked, it might also work on the progeny of infected dogs and cats.

It might also help get rid this contaminant that had taken over his facility, at least two of their homes and cars, and had settled on their skin and in their saliva—facts he failed to relate to anybody else at RCR, and not without guilt.

Jason opened the briefcase and pulled out photographs of the virus. He handed them to Shenero who examined them and commented, "You told me on the phone you wanted to grow a large quantity of this. That's not an unusual procedure when you want to study its metabolism via its growth byproducts. We do that all the time with unknown molds I find in the jungles of Asia and elsewhere. "It is a virus, right?" Shenero had guessed his motive in a roundabout way.

"Or so it seems. It is able to self-replicate," replied Jason.

"That's odd. What can you tell me about how it does that?"

"We don't have a clue, except that it divides lengthwise," Jason admitted. He knew he was being evaluated for the accuracy of that statement.

"That's very odd," Shenero replied and remained quiet for a long moment. "Are you familiar with industrial fermenters?"

"Fermenters in a general sense, yes," Jason gave a quick shrug.

"They're large machines, vats, if you will. The brewing industry uses them to make alcohol. We use them to grow mold and bacteria for mycotoxin and antibiotic production. Let me show you one and see if it's what you have in mind."

He led Jason down a lengthy hallway. On the way they passed one lab where two men were operating a reflux condenser, as though they were distilling alcohol. "They're concentrating fungal toxin. Once it's purified, we combine it with antibiotics to get a greatly enhanced effect," Jason's host commented.

A number of questions flooded Jason's mind about what Shenero had just said, but he would save those for another day, if that day should come. Three more labs contained one or two white-coated researchers each, taking notes, injecting fluids into machines for analysis, cleaning glassware and counters.

They reached a room with a humming machine measuring six-feet deep by eight-feet long by seven-feet in height. Jason noticed a catwalk in the front upon which an operator might stand to use various switches; ostensibly to control temperature and other variables of the liquid contents within a bell housing. This was a heavy metal 20-gallon container hoisted by a hand-operated forklift and bolted in place.

Shenero smiled. "I like to call this my space-time machine because of its appearance." He stepped onto the catwalk and explained as he demonstrated. "You turn on the power. Triple distilled water flows into the tank while your workers weigh out the exact proportions of ingredients needed for a 20-gallon volume. You add the ingredients, sterilize it, let it cool, and set the thermostat. After it reaches the set temperature, you add your microbes and check it periodically by drawing off samples."

Jason stared in awe at the huge device, definitely larger than he expected.

Smiling, Shenero confessed, "I must admit this one is a dinosaur. We're planning to get rid of it and install two new models with twice the volume for a fourth the cost. Technology and all that. We don't use them very often, but when we do, we need something reliable. We haven't quite decided yet which ones to buy. Working with this one is like the working with the first phones or cars or planes compared with what's out there today. If you'd like, I can show you a catalog that describes fermenters that can hold anywhere from five gallons to 1000 gallons. Some are even made in China. Can you believe that?"

Shenero stepped off the catwalk and continued speaking, "

Let's look at some pictures of what we're thinking of ordering. The newer ones are a lot easier to work with and stand at ground level; none of this catwalk business."

Shenero grinned, "You can be the guinea pig. Try one and let me know how it works. If it doesn't, I'll buy something different."

Jason had to ask, "What are you going to do with the old one?"

Shenero shrugged. "Probably part it out. For the cost of moving and reinstalling it, you can buy two or three new ones."

"Probably won't last as long as the old one," Jason offered.

"Definitely won't. Throw-away types anymore," Shenero admitted. "In any case, depending on your needs, you can expect to get several pounds of microbes. That's for bacteria and yeast. I don't know anything about what you're trying to grow. Viruses aren't my area. We use ultra-sound on ours to bust open the cells or the mold mycelium. Sonication causes them to release a lot more of the antibiotic or toxin we're looking for."

"Doesn't it excrete those byproducts into the liquid growth medium as its growing?" Jason asked, probing, thinking about red luminescence.

"Correct. Using ultrasound gives us a much richer yield."

"I definitely would like to see the catalog," Jason said, beginning to get excited.

Shenero paused and queried, "By the way, you are familiar with microbial growth cycles are you not?"

"Only in the general sense," Jason answered, sheepishly, "I'm a molecular kind of guy."

"Then let me give you some basics." Shenero explained the fundamental principles related to growing and harvesting microbes in a vat, or the behavior of any species of life in nature.

As the scientists exited the room, Shenero noted, "You will need a serious centrifuge to spin out the particles, of course."

"Understood," replied Jason, not at all understanding.

"Wait a minute." Shenero halted for a moment. "I'm thinking old school. There's a new combination unit that people swear by. It's about the size you'll want. You grow your microbes in the centrifuge itself. It's like a washing machine tub with a spinner, thermostat, oxygenator, sampling port. It's the whole shootin' match under one roof. When you're ready to harvest, you begin the spin cycle. When it reaches sufficient speed you open the drain to allow the liquid to escape. All you have to do is to remove your mash, which is stuck to the walls. Then you clean and sterilize, ready for the next run."

Once the men reached the office, Shenero pulled out thick catalogs and the men perused them for several minutes, paying special attention to the combination unit. Jason took notes and prepared to leave.

"Here, take these with you, Jason." Shenero held out one of the books.

"Are you sure?"

"Of course. I've got too many. They load up my mailbox quarterly." Then he added, "You'll have to invite me up there sometime to see your place."

That was the last thing Jason wanted. He deflected the question. "Okay," he replied simply. Then, "What projects are you working on?"

"Right now we're wrapping up a big one on a damn good antifungal agent. We took one of the common anti-fungals on the market and combined it with a low dose of fungal toxin from a black mold. We're getting tremendous synergistic activity, at least in animals. The enhanced multiplier effect is working against Valley Fever, histoplasmosis, farmer's lung, and several other diseases caused by a variety of mold species; some are quite exotic. We're going to human trials within a couple of months. By the way, do you fish?" Shenero quickly added.

"Do I fish?" Jason repeated, trying to grasp how that fit into their conversation. Could it be a trick question? Was this a lie-detector test where they set you up by asking you to give your address and phone number and then hit you with, "Did you murder that man?"

"It's called a question out of context. So, what's the answer?" Shenero asked.

"Yes, I know a few things about fishing. Why?" Jason replied, looking suspiciously at the other man.

Shenero stood and took off his lab coat. He hung it on a clothes rack and said, "I need to get out for a while. There's a lake not far from here where I go when I can, but I really don't know much about what I'm doing. Do you want to join me and give me a few pointers?"

Jason wanted to run back home. He had catalogs to peruse, a business to run. He mentally slapped himself. Don't second guess. If you look a gift horse in the mouth, you could soon be looking at the other end, if not become the other end. There could be worse things than teaching a man how to fish, as long as you weren't the bait.

Jason admitted, "I'm not really dressed for it. Otherwise I'd love to," trying to get over the no-time-for-enjoyment-syndrome. He added, "You must have known I like to spend time outdoors."

Shenero grinned. "I presume you researched me before calling. Background checks can go two ways." Without waiting for an answer, he looked over his guest and commented, "We're similar in size. Hang on." He went to a closet Jason hadn't noticed and found two pair of jeans along with two clean tee-shirts and tossed a set to Jason. "Here, try these on. Can't do much for the shoes. Doesn't matter. Where we'll be we can take off our shoes and socks."

As though they were old friends in a locker room, the men changed clothes in the office. "Tell you what," Jason offered, now feeling looser than he had felt in a long time. "If you're a good student, I'll give you my autograph."

"That's generous. And if I'm not?"

"Then I'll give you two them," Jason gibed.

The two men laughed and bonded and headed out to Lake Thunderbird. Shenero picked up a cold six-pack of beer along the way and put it in the plug-in ice chest he carried with him in the trunk of his car.

Poles in hand, their discussions alternated between the capabilities of different species of fish to smell and see bait, to combination drug therapy, to what the hell was somebody as beautiful as Carmen doing around a guy like Jeff.

Jason caught the last flight to Lincoln at 8:00 p.m. He held a briefcase containing photographs of a virus from outer space, two catalogs with dog-eared pages, and the memory of a man who may have given him a new life. His mind was awash in ideas— virtually an endless array of products that could be made from an invincible microbe: long-lasting clothing and shoes, lightweight aircraft, spacecraft, reentry heat shields, buildings, bulletproof vests, thousands of applications.

The next morning Jason sat in his desk chair reading a scientific paper on-line relating to the rampant spread of the two new diseases. The first, dubbed the New Flu by the article's author, was characterized by ongoing cold-like symptoms similar to those encountered by Jason's team. The second disease involved abnormal births appearing in numerous cities. Curiously, those births followed the onset of the New Flu into each community. Experts believed the two diseases were linked in some manner.

Don walked in and Jason left nothing out as he related to him the horrific discovery about the mice, including his conversation with Linda the night before he left for Norman. Don looked over at the cage of controls and, bending over for a closer look, shook his head back and forth several times. After a moment's pause, he turned back to Jason and said, "Man, it hurts to tell you. We ran samples of DNA from the adult mice and their offspring. We sampled my own skin and Linda's. The DNA from our virus is binding with the DNA in absolutely everything we checked. Linda left after she found that out. She said she'd call you today. She wanted to take another look at the mice first and said she'd stop by about six or seven this morning and check on them. Guess she didn't stick around."

Now another round of guilt overtook Jason's fear. Why hadn't he dumped the samples down the drain when he first thought about doing it? The answer was that he would have had to open the flask in order to empty the contents, so nothing would have changed. If he had run up the flask in the autoclave first in an attempt to kill whatever was growing in it before dumping it, nothing would have changed because steam heat wouldn't have done a thing to hurt it. Furthermore, if he had tossed the sample before looking at it, they would have no idea at all what they were dealing with. Now they did. In the grand scheme of things, did it matter what they knew? After a slight cough, he managed to say, "Hold on, Don. If the DNA is binding with our DNA, why aren't we changing?"

Don had a smile on his face, but his eyes were sad. "The day is still young, my friend."

Jason thought hard. "Well, there are a couple of things we can do. First, this binding business is our secret within these walls. Only our people know. Second, we have to see if we can make this work for us."

"How do we do that?" Don asked.

"This idea came to me a couple of nights ago. We grow a super batch of virus. If this sucker is as tough as it appears to be, maybe we can make something useful out of it. And, we must continue with the animal studies."

"Useful? Like what?" Don prodded.

Jason began to jabber. "If this virus can self-replicate and had gone through all that June had alluded to, I'm set to buy an industrial fermenter to grow a large batch of it. We don't know for certain if it got loose. Colds are common. Maybe it's a new strain of virus that's going around."

He stopped speaking as he realized the truth of his last statement.

"Did you check the air in Linda's home or your own?" Don inquired.

"Well, we were checking the glow," Jason said sheepishly. "Besides, I didn't have the pump with me."

"I agree. Colds are common," Don declared facetiously. "Mutations are also common in a hundred percent of new babies and everybody's steering wheel and footprints always fluoresced red in the dark. None of that ever happened until that night when we took samples from the flask. Why didn't I think of that?"

"All right, you don't have be sarcastic," Jason shot.

"Hey, I'm not a dog you can yell at. I'm your friend," Don shot back.

Jason backed off without apologizing, frustrated that Don viewed the issue in a more balanced approach than he did. "All I'm saying is that it may self-cure. Besides, what good will it do to tell the world this life form we discovered is spreading out of control? Do you have any idea what kind of panic it would cause? It's not our fault," he summarized, childishly, voicing words opposite of what he felt, as if claiming or disclaiming fault would change an outcome. For a moment he felt as if truth belonged to the person who could win an argument when real truth watched and laughed.

He wanted to make products. Forget the fact that every product would be made from a space virus that turned newborn mice and domestic animals into something not quite right and scared women enough to consider aborting their baby.

The morning meeting was somber without Linda. Had he been too cold to her? Was she angry at him? Why shouldn't she be? Maybe she had packed up and cleared out.

"It would be nice if we could get more help," moaned Tomás, coughing. He'd heard his employer had backed off looking for additional help, informing applicants the positions were filled and thanking them for their interest.

Now the time had passed for the hiring of additional help without revealing a simple fact: RCR had possessed this virus from the beginning of the epidemic. No one knew anything about its physical nature, only what it was doing to animal life. If Jason permitted outsiders to view the virus, all the cause-and-effect dots would be connected. He couldn't think of a plausible story he might relate to the CDC, if he sent them a sample for their opinion, without lying at some point about where he got it and how long he'd possessed it, and what he was doing with it. The lie would be the worst part, if it were found out. Once again, he chastised himself for not listening to Don months ago, to man up instead of wanting to learn more about it; yet, if he had told the truth, the epidemic would still be in progress, wouldn't it?

Jason viewed this new virus as a bad relative who suddenly showed up on his doorstep with suitcase in hand. He agreed to let the relative stay for a couple of days and then he got weak and allowed him or her to stay a little longer. After that, the entity refused to vacate his premises, leaving him with no one to call for help, as they cause him to reorganize his life. Unquestionably, this present circumstance was not one of those situations people encounter where it made one into a better person for the experience.

Five years earlier, after Jason had acquired the necessary permits and passed inspections, he sent out ads. He had hired Linda Beaufort and then interviewed Tomás Angel Rubio. Originally from Mexico City, he bragged a Harvard degree. He currently worked in virology at the Frederick National Laboratory for Cancer Research in Frederick, Maryland, an exceptionally high quality facility that claimed Nobel Prize Winners. The Frederick facility also included the National Cancer Institute. And yet, Tomás wanted to work for Jason's startup company in Lincoln.

Jason walked leisurely to the outer office to greet the man after his first secretary had called to announce the applicant's arrival. He stood the same height as Jason, but weighed some twenty pounds more and appeared to be his reported age of fifty with straight black hair cut short, dark eyes, brown skin, and genial smile. His nose was small and his ears lay flat against his head. He wore a dark blue business suit and a blue and red tie with school buses depicted on it.

Jason led the visitor to the conference room where they took their seats opposite one another. A large white board was mounted on one wall. A pitcher of ice water sweated on a coaster between them.

During the interview process, Jason wanted to get a sense of the personality he would be dealing with. The individual wouldn't be there if he or she wasn't highly qualified. He also wanted to see if the gust inquired about the people he would be dealing with at the institute. Hiring was a two-way interview process.

Jason asked, "Tomás, the first question that comes to mind is: Why do you want to come here? This is a startup company and a long way from Maryland."

"That's true," Tomás replied, comfortable in the interview process. "I love my job and the people I work with at Frederick. It's the crowded coast I've been complaining about. I grew up in Mexico City, then went to Harvard in Boston, then to Maryland. When my son got football scholarship offers, he decided that Nebraska would be the best fit for him. When I saw your ad, everything clicked. "

"I can certainly relate to going from big to small.

In fact, that's why I left Virginia and ultimately ended up here," Jason offered, honestly. He looked down at the file in front of him. "Does your wife work?"

"She's an elementary school teacher," answered Tomás. "Her former name was Alice Harris. I met her at a coffee shop during one of her school vacations. She's fine with moving, if I get this job."

The men began talking salary and other terms. They discussed technical molecular biology and, having good vibes of the man, Jason gave him a tour of the facility and after discussing salary, Jason hired Tomás.

One month later, Jason interviewed Dustin Jones. The man wore dark slacks, a dark long-sleeved dress shirt open at the collar, and a light sport coat. All the clothes appeared to be of cotton; not rayon, nylon, or polyester.

The tall man stood six-two with dark brown hair spiked to a peak in the middle. He had a thin face and thin nose, but overall wasn't bad looking. His ears were pierced, but no earrings adorned them at the time. According to his résumé, he was in his mid-forties and single.

Born in Seattle, Washington, Dustin attended The University of Washington where he graduated top of his class a year-and-a half early. He had never known a grade lower than A during his entire life, including the quarter he had taken six classes. He had a side interest in magic and, reportedly, had taken private lessons in the art while attending school.

After his Bachelor's degree, Dustin went directly into a PhD program at The University of Massachusetts. He loved pure research and disliked the pressures of a big university. After seeing Jason's ad seeking experts in genetics as applied to the study of cancer, and researching Randolph, who wanted to start a research facility named after himself, Dustin took a chance and applied.

To Jason, this Dustin character was totally off-the-wall, space-case brilliant and eccentric, spiked hair and all, but harmless and very loyal. His values were solid. Opening the file in front of them as the men sat in the conference room, Jason began the interview with a potentially problematic issue, "You describe yourself as an environmentalist. Could you explain to me your views on that topic?" Dustin's response could be good or bad: Would he take off work to join some street march? Would he balk at being involved in certain lab procedures?

"I'm just a natural type of guy," Dustin replied, relaxed in his seat. "I grow my own vegetables in my home garden and, if I bought a place here, I'd build a greenhouse. I don't hunt because I don't like to kill animals. That said, I understand experimentation on laboratory mice, but it really hurts me to see them used. I wish there was a better way to check the response of medications on biological systems. Personally, I won't hurt the mice. I understand it's the field I got into, so I have to take some bad with the good. I don't believe that using less paper will save trees, because we'd still find a way to ship a billion tons of lumber to China or Japan each year. I don't buy farmed fish. I mean, if you carefully read what is printed on these really nice packages of fish in the market, you find that the fish are really farmed in China or Indonesia. No thanks. I don't do pesticides or contaminated grains. Those are my personal views and I don't impose them on anybody."

Dustin went on. "I also know there's not a thing I can do to stop global warming, man-made or otherwise, and I choose to live conservatively. Waste is one of my hot buttons."

Dustin's comfort with himself impressed Jason. Was there a curve-ball he wasn't seeing about the man? Or was he one those 'what you see is what you get', kind of person.

"Are you interested in sports at all?" Jason asked.

"No, sir. I'm okay in the lab, but if you put me on a stationary bike I'd probably fall off."

Dustin's use of the words "okay in the lab" was the wrong usage of the words "extraordinarily brilliant." His expertise in the field of gene mutations stood out in his publications. Another one of his strengths lay in the detailed operation and construction of the scientific equipment used in today's research. A person skilled in that area was always a valuable asset to any lab.

Dustin asked, "How many are you going to hire, sir?"

Jason responded, "There will be four of us until I can hire more. You'll be working with me, a woman named Linda Beaufort and another man named

Tomás Rubio who will be coming on. He's joining us from Frederick."

"Impressive. Is there anything I need to know about you, personally, sir?" Dustin inquired.

There it was. "Of course. Unlike you, I enjoy hunting for food. I also like to fish. I'm a perfectionist in my work and I expect others to be that way. I enjoy running, but only on a treadmill. Call me an introvert. I want results in triplicate when there is something worth going after. I run a tight ship."

"Is there any other way to run one?" Dustin asked.

Jason liked Dustin and asked him what he presently received as a salary, then said, "The cost of living here is much less than it is in Massachusetts. But I'll start you at the salary you were earning there and that will remain in place for three years. After that, we'll talk. If that works for you, I'll show you the grounds."

Jason waited a long day for Linda to call. He phoned her that evening both on her landline and cell phone. A mechanical voice greeted him coldly stating she'd be out for a couple of days and to leave a message.

Her lack of direct contact worried him. Linda was a true workaholic. That she hadn't touched base with him hurt. He never felt closer to another woman as he did to her. She always let him know in the past if something came up and she couldn't get to work.

Two days later Linda returned. She made no

mention of the dozen or so messages Jason had left. She was distant and hurting. He didn't really understand what he had done wrong, but whatever it was, he needed to make an effort to fix it.

That evening at his house, Jason broached the subject by simply asking Linda if she felt like talking. She understood his intent and simply declared, "I told you, Hon, I didn't want a baby to look like those animals."

He could have argued with her about his own feelings, but to what end? She changed the subject and said, "The other morning at x-ray, Don and I talked about a lot of things. He wanted to know if you needed any more full-time help and was thinking about asking you."

Jason felt a little embarrassed that he hadn't asked Don first, as he had planned to do. "What did you tell him?"

"That we definitely needed help and he would have to ask you," she replied.

The next morning Jason, while Jason donned his lab coat. Don walked in. "Hey, Jace, how's it going?" Don beamed.

"That name is reserved for certain people and the answer is yes, you have a job if you want it," Jason grinned back. "We'll start you at minimum wage and you can work your way up. Unfortunately, I can't hire you as a full time employee."

Don looked confused. Jason announced, "I can, however, hire you as a partner." Don had a good idea of what his salary would be as an employee and wasn't worried about it. He knew Jason paid very well. As a partner, well, the pay would likely be a lot better. Like Jason, Don didn't need the money. What he wanted was to be involved in the project that had originated from his own meteorite and to be part of this small clique of elite scientists.

After the new hirings, Jason had a small wing added to the east side of the lab, which would eventually house several combination 20-gallon fermenter-centrifuges along with water lines to provide distilled water and drains. The cost came out of Jason's pocket because, to those agencies supplying RCR with grant money, he couldn't justify the use of this device in his research unless he changed his investigative approach. Still, he still couldn't hire additional outside help. Feeling trapped, the only option was for him to go forward.

August of Year 1

June began the morning session. "Doctor Randolph expressed concern about the abnormal births we've all heard about and asked me to put together a timetable based on a worst-case scenario. Several species of animals are involved, so far. Let's look at how many other species might become involved and when might this happen. I have some time frames on gestation periods and locations. We all know the generalities, now we need specifics.

"Gestation periods: horses, 11 months; cattle and humans, nine months; dogs and cats, two months;

mice six weeks; birds, roughly one month gestation and three-to-five weeks for eggs to hatch, depending on the species.

"The gestation period for white-tailed deer, elk, moose, Alaskan and Siberian caribou is about eight to nine months. For the various species of bears, including black bears and polar bears, it is in the range of seven months. The Antarctic penguin hatches two months and the Bengal tiger gives birth in a little over three months. All known offspring of these creatures were becoming children of the New Flu.

"Dog and cat abnormalities first began in the four cities in question at about the same time, five if you want to count Omaha, thanks to my husband's travels there for teaching duties."

June continued, "The disease appears to be spreading remarkably fast. A given city can get hit hard within four weeks given variables of density and movement. If we're looking at dogs and cats, we can expect births to occur some three months later when we factor in the lag time once the virus settles into the host. For us, it was about two weeks between when we discovered the virus and when we began to have our cough, headaches, and other symptoms. Horses will show up last, after humans; probably some three months later.

"With animals, their abnormal births are appearing first in the primary cities in a rough order of their gestation periods. That's why we probably won't see all animals affected at the same time, unlike an outbreak of, say, dog distemper, whenever we're able to trace the flow. If birds become involved, their number and type will tend to throw off the calculation. False reporting is not an issue. It's pretty hard to false report something like this."

June went on with her presentation. "Here's another interesting factoid. Populations: London and Mexico City 9 million each; Seattle 700,000; Omaha near a half-million; Lincoln, less than 300,000; Richmond, Virginia maybe 225,000; Norman, Oklahoma, less than that."

Linda said, "Which ties in with what I have to say. Doctor Randolph and I believe that after the incubation period, there is an adaption period in which the virus spreads throughout the host's body. We believe this may take about one-third of the gestation time. For humans, we expect reports of the first abnormal births about a year after exposure, that is, this coming November in the cities June mentioned."

Jason raised his hand halfway, as if requesting permission to speak in his own institute. "Yesterday evening I listened to a radio talk show host interviewing somebody from the local health department who asked the question: 'If it's a human carrier, why would anyone from one of those cities visit the others? They have nothing in common. So maybe it's not a person. Maybe it's an airplane'. Then the host answered his own question by saying they had checked it out only to find out the airlines use totally different jets for international flights. Which left them with no solution at all."

Tomás offered, "The argument against this happening is that viruses are species specific. Dogs transmit dog viruses, humans to humans, birds to birds. Viruses can overwinter in pigs, so a strain can hang out there and come back for another round of infection, without infecting the pigs. Believe me, they have their own swine flu that can wipe out an entire country's worth of the animals. So do chickens. I don't see this happening. Something else is occurring that has nothing to do with us."

Jason's heart sank. He believed differently. "Unless, what we have is only a look-alike virus; one capable of infecting any species of animal and it's not a virus at all."

Once back in the fermenter room, Jason added his special blend of nutrients to the sterile water in the container to begin the mixing process. Two hours later he added a batch of fibers that had been grown in a flask, double-checked the settings on the machine, and walked away. As the days passed, he checked samples occasionally by collecting a small amount of the liquid in a flask. He used a light meter to check the intensity of the glow. When the glow appeared to reach its peak in the growth cycle, he stopped the machine's operation.

Bringing the flask back to his lab, Jason gave it to Tomás who inserted a probe that emitted high-frequency sound waves, as Shenero had suggested. After using the probe for several minutes, Tomás took a sample from the flask, checked it under the microscope, and motioned for Jason to have a look.

The virus particles were intact. They looked as they always had; dark, foreboding, and ominous. The red glow had not changed in intensity after sonication. This entity did not follow the rules. It was supposed to rupture and the glow should have increased.

Jason centrifuged the medium, then spread out the black mass onto sheets to dry in an oven. In the end, he had nearly four pounds of glowing shiny black powder. Would it burn? Could it be frozen? Could it be made into thin sheets? Could it resist acids? What were its insulation properties? Was it still infectious, or did that matter anymore?

Jason was a biologist, not an engineer, but Don knew people over in engineering at UNO while Jason knew people at UNL in chemistry. Those departments would have a much better idea of what tests to perform from their end. All he had to do would be to supply them with the material without telling them where it came from.

With Linda back at work, the lab was now at the full force of six including Don and June; seven counting Rick. During one of the morning brainstorming sessions, Dustin, Jason's tall thin eccentric genius from Seattle, suggested, "All we have to tell chemistry and engineering is that we were trying to make a big batch of growth formula from basic chemicals and we got this black stuff and could they run some tests? Don't great discoveries come from fooling around, straying from the well-worn path?"

Dustin's explanation sounded silly, yet reflected the absolute truth and therefore, would be easy to remember. Omitted would be the tiny part about their alien friend being in solution in the first place. Everyone knew the people who were going to receive the samples would soon figure they hadn't been told everything. That's the nature of science when you don't want people to know more than you want them to know—the kind of thing one leaves out of a scientific paper so others can't quite reproduce your results, unless you want them to.

The departments of chemistry and engineering received a quarter pound of black powder each. Don made it clear he would pay double for results in half the standard 90-day reporting time.

During the time the baby mice grew, the adults also exhibited changes: learning improved, their upper thighs appeared to thicken, and their speed increased. Linda purchased several wheel-o-meters and found that the average mouse ran inside the wheel at 1.7 miles per hour, some 18 percent faster than the standard rate of 1.4 miles per hour. The rate for the mutated next generation mice averaged 1.9 miles per hour at maturity, an unheard of running speed; the equivalent of an average human running any given distance at world record pace.

Linda prepared a complete set of mouse tissue sections from original mice six months old, one-third into their 18-month expected life span and sent them to a scientific pathologist for analysis. She needed to know what abnormalities, if any, might be found in muscle, cartilage, lungs, skin, joints, brain and various organs.

Meanwhile, the daily news described a new strain of cold virus reaching pandemic proportions. Hot spots included Lincoln, Omaha, Norman, Seattle, Richmond, Mexico City, London, and a dozen other cities with possible cases in more distant parts of the world. Couldn't anybody come up with a cure for the common cold? And what was going on with these crazy animal births? Over-the-counter and prescription medications for colds, allergies and pain were in short supply, while businesses that promoted naturopathic medicines flourished.

Health authorities described the current epidemic as highly unusual. "A new strain of virus has appeared that does not follow the normal pattern of distribution, nor do the symptoms match records of previous cold and flu outbreaks. As of this date, health authorities are unable to isolate the causative agent of this disease to determine how it compares with known strains of cold and influenza viruses. However, the CDC confirmed the findings of other laboratories. Experts hypothesized the infection might be the cause of the abnormal births that followed the cold symptoms."

September of Year 1

Jason's relationship with Linda returned to normal. Staying the occasional night, she enjoyed his large house, neat as a hotel room, with little warmth, not even the occasional personal item strewn about. There were no forgotten items on the floor needing to be picked up, just his easy company and his taste in music. His lack of interest in television served as a big plus in her regard for him.

Early in their relationship, he had informed her of his love for classical music. He laughingly joked about a conversation he'd had once with a psychiatrist friend whom he had asked if it was normal to listen to harpsicord music for an hour straight. The psychiatrist told him that he didn't know because he'd never heard of anybody doing it before.

One Monday evening, Jason put down a book on infectious diseases, realizing he hadn't invited Don and June over for some time due to the state of agitation at the lab. He thought the upcoming Friday evening would be a good time for a visit and dinner, if they were so inclined. He missed Linda because she provided him with intellectual challenge, while respecting his space. All right, she also added a sense of warmth and security, human factors he seemed to need more frequently as time went on. As it turned out, all three consented to come to dinner.

That Friday, the foursome lounged outdoors on lawn chairs in Jason's backyard, the sky clear of clouds, and a warm light breeze blew in from the west. The topics of conversation avoided work, politics, and religion. Off-handedly, June suggested, "You should cut your lawn, Jason. Critters are going to start hanging out there."

"Thanks for the tip," Jason retorted. "The gardeners did it last weekend. They probably added fertilizer."

"Must be good stuff," she responded. "You think your lawn's bad, try plucking strawberries and blackberries once a month. I've got a freezer full."

Linda laughed, "Maybe it's our little friend making them grow faster."

"Sure, Linda," Jason offered. "It's making my lawn grow faster, too."

Linda gave Jason a quick glance and nodded to June who got up to retrieve her purse. She pulled out a little baggie and handed it to Jason.

"What's this?" he asked. Take a look at your lawn, too. At that, she reached down and pulled up several blades of grass and stuck them in the baggie. Jason shrugged, took the baggie, walked indoors to put it in the freezer and returned to his chair. "If you think the virus is in the strawberries and the grass, well, that's just a bit off, don't you think? After all, I don't see them having funny looking faces." He was the only one who smiled.

Three days later, Jason and Linda were reviewing mouse data at Jason's lab desk when he pointed to a row of numbers. "This seems to confirm our suspicions. Once the mice arrive in our building, there seems to be an incubation period where this virus has to settle into the host for a period of time; no different than any other infection. If mating occurs during this incubation period, there is no effect on the offspring. If mating occurs after that time, the offspring will show deformations."

Linda noted, "We got our first symptoms maybe two weeks after exposure. My guess is that it takes a lot longer than that to affect the reproductive system. Based on our mouse study, it could be as long as three months in a human. If mating occurs before three months, the babies will be fine; if after that, not so good. Less than a week had passed after you discovered the glow and found the building contaminated. It got loose and multiplied like crazy. We all carried it out with us. It takes time to get transferred in a city to the point when deformities in animals are reported. My sense is that it is accelerating its rate of infectivity, similar to most diseases."

Jason offered, "I came in Saturday hoping to receive the findings from the chemistry and engineering departments. They arrived on the date they projected. The chemistry report says there were trace elements and simple molecules in the batch of black powder they had received."

Linda suggested, "That's probably from residual traces of the original growth formula after you washed it. Right?"

"Right," Jason confirmed. "The report also states that the sample could not be dissolved. A complete listing of chemicals used is provided in a lengthy list of items."

He reached into the desk drawer and handed Linda the reports. She read the one from engineering that noted the sample of black powder they received couldn't be ground down any finer. They found it to be several times harder than a diamond in a crush test and each of the powder particles consisted of countless fibers. Furthermore, a solid piece would be needed in order to ascertain its tensile strength.

"What are you going to do now?" Linda asked.

"Give them a solid piece, what else?" he answered.

Now, after several generations of mice, all doubts were gone. Each new generation retained the deformities; hunched shoulders, muscular legs, eyes and ears offset, nose and mouth canted, none of which appeared to affect their eating pattern or what came out the other end. Most importantly, it didn't seem to affect their survival or adaptability to new situations.

The workload became massive. Jason assigned each team member a different aspect of research: chemistry, DNA analysis, histology, and animal studies. Each wrote mini-reports, as data became available, and gave them to June, who prepared a general summary for the team to review each morning.

More samples were submitted to histology which confirmed their observations. There were more compact muscle fibers throughout the bodies, with larger ligaments and tendons around the shoulders, elbows and knees.

Histology also found the entire respiratory tract to be inflamed in the parent mice which was labeled sample Gen. 0, but not in their offspring, which were samples labeled Gen. 1 or Gen 2. The neurons in the central nervous system were both thinner and more numerous. (A footnote suggested that electrical firing might be faster as a result of this.) Other organs appeared to be normal, with the exception of the lungs. Finally, the meninges, the membranous covering over the central nervous system, including brain and spinal cord, exhibited slight swelling.

Given the findings, a sequence of events began to unfold in Jason's mind. The virus entered through the nose and lungs affecting the respiratory tract, then headed to the central nervous system, resulting in coughing and headaches. It progressed to cells that affected certain muscles, including those of the shoulders, legs and parts of the brain. Every cell of the body they tested had the virus. What else didn't they know about?

In addition to his unshakable guilt, Jason felt sick with the knowledge that, thanks to this invasion, his beloved RCR was completely ruined. How could any medical research be conducted with the fibers loose in the building to bind with every piece of DNA it touched? If research did not entail the use of human, animal or cultured cells, he had no idea what might happen once the fibers or the glow chemical contaminated any experiment, whatever it might be. Could it spell the end of biological research altogether, anywhere? Would it substantially change the results of basic chemical reactions? Would it affect experiments in physics and other fields of research? How many jobs might be lost, how much medical gain might not be achieved? Would the production of pharmaceuticals be affected?

So much for building a bigger and better research center. What do you do for the rest of your life when your primary source of income and joy is taken away? Certainly, finding a way to neutralize its rapid spread into the world at large seemed like an impossibility.

October of Year 1

Retaining his vision of trying to make use of the virus for some good, Jason contrived a plan with Don that called for the use of a superglue epoxy spray. Because both wanted to be around to finish what they had in mind without their lungs becoming glued shut, he would use the hood in his lab to do the work.

Jason's mind flitted in a different direction, resulting in an online search. Finding what he wanted, he asked Don to locate and order a compression press—one with a timer-activated pressure and temperature gauge that engaged when the pressurized metal plates were closed. Once the unit arrived, the installer instructed both men on its usage.

Jason now possessed a mass of virus powder with fibers thinner than a bacterium. He envisioned a reinforced sheet made from that powder. With Don assisting, he cut numerous pieces of thin plastic one-foot square into fours and placed all of them in the hood, along with a can of epoxy, a tablespoon, salt shaker, forceps, and a flat pan of black virus powder with a cover on it.

Having only a vague idea of what he was doing, Jason reached into the hood using the built-in gloves and filled the salt shaker with powder, then sprayed a single square with epoxy. Using the forceps, he picked up the sheet and laid it onto the pan of powder, removed it, and with the use of the flat edge of a plastic knife blade, tried to smooth it to 1/16" in thickness. He used the salt shaker to fill in any gaps, while Don hovered over his shoulder watching him work. He quickly sprayed another sheet of plastic with epoxy and, again using the forceps, placed it over the waiting square with glue-side down. Aside from the color, the sandwich looked more like it had been spread with cold peanut butter. He removed the sandwich from the hood and handed it to Don who carefully set it in the compression press, setting the pressure to 500 pounds per square inch for one minute at 200 degrees Fahrenheit. They had selected all three values as a place to begin, as suggested by the technician who had delivered the machine.

After several tries, the men still ended up with a lumpy mess. Jason asked Don to tell June to run to the corner store for a large bottle of white household glue. Within fifteen minutes, she returned with the bottle. Jason repeated the process using the plastic knife to spread the white glue. Don placed the sandwich in the press, this time setting it at 500 pounds and 500 degrees with one minute of pressure time. He opened the press, gave the sample time to cool and removed it. It felt like a lightweight steel plate.

Using a micrometer, Jason found the sample measured 1/64th of an inch, four times thinner than what he started with and only four times thicker than a sheet of paper. Both men believed it could be easily reduced to paper-thin proportions. Jason did not feel like congratulating himself. The exhaust fan connected to the hood super-heated the escaping air, a technique meant to destroy known microbes, not those surviving a volcanic eruption or a meteorite that had encircled the sun for eons.

Taking contaminated material out of the hood also added a ridiculous element to the procedure; and what do you do with the bad samples, throw them into a plastic bag for the trash man to pick up? Furthermore, how does this stuff get mass produced? One step at a time.

A few mornings later, Jason passed around the samples he and Don had prepared. He did not delight in the thought of a new facetious Chinese proverb of his own creation: Doing many wrong things may lead to boundless joy.

"You might do better with thinner plastic and work out a way to go back to the epoxy," suggested Dustin. "And maybe little more heat. You want the plastic to heat fast and evenly on both sides. Also, you might make certain to place the sample in the center of the press."

Tomás sat still, seemingly disinterested.

Jason's mind spun with advanced calculations including temperature, pressure, and melting points. He could find thinner plastic and use different colors to cover the blackness. He went online to locate stores selling sheets of film thinner than those he had previously used—not so thin they wouldn't lay down flat.

Two days later he presented the team with a number of red and yellow variations of the squares now measuring eight times thinner than the original with a thickness of half that of a sheet of paper.

"Anybody here a shooter?" he asked during the session. Silly question. A large percentage of the state's population could shoot. He didn't expect Dustin or Tomás to raise their hands, but knew Don and Linda possessed weapons, in addition to himself. Jason held the sample in the air. "All right. You two take the morning off. I'm going with you. I know an open range out of town so bring your weapons. Let's have some fun. Hopefully, we'll have more of these we can give to engineering."

Dustin typically used the morning session to eat his breakfast. He set down his sandwich of tomato, avocado slices and bean sprouts, He said, "I'm down with seeing the results of that; like what force would be necessary to tear apart this virus compared with braided rope, steel or some composite metal? Did it have resistance to heat or cold? Could it be sand-blasted? Could it be cut with a laser? If so, could it be laser-heated back together again?"

Jason wondered: Is this a trade off? Are we trading contamination of life on our planet in exchange for the betterment of the human race; a race that is being eaten alive from the inside out?

Linda asked, "Don't we need to patent this?"

Dustin asked, "Why bother with the patent? I

mean, nobody is going to copy it."

Jason thoughtfully replied, "Agreed. Frankly, Dustin, this is out of my department as to whether we can file for a utility or a design patent for this sandwich-making process. We may not have to reveal the source of the innermost layer, but an attorney would know that part. As far as a design patent, we would have to make our product similar to what is out there, but differ in some way. Functionality has a lot to do with it. I'll have to think about it. Meeting adjourned. I'm anxious to get out to the range."

"Can I watch?" June asked, with a lascivious tone to her voice.

Jason smiled. "All right. We'll all go. Here are the directions. We'll meet there in an hour."

"Sorry, sir, I'll pass. I've got data points coming up in about 90 minutes," said Tomás, happily. Apparently, shooting did not interest him. He'd settle for the results.

Later that morning, after returning from the range, Jason worked at his desk comparing data from the mouse experiments when Tomás came in and requested a private audience. Jason told him they could meet in the conference room in a half hour.

The meeting had not gone well. Tomás began, "Doctor, I don't understand what we're doing. This is supposed to be a cancer research center, but a large part of our time is spent on working on this virus. You said you were going to hire more people, but you didn't, and okay, that's your business. We are all concerned, but Dustin and I are the only ones working on the genetics of this thing and maybe Linda is on occasion. You expect us to divide our time and we can't do justice to two different projects simultaneously. This virus appears to have gotten loose and so be it. In my opinion, we should be spending our time either on cancer, or trying to figure out ways to stop the spread of the virus. Instead, you're making square plates to shoot at."

Jason felt like a sitting duck in the cross-hairs of a man who came from the Frederick National Laboratory. Jason's father once told him that if somebody calls you out and their statements approximate the truth and you admit to their statements, they have nothing left to say. "Tomás, I can't argue with anything you said. Had this new virus originated from somewhere else, I still would have shifted our emphasis to it because this problem is more imminent than cancer."

Jason paused a moment and continued, "There are ten thousand cancer researchers out there and a few less for a short time won't be noticed. The reason we shoot bullets at it is because there is a chance to make something good come from this while we're trying to study its genetics and its physical characteristics. I don't want to lose you, Tomás, and I'm asking you to stay with me and see this thing through. I'll put you back to working on our grant full time."

He omitted telling Tomás about the shame he

couldn't face once the truth came out that the virus had originated from them or that the lack of operating money might become a problem. Jason was obviously skirting the issue; deflecting it by changing the subject. He understood Tomás would pick up on that and trusted the man would keep it to himself and wouldn't challenge him.

"You're not going to lose me, Doctor," Tomás replied. My son is in college here and my wife is working. We're a family. I can't speak for when he gets out of school, so if you'll have me, I'll stay on and we'll see where we're at when it is time for him to graduate."

Tomás was right. The ongoing grant money from the government would not be forthcoming unless they reported progress. As it was, it barely covered costs, but at least he wasn't bleeding money. That would happen if the grant wasn't renewed and more money wasn't forthcoming. Without a cash flow he would be broke and out of business within a couple of years. The future did not look bright, unless, of course...the inspiration came to him to apply for a research grant to investigate the New Flu. He could say they found it entangled in everyone's DNA. At least, they would come up with something original. Hell, they knew ten time what anybody else knew. With new equipment they might be able do something he couldn't define at the moment. He'd have to think about it.

The next morning Jason came in with the samples in hand as the others took a seat. He began by holding up one of the squares. "Let's name some variables in the production of this item."

Linda named several. "Temperature, pressure, thickness of plastic, thickness of powder and time of pressure"

Don said, "Add type of epoxy and amount of pressure."

"Too many variables. It'll be impractical to vary them all," Jason replied.

Don added, "Use mid-point in the thickness. Increase the pressure to say, 1000 psi. Up the temperature."

"Why do you think more pressure would help?" Tomás asked.

Jason was pleased. At least the man was participating.

Don said, "It's like putting pressure on a stack of logs. They would roll over one another to fill in the spaces between them, thus increasing the strength and the insulation ability of the sandwich. More heat will melt both sides of the sandwich better so it should coat the insides more evenly."

Jason nodded, "That makes sense. It would explain what happened at the range yesterday when one of the rounds from my .22 long-rifle punched a hole through the thinner sheet, but no rounds from Linda's .38 made any dent at all. The .22 round must have found a weak area in the preparation; the space between the logs. Rounds fired from Don's .45 and .357 Magnum failed to penetrate a thicker sample; neither did high velocity rounds from my own 30.06

hunting rifle or my 12 gauge shotgun, but they did penetrate the thinnest sample."

Several days later, sixteen samples were in hand, some of which were duplicates. They stacked less than an inch and a half in height. Don discarded the rare sample with the bullet hole in it and placed a random number on each of the others with an indelible marker. He held onto the code so the engineering department wouldn't know details about them. The department would assign a couple of graduate students to work on the project. They could have it done inside of a month. The money they receive would go into the department research fund.

Jason directed Tomás back to work full time on cancer. The others turned their attention to trying to figure out a way to reverse the binding of the virus from the host DNA while they waited for the engineering report to come back. The problem was several-fold: What chemicals or antibiotics might they use to conduct those experiments on separation? How would they determine if separation had occurred? How could they make it work for practical purposes? DNA couldn't be seen with the standard binocular microscope and the electron and x-ray microscopes at the university were in currently in use. Then the electron microscope went down. It would be out of commission for some time until a technician could be flown in to repair it. Jason had never felt so helpless.

December of Year 2

When the results did come back from engineering, Don and Jason decoded them and enthusiastically presented the data to the team that same afternoon. Holding the pages in front of him, Jason began, "All right. Here it is. The best laser they have will cut through the thinnest sheets. For the thicker ones, it will be necessary to use a very high intensity laser. It turns out there are only a few instruments in the world at the present time that can generate enough energy to make those cuts.

"A separate report addresses the issue of tensile strength. It reads as follows: 'Unit for unit, the lightest sample you sent weighed one-half ounce, or 14.2 grams. When extrapolated to ensure the equality of numbers, this compares with a weight of four pounds of Kevlar® (Aramid) used in bulletproof vests. Both products have flexibility at this thickness.

'Your samples have ten times the compressibility as does Kevlar® and ten times the tensile strength; thus, it has fifty to sixty times the tensile strength of steel. Therefore, it is potentially usable in the construction of bridges and buildings and for the lining of tires. There may be possibilities for numerous other uses, such as in the manufacture of aircraft wings and hulls of surface ships and submarines. Your product is much more resistant than Kevlar® to heat, cold, ultraviolet radiation and other factors. (Please refer to raw data enclosed in this report.)

'When compared with the official US National Institute of Justice Body Armor Classification, it is equal to sixteen layers of Kevlar®. It may be suitable for use in rockets of all types, both in their framing and engines. Its best attribute may lay in its soundproofing ability.

'A thinner version of your thinnest sample is requested for further comparisons.

'Finally, all samples submitted are much less breathable than Kevlar, but are more resistant to water intrusion'. Significant improvements to the product design may be implemented at the discretion of the inventor."

"Holy smokes," Tomás declared, smiling and obviously impressed. He understood that, without his help, there would be no money coming into RCR, yet he felt an urge to turn his talents toward this new discovery.

Jason was pleased with the report; not elated. Because the pendulum always swings two ways, he made an effort to remain emotionless, in order to avoid highs or crashes. At least his intuition turned out to be correct. In a way, he felt like a date who had slapped him at their first meeting just because she felt like it; one who came back later trying to make it up to him even while further mischief lurked in her dark heart. He might expect another slap at any given time.

Included with the report was a short note from Dr. Wilbur Gottlieb, Chairman of the Department of Engineering, who wanted to talk with Jason regarding the samples. They had briefly met at one or two faculty functions where Jason found him to be tall, clean cut, well-dressed, and engaging. His eyes were dark and penetrating, his black hair full and razor cut.

If nothing else, Jason could recognize people who had money. Gottlieb might be what his parents called nouveau riche, or, of money earned during his own generation. Unlike others of his type who tended to be ostentatious, this man had distinctive class. For the moment, Gottlieb could wait. Jason had more work to do. At the moment, it looked like any possible deal with Gottlieb could be considered ifcome and wishcome rather than income. He thought, How weird is this? Gottlieb was the name of the mentor of Doctor Martin Arrowsmith. Unfortunately, in that novel, Arrowsmith's loved one died of the plague. Let that not be so here.

January of Year 2

The first deformed human babies were born: first in Lincoln, then in Omaha, then in Norman. These births upped the ante by an order of magnitude in terms of fright. The disease was becoming more recognized in the Western World. Would it spread? How could a disease that affected animals also affect humans? There has to be some common factor causing the problem. Could it be caused by a new pesticide used in grains? Two pesticides might have interacted in some crazy fashion in the mammalian body. It wouldn't be the first time that had happened.

There was nothing new about occasional abnormal human births. These would include Siamese twins, babies with enlarged heads from encephalitis and occasional tailed humans or those born with six fingers. Most horrific were the Thalidomide babies with malformed limbs and a wide variety of other defects born to 10,000 mothers who had taken the sedative in 46 countries in the late 1950s and early 1960s. Originally used to treat leprosy, it was prescribed to expectant mothers as a cure for morning sickness, insomnia, and anxiety. Obviously, the clinical trials were insufficient before the drug had been disseminated.

New Flu babies were different than babies born with other abnormalities. There were no clinical trials. The causative agent was on its way to include possibly all humans and animals in its trial run. The appearance of human babies matched that of newborn animals. Demands were put on authorities, moneys were shifted and the New Flu became an international priority. Hospitals and doctors were of no help. This was not a disease that could be cured, at least, not once the child was born. Statisticians found that normal human babies were also being born. These belonged to parents who had not yet caught the contagion, or had caught it after the start of gestation.

Early one evening, Linda and Jason sat in his living room, his arm around her, her head on his shoulder. Tchaikovsky's Overture of 1812 played in its all its dynamic glory. Linda thought the music an odd choice for the occasion in which a Braham's gentle lullaby might be more fitting. Either Jason maintained some enthusiasm about which he had failed to mention, or he was using the music as a means of distraction. She did know one thing: Loud sound overwhelms the brain and cancels pain. To her recollection, he hadn't played Brahms since before the first glowing flask of red liquid appeared.

As the bells of the final movement completed ringing and the canons began to fire, Jason mumbled a few words unrelated to the music. "We might be able to revolutionize the world while losing what we recognize as humans; maybe recognize as any animal—a bad tradeoff in my book."

Linda put her hand on his arm. "Like the mice, aren't we smarter, too? Maybe we're smart enough to find a way to get it to let go."

Jason could think of no apt reply.

Before becoming Chairman of the Engineering Department at UNL, Gottlieb spent years in R&D at RX Missile Defense Systems. He had filed for scores of patents, all owned by the RX Corporation. Gottlieb still retained a trace of German accent; an accent he purposely retained after his parents' immigration from Germany. His grades were so high, his work so meticulous, that he received a full scholarship to MIT, thus saving some $25,000 in annual tuition plus another $7,500 for room and board. That was decades before. Double those fees today and then some.

Growing impatient about an unreturned call or a

reply to his letter that accompanied the engineering report, Gottlieb telephoned Jason who apologized for not getting back. On the plus side, Jason told of they had made to the plastic squares, wanting them finished before he made contact with Gottlieb. As well as being soundproof and resistant to both radiation and temperature fluctuations, the flexibility of the thinnest could probably stop virtually any rifle bullet. Jason further expressed his certainty that its high resistance to radiation, temperature, and sound also improved proportionally. He then asked if there was some way to market it.

Gottlieb had a deeper understanding of what Jason had told him than Jason did—intimately more so. Gottlieb had overseen the tests. He was not interested in the man's naiveté, only in his talk about marketing this invention. Gottlieb offered to buy lunch three days hence. Jason mentioned that he intended to bring a couple of people with him and if lunch cost too much he'd be happy to loan Gottlieb the money. Gottlieb laughed. The man had a sense of humor. Jason invited Don and Linda to the luncheon; Don, because he was a partner, and Linda because of her ability to see to the core of a person.

During those three days before the meeting, the news reported strange hatchlings emerging from various birds' eggs in different countries. Because the deformations were consistent with the recent births of other creatures, the press attributed the mutations to the New Flu. In June's opinion, birds could transfer the disease more rapidly and through greater numbers when compared with the movement of humans. She related her own observations which concurred with those reported by the media. With the newly-hatched birds, their eyes were not aligned. Their wings were hitched up a little higher. They could do what they did before and could do it longer. Some birds were able to fly straight up for hundreds of feet while others hovered in one place or go backwards for lengthy periods of time. Ducks could keep pace with a human freestyle swimmer. Everything was evolving into upside-down madness—the new norm.

One scientist enjoyed his fifteen minutes of fame when he speculated that a Proboscis monkey, newly acquired by the Henry Doorly Zoo and Aquarium in Omaha, was the cause of the disease. In his view, the monkey, supplied by a shipper in Borneo, probably carried the infectious agent. Somebody better check out what is going on in that country, so the CDC sent an investigative team to Borneo to find out the truth.

A major news outlet claimed the CDC screwed up when they prepared the latest batch of flu vaccines. They'd better recheck the identity of their workers. Terrorists might have infiltrated the establishment. The FDA debunked the report, clarifying that the CDC does not prepare vaccines. Instead, it works in concert with the FDA to monitor the complex elements involved in their preparation. Private companies normally develop vaccines based primarily on basic research conducted with grants awarded to universities.

At last, an investigative reporter uncovered the actual cause of the disease. A reliable witness (shown on camera with a hood over his head and voice altered), confessed he was part of a biological lab in Russia experimenting with a new bacterium to be used against the Americans. In his own hands a vial broke because of cheap materials due to the rampant corruption in the country. The vial contained the deadly agent. Budget constraints did not permit the rigid controls he repeatedly demanded of his government and the bug got loose, thanks to the poor containment barriers at their top secret research facility. The U.S. briefly considered hostile action against the Soviets before pressure on the reporter forced him to reveal the prank. Reliable sources noted that the investigative reporter and his hooded brother would soon be applying for food stamps after being released from jail for violating the Yelling Fire in a Crowded Movie Theater statute.

Jason wanted to call out to those who would listen, "Here I am—the cause of it all—and I can prove it." On second thought, he came to the conclusion that getting caught by accident would be much less painful than having to go public and openly admit the truth. If it came to that, he might be able to do it on camera and not have to embrace his deepest fear of speaking before the masses.

There were a lot of very smart people with their own microscopes, but they wouldn't find the fibers in cellular tissue. In point of fact, the entire fiber never entered a cell. The viral DNA directed itself straight for the DNA of the host. After hard searching, all the very smart people might discover would be some very messed up genetic codes. None of those codes would reveal their past life—having their origin on the planet Mars, or worse, lay claim to being from Randolph Cancer Research. Would they?

Lincoln's historic downtown Haymarket district normally saw a busy lunch hour at many of its score of eateries. This weekday, business was slow. Although no snow fell at the moment, the leaden sky threatened to add more to the three inches that lay on the ground. A cold wind coming down from the north provided a wind chill into the mid-twenties.

Jason slowly drove his SUV down Q Street with Linda seated next to him. Don sat behind her enjoying the feeling of being chauffeured. They passed a store that sold licorice from countries across the world as a family of five, just leaving and bundled up in winter clothing, checked out the others' purchases.

When Gottlieb had called about the lunch appointment, Jason had hoped he would select a Czech restaurant noted for their liver dumpling soup or boiled beef and kraut. Instead, he chose one that featured southern cooking, also fine with Jason, happy to leave his practice of usually eating lightly when alone.

Jason continued another block to 8th Street, passing a bar and grill, Irish pub, and a coffee shop. He found a parking slot directly in front of the restaurant Gottlieb had chosen for their rendezvous, pulling next to an expensive late model Audi.

The establishment was renowned for its gumbo and southern flavor. They were all familiar with the place, having patronized it on occasion. The popular eatery threatened sensory overload with its rich décor of wooden floors and wooden center islands resplendent with canned and jarred products for sale imported from around the world. Most of those dining there were professionals or retirees, with prices well above what the average college student could afford.

Gottlieb sat at a window table for four with a glass of ice water in front of each of the place settings. He stood when he saw the trio walk toward the door and stop beneath the overhang outside. Don had pulled a comb from his pocket, trying to work on his wild white hair that had blown straight up in the wind. Linda was miffed at having to pat down her carefully tended fashion statement; she had refused to wear a baseball cap or something more ladylike for fear of messing up her laboriously coiffed hair. Jason grabbed Don's comb from him and ran it through his own hair.

Don held the door open for the others to enter the restaurant. Gottlieb recognized Jason and waved them over. The trio exchanged greetings and introductions. Linda and Don took their seats next to the window opposite one another, Gottlieb slid in after Don, and Jason sat next to Linda, directly opposite Gottlieb.

The décor in the restaurant was ocean-oriented. Pictures of trawlers on the high seas pulling in baskets of lobsters while fighting the elements adorned the walls. Discussing the weather of the day occupied the conversation until a young blond-haired waiter approached the group. He may have found part-time employment to work his way through school. He wore a white shirt one size too large and a black clip-on bow tie. A tag on his shirt identified him as Jimmy.

With everyone's consent, Gottlieb ordered four shrimp cocktails as an appetizer and the group engaged in light conversation until the waiter reappeared carrying a tray supported by his left palm. When the glass-filled bowls were delivered, the waiter's right cuff briefly dipped into the last of the cocktails when he placed it onto the table. Jason noticed that he also picked up the glass cocktail bowls from the top rather from the sides. His thumbs were on the inside of the bowl.

Jason called him on it. "Excuse me, sir, you might check the cuff of your right sleeve and please bring us four fresh cocktails. Also, you might want to wash the sauce off your shirt. And please don't place your fingers inside the bowl itself."

The waiter looked at his cuff, blushed, and said, softly, "Yes, sir," removed the four cocktails and turned to leave.

"Make certain they're new cocktails and not the same ones," Jason called after him. Linda and Don didn't bother to exchange glances. They were accustomed to Jason's correctness.

The youth had taken but three steps when Jason stopped him a third time. Frustrated and confused the waiter turned to face him. Jason softened his tone and queried, "Pardon me, Jimmy, let me ask you something. What do you think about this disease that's going around?"

The youth paused in thought, then pontificated, "Well, sir, if you want to know, my mom and I are with our pastor on that one. We were all about due for a shakeup. You know, bad people and all. The Lord is making his will known. My pastor says this is only the beginning. He says it's like a hurricane where you first get the cloudy skies and light breezes and choppy water, then comes the monster wind, the torrential rain and the storm surge and the flooding and the deaths and devastation over the earth. He says this is just the first light breeze part of it."

Jason swallowed. "Did he say anything about recovering from the hurricane?"

"Yes, sir, he said it would be long and slow and very expensive. And not just in terms of money?"

"What does your father think?" Jason persisted. He needed to know.

Jimmy replied, "My dad thinks these animals with the funny faces should be put out their misery." He turned and walked back into the kitchen.

Jason wanted to ask the boy why he thought the animals might be miserable, because of the anthropomorphic nature of that opinion, but let it go. Gottlieb ignored their exchange and got to the point, coughing slightly, as they all did. "Might I ask the source or your material, doctor?"

"It's Jason, and the source is proprietary," he answered.

"If I may be so curious, is the source American or foreign and is it legitimate?" asked the engineer.

"It is definitely foreign, and legitimate is a funny word. If you're asking if we can be prosecuted for possessing it, the answer is maybe," Jason answered, vaguely. He didn't know how to respond. Yes, he would be prosecuted for a lot of reasons, if it were shown the virus had come from his lab. It might be claimed that he was careless or reckless. It might be claimed that a man of his quality and education should have known how to contain the creature, never mind his ignorance of its nature the time. And yes, the virus was foreign. It came from outer space, didn't it?

Don came to the rescue. "Wilbur, we are absolutely the only source of this material. I discovered it in Antarctica and it is natural. I can guarantee nobody else can find or duplicate what we have and we can provide you with however much you need."

Gottlieb seemed satisfied with Don's answer. As far as Jason, he wondered about why the man was weaving in and out, talking like a politician afraid to say the wrong thing. Would Jason be able to tell him where to find the bathroom without providing useless directions that led to nowhere? He knew a number of well-educated foreign diplomats who had developed this level of cryptic communication to a high level. He called it crypto-speak, where they structured every single word not to offend—an offensive action unto itself.

The waiter returned with four new shrimp cocktail bowls and took their orders. Jason didn't challenge him regarding their freshness, having received a squeeze from Linda's hand as the dishes were placed on the table, sans thumb. They ordered seafood gumbo and jambalaya, while Gottlieb and Don chose the blackened catfish and crawfish platter.

Linda added, "What we need is somebody with an engineering background and good connections to turn our ideas into useful products."

Gottlieb looked at each of them in turn, wondering if he should have misgivings. These were not brilliant inventors who had created a new type of computer in their home garage, yet, the data obtained from his own department's tests on the samples these same people had submitted were absolutely locked-up-tight and 100 percent irrefutable. He had personally overseen the work and had been astounded. As per standard procedure, the equipment was first compared with known standards. The chain of custody was intact. The details he required to create a business out of this potential new product line would not be needed at this preliminary meeting. At the moment, the element of trust had to be developed.

"This will take time. Here is what I need from you," Gottlieb directed in a firm voice, looking from one to the other, uncertain as to who actually ran the show over there. "I need more samples of various thicknesses, some as thin as possible. I can have one my engineers work with you to improve on the very crude samples you provided for testing. That must be done. Once we've seen the improvements I expect to see, I can try to raise the necessary money for this enterprise. Also, I want to own any patents we obtain."

"That's nuts, man, it's my product," Jason argued. Gottlieb had touched a nerve.

"True, but I take the risk and I take the liability," Gottlieb retorted, business-like, unemotional.

The two men talked percentages, and by the conclusion of the luncheon, all agreed that a lot of work would have to be done before any papers could be signed.

Gottlieb said he would have his attorney draw up a preliminary contract, conditional upon his obtaining suitable samples, finding suitable methods to go into mass production, and finding enough money. The last part might be the most difficult.

Jason looked at his friends and began to smile, as they looked at him with some concern. "Sorry, private joke," he muttered. He didn't trust Gottlieb, but there was nothing for Gottlieb to steal. In a real sense, Jason owned the virus. With a sick sense of humor, the part that struck him funny was that, not only did the virus live inside his own house, it lived inside of him and evidently, considering Gottlieb's cough, also lived inside the engineer.

With lunch completed, Gottlieb picked up the

check and the group left the restaurant. The temperature had dropped further during the time they had been indoors, but the wind had lessened. Jason pushed the unlock button on his key fob, the three stamped the snow off their feet, and took their respective seats in the car. Adjusting their seat belts, they watched as Gottlieb got into the Audi next to them and backed out.

"Well, what do you think?" Jason asked to anyone who would listen. Linda was fumbling in her purse for a comb and had pulled down the sun visor to use the mirror.

Don said, "I think he's going to be good for us. I don't see any way he's going to cheat us, but it depends on who hires the bookkeepers."

"True," replied Linda, gently smoothing down her hair. "It also depends on the honesty of the auditors who will be monitoring the bookkeepers."

"Well, that's down the line a ways. I'm sure we can find more trouble to get into before that happens," Jason philosophized.

When Gottlieb's department first received the request from Jason's lab for testing of the sample squares it was an average day. The department frequently conducted independent testing requests from outside sources. Compared with outside engineering firms, their prices were lower simply because there was no cost of labor. Graduate students were on scholarship and craved experience. It also brought a flow of income into the department. He did find it interesting that Jason's lab had put a rush status on the job, but gladly accepted the down payment once he consulted with one of his professors who operated the materials lab. Fortunately, the lab awaited another project some three month hence and was currently available to pursue this particular one.

The first sample squares were found to be terribly crude and unquestionably amateurish in their production. He was surprised they had come from Randolph's institute. What they had provided under terribly crude manufacturing conditions was nothing less than earth shaking. When the second set of squares was tested and the results were found to be significantly more impressive than those of the first batch, the time had come to contact Jason.

New inventions and new discoveries were fine. He had more than a few to his own credit. Some were quite ingenious, he had to admit. But this was different. This was magnitudes above man's understanding of the behavior of materials and, shockingly, came from a cancer research center located only a few miles away. How had he not heard anything about it up to this point? His engineering mind spun with possibilities and modifications. He lost sleep. He had to be part of whatever this and wherever it might be going.

Now that he knew the story, he wasn't sure he believed it. But why would they fabricate such a tall tale? Had they stolen plans from someone else? Everybody he knew of was decades away from anything close to this including the body-armor people.

There were no breakthroughs and none pending. Improvements, yes, breakthroughs, no.

And this Randolph character, who couldn't speak English, was a dyed-in-the-wool cancer man not given to thievery. That also held true for Jennings. To what end? Neither of the men needed money or to further their reputation. So what was going on over there?

He also had questions about Linda. Other than her being sharp, clean, good looking and very intelligent, who was she? Some might call her hot. Did she have Jason by the nose ring? If so, for what purpose? He didn't think that to be the case. She had a clean background and Jason seemed too independent to fall for a trickster. His people told him her background included a conversational ability in French. He'd have to introduce her to his wife, someday. So far, Gottlieb sensed that Randolph absolutely needed her in the lab and that might be about as far as it went.

Personality issues and backgrounds aside, the data didn't lie. Until he knew more, he would have to ride the river and begin making contacts to line up the money. He'd have to tender this resignation to the university if he wanted to spend time on this new endeavor. It's never easy to convince investors to fund a hundred million dollars in set-up and marketing charges. He hoped to put together a package that would convince them of the validity of tale. He had an idea about he might do it.

An hour after returning from their luncheon with Gottlieb, Jason sat at the microscope attempting to disprove his own findings: the fibers were not visible in human or mouse tissue; not with the normal light source, not with dark field, and not with polarized light.

Dustin walked in and hovered over his boss until Jason looked at him, away from the computer screen that held a manuscript he'd been preparing. Dustin would stand there for a half-hour, if necessary. Jason nodding upward, as if to say, "Go ahead."

"Sir, we have got to get some new sequencing equipment. I hate to say it, doctor, our stuff is out-dated. Tomás says he saw better equipment last time he was home in Mexico City at the university where he visited. It's also better back in Maryland."

"How much is the new one?" Jason asked.

"One-fifty," replied Dustin.

That caught Jason. "I bought ours several years ago before you joined us. I paid $250,000 for a used one."

Dustin shook his head. "Yes, five years ago. A lot has changed. Five years ago HDTV was a the-ory. Now they've got super high-definition smart TVs with voice command soon to be 3-D TV. Plus, they're getting cheaper all the time. Look here." Dustin pulled out a catalog from behind his back that he had dog-eared to a page.

Jason took the book from him, read over the de-scriptions and examined the photographs. In truth, some nice new generation sequencing equipment beckoned those with money. In a fraction of the time it took them now, any one of them could more rapidly read the codes within specific genes to see if they were normal or abnormal, especially since the human genome had been completely mapped. Now they might make some real progress.

The billions of individual nucleotides in DNA are aligned in a particular order to make up individual genes for each species. The sequencer can easily identify many of the commonalities and differences. Jason likened the technology advances in their field of research to a mechanic who first worked on flathead car engines and then had to learn the complicated electronics found in today's models. Today, instead of a few enzymes and chemical separations, one used radioisotope labeling, nano-filtration, ionic charges, and smaller equipment that could provide the investigator with the proper order of DNA base pairs. In a few years, a person would be able to do their own DNA analysis at home. All of which made men like Dustin and Tomás invaluable. Jason relied upon Dustin to keep him informed about the operation of new equipment once it became available.

Unfortunately, so far, they could only detect a number of confusing sequences, when using standardized tests on pieces of DNA that had been figured out a long time ago. In Dustin's words, the virus had created some pretty messed up DNA.

"Do you know anybody who has one of these?" Jason asked.

"Yep. Berkeley, for one," he answered.

Jason felt slightly embarrassed. That's where he'd come from. "Call somebody over there. Tell them you're from my lab. See if they like their new equipment," Jason directed.

"I already did."

"And..." Jason began.

"They said it's like night and day."

"Okay. Order it. But first see if anybody wants ours," Jason concluded.

"I did that, too. Johnson over at UCLA will take it for a hundred thousand," Dustin reported. "He doesn't have the one-fifty for a new one."

"I'll lose a fortune," Jason groaned. He was surprised Dustin didn't say he'd already ordered a new one until Dustin admitted, "I put a new one on hold for us, pending your approval."

Dustin turned to leave, but stopped short. "If you want to wait a couple of years, they'll be demonstrating a hand-held unit that will sequence a virus in seconds and all three billion base pairs of human DNA within hours."

Jason stared at him in such a way that the taller man asked, "What?"

Jason slowly shook his head side to side. "Dustin. It does not make any sense. It's supposed to be a virus; in fact, I'm sure it's a virus, but it's not what it seems."

Dustin gathered his thoughts and replied, "Not to be philosophical, but for all we know the universe gets along just fine without humans trying to analyze it and put their own twist on things."

Not understanding Dustin's comment, Jason cocked his head. Dustin orated, "You know I'm one of these health guys, so I follow a lot of trends. Do you know that much of what we're told to believe is not what it seems? I mean, tens of thousands of people are tested, up to as many as a hundred thousand or more in each study conducted by the Brits, Aussies, Swiss, Norwegians, Americans and others, and the results of the studies are disconcerting. It's a good size list of studies: Vitamin C or any ingestible or inhaled product claiming to cure the common cold, probiotics, calcium supplements in milk to strengthen bones in adults, Omega 3s, antioxidants, sports drinks, and cholesterol content in foods. How about organic versus inorganic, brown chicken eggs versus white eggs, and free-range chickens versus caged chickens. If you want, we can go into sacred territory and talk about the efficacy of ozone machines and air purifiers. None of it can be proven to do what it claims to do."

Jason threw his hand up in the air. "Stop it. You're killing me," he implored.

Dustin forged onward in one of his rare moments of discourse. "I could easily name another twenty. The point is, it makes total complete sense that all of these should do what we expect them to do, but, to me, not a single one of them does what it claims to do or what we expect it to do; with the exception of rare cases, of course, where a person is shown to be lacking in some vital nutritional element."

"Maybe we're measuring the wrong thing," Jason hypothesized.

Dustin dismissed the comment by saying, "I do believe in the placebo effect where it will do what it is supposed to do if you believe in it enough."

Jason countered, "Maybe, on an individual basis. On the large scale, placebo is counterbalanced by those who believe something won't work and it doesn't. So you're telling me not to take any supplements?" asked Jason.

Dustin responded, "I'm not telling you to do anything. According to my own blood tests, I'm low on potassium and magnesium, so I eat a lot of foods with those elements; bananas, potatoes, beans, squash. Now I don't get leg cramps at night. But I don't have an answer for what the studies tell us, Doctor. I know people need something to believe in. All we can do is our best."

With a wave of the hand, Jason resignedly concluded the conversation. "I have an answer. Don't have any expectations." He turned back to the microscope with a sick feeling about having to spend so much money. On second thought, unlike the relatively inexpensive fermenter, there was no legitimate reason why he couldn't build the high cost of the sequencer into a new grant application to study the New Flu. He looked up to stare at Dustin's back as the man left, pondering. If none of our beliefs work like we think they should, why is it something like their new virus that wasn't supposed to work actually did? And it didn't have a damn thing to do with placebo.

Jason turned back to the microscope when Don entered the room and asked, "Did you see the TV when we were at lunch with Gottlieb?"

"Sorry, my back was to the entertainment center," Jason replied, sarcastically." This was turning out to be one of those no-work days despite one's best efforts.

"Maternity ward in London. Two infants; one black, one Caucasian. Both deformed."

Jason snorted, "Deform is the new norm. London is where Linda went on vacation."

"Damn stuff moves fast," Don proclaimed.

"So would smallpox if it ever got loose, what with air travel and today's mobile population."

"Better load up, Jason. The fallout is crazy. Gun stores and liquor stores are running out of stock," Don advised.

"Maybe this will boost the economy," quipped Jason, wryly.

Don departed, passing Linda walking in. Jason looked at her with a bemused smile. Okey dokey and honkey donkey. Next. He turned off the power to the microscope, placed the dust cover over it, stood, and hung up his lab coat. "Let's take a walk."

Linda looked at him quizzically. "What's got you laughing, love?" she asked, as they left the building, grabbing their winter down-filled parkas on the way out.

"I haven't got the slightest idea," he confessed.

They got into his car and drove catty-corner to Holmes Lake. Jason parked and they got out, casually strolling the walkway sided by an expanse of snow-covered lawn. There was no scent of freshly mowed grass to add to a lazy day of Frisbees or the occasional seated person leaning against a tree reading a good book. Finding an unoccupied bench beneath a cottonwood, they brushed off the snow, relaxed, and looked out at the cold water of the lake glittering as it began to freeze over.

Three dogs playfully chased one another on the snow, their master carefully overseeing their activities. One of the dogs, a smaller Cocker, was noticeably faster than the two Jack Russells with which it played, escaping at will.

When the dogs turned toward the couple, Jason saw the abnormal appearance of the Cocker pup—a Sider as Jason was beginning to call them—adding to the feeling as though it belonged to the lazy day as much as anything else. The dog saw them and ran over to Linda who bent down to pet it. The dog looked up at Jason and they locked eyes for an instant. He thought about Jimmy, the waiter. This dog did not look miserable, in fact, of three dogs, this one seemed to be the most friendly.

The whine of four turbofan engines powering a giant Boeing C-17 Globemaster flying low broke the silence as it gained elevation. Jason surmised it might be traveling the U.S. Strategic Command out of Omaha. It may have been heading to McConnell Air Force Base in Wichita, Tinker AFB in Oklahoma City, or further south into Dallas or Houston. Military planes and helicopters frequently traveled the route going in either direction with almost a straight-line between the five cities. Following that same line straight north would take the plane to Ellsworth AFB in Grand Forks, North Dakota, 500 miles away. Jason also surmised that most, if not all the bases had nukes in the form of underground missile silos and bombs of varying yields. He did not voice the thought that if humans nuked themselves out of existence, only the virus and possibly cockroaches would survive.

After the noise of the C-17 receded into the distance, Jason had another thought. He pulled out his phone and asked questions to a female robot. She replied, "A total of 102,000 commercial airline flights around the world occur daily with another 50,000 private plane flights. Last year, 700 million passengers traveled by commercial airlines in the U.S."

He'd have to discuss this with June who maintained that birds migrated more than humans. He lost track when he began to compute the number of people carried by cars and boats leading him to think that the disease wasn't communicable. One caught it by inhaling virus particles, but they never left the body in the normal sense. Unlike the cold or flu, it couldn't be caught when someone sneezed, or touched something or drank from a contaminated object. The virus didn't reproduce in the mucous membrane like the cold and flu virus or inside the gut like Salmonella or in mayonnaise-laden potato salad like Staphylococcus or E. coli, or in the lungs like TB or pneumonic plague. In fact, the damnable things didn't reproduce inside the body at all, they reproduced outside of it. If the particles were on the skin and clothing of one airplane passenger, they would probably be on and in everybody else in the plane by the time the plane landed.

Contacting the cell phone's robot again, Jason found that, everything considered, approximately 200 million miles are flown throughout the world each day with public and private transportation combined. At roughly a mile per gallon of fuel used, that came to 200 million gallons of jet fuel used each day, much of which goes into the upper atmosphere. Roughly 20 pounds of carbon dioxide are released into the atmosphere with each gallon burned, not counting other particulates and pollutant gases. For carbon dioxide alone, that converted to four billion pounds added to the air. Per day. Over a trillion and a half pounds a year—nearly a billion tons.

A final cell phone inquiry made a bad situation worse. The automobiles of the world released 2.4 million pounds of carbon dioxide per second which comes to nearly 40 billion tons yearly. He'd better not tell any of that to Dustin. The man would have a stroke. They were being attacked from the air above them, from the air they breathed, and from within them all. Any way you sliced the pie, whether the travels were one way or round trips, the worldwide spread of this new strain of influenza looked to be inevitable and extremely rapid.

Jason shook his head, as he ran more numbers through it. The flu pandemic of 1918 affected one-third of the world's population of 1.5 billion without airline travel amounting to anything during those early years of flight. If that occurred today and at a percentage of one-third of the people being affected, closer to two billion could be counted, not a meager 500 million. The good news? Maybe nobody would die from it. At least not directly. Indirectly might be another story altogether. At the moment, he didn't want to think about how that might come to pass.

Linda broke into his reverie and his phone calls. Seemingly, he had forgotten her presence. "Dustin told me you ordered the latest sequencing equipment."

"It was more like he ordered it. I merely okayed it," Jason snorted, putting his phone away, his frosty breath coming out like puffs of smoke. This time she chuckled.

They spent a few minutes in the cold, knowing a single secret privy to only a handful of people on a world of almost eight billion. Finally Linda asked, "Gottlieb's proposal does seem to have merit. What do you think? I say the man's got serious connections."

Jason shook his head quickly side-to-side. "Why should he hold all the patents?"

Linda looked at him as though he didn't have enough brains to pass a class in basic stupidity. "For a whole lot of reasons."

"Like?"

"Like, he's lining up a ridiculous amount of money for the venture. He's making, marketing and selling the products, taking the risk, shouldering the responsibility and turning you into a multi-zillionaire. Like, you've got nothing you yourself can use to file for a patent, even if you wanted to. You said so yourself. So, sell him the rights to the material. It's called licensing. Hey, you're the one who wanted to make products. Now's your chance. Do you have the time to shop around? Go for it, because I really don't care either way. Furthermore, the next guy will tell you the same thing. In my opinion, you're not doing very good job of hanging onto your own nuts, so let the next guy do it for you and you get paid while he's the one doing the work."

Jason's eyes widened at Linda's words. He relented. "Got it. Anyway, I'm thinking of selling twenty-five percent. The remaining money will be split with Don and me with each getting twenty-five percent, and for you, Dustin and the other three to split equally what's left. Don can take care of June."

"Five percent each," she quickly computed. "That'll pay a lot of bills."

"We'll discuss it with the others in the morning. I need to sleep on it first. Casual dining and relaxation at my house tonight, babe?" he asked.

"You got it, boss," she grinned, mischievously.

They both stood, strolled to the car, and drove back to the place where it all started. More correctly, it all may have started 250 million miles away and a close to a billion years in the past.

The image of the Sider dog looking at him

wouldn't leave Jason's thoughts. Completely fatigued from half-dreams about millions of mutants traveling the skyways, each wearing new clothing made from the virus, Jason drank his first cup of coffee at 3:45 a.m. He had no desire to look in the mirror in case he'd made the conversion to a mutant during the night, similar to turning into a zombie in the Living Dead television series. Stage fright panic surged through him.

Mirror mirror on the wall, what the hell went wrong? Wait a minute. Curious about a piece of random information, he went to the computer and looked it up. Stagefright was the name of a computer virus that infected certain operating systems. When he read that he began to laugh out loud.

Jason broke one of his own rules and purchased a TV for his home. For him, there is nothing like graphic images to infuse one's daily or nightly thoughts with negativity. He couldn't decide whether the purchase satisfied a need for self-flagellation, or if it reflected a curiosity about the state of world affairs.

Arriving at work by 7:30, he met the group at 8:30, and by 9:00 the team had made two key decisions. First, they decided to maintain the animal studies. You can use a test tube to get a lead, but biological systems have a way of destroying that lead in nothing flat. Or that lead could be supported. Then you expand the experiment to include a larger number of biological systems, mice in this case, then go to a small trial in humans, which could expand into a larger trial. All of this takes years under normal, stable, FDA regulated, peer reviewed, medically approved, circumstances.

None of that applied. This needed to move on the fast track. Rick, their animal keeper could be trusted. Everyone agreed on that. Simple common sense on his part would be needed to match the warped mice in his care with what he was viewing on TV. He had to know a lot and still kept it to himself.

The four biologists also agreed to purchase a new DNA sequencer, recouping the expense with the next grant application. More work would be done in a fraction of the time it took them now. Jason wanted Don to work with June correlating data as Linda went over more advanced microscopic photos in an attempt to make further discoveries about the virus in their midst. The others would continue with their various research duties until Gottlieb called again. Dustin laughingly noted that Gottlieb wasn't the only player; only the first who might make an offer.

When working on the New Flu virus and using basic techniques of virology, Dustin and Tomás worked on human cells grown in tissue culture in Petri dishes, while Jason and Linda worked on tissues taken from the mice themselves. How did the virus get into a cell? How long did it take to bind to the host DNA? What happened to its outer coat?

Two weeks later, $150,000 worth of genetic sequencing equipment arrived from Minneapolis accompanied by a coughing technician to update the users on new settings the old device lacked. Perhaps now the team could make some serious progress.

18 May of Year 2

It didn't happen that way. As the months passed, work became the dreaded routine of basic research, offering an occasional exciting moment of false discovery randomly inserted between endless hours of tedium. Jason felt as though he might as well be trying to whistle into the wind to indicate their lack of progress. He decided to publish what they had found on the virus—entangled DNA and mouse data, complete with photographs. That would be acknowledged a breakthrough. The data would be quickly reviewed, published quickly, and would bring in fast money. He also decided to reapply for more money to continue Tomás ongoing project that.

Jason forced himself to watch the TV he'd purchased to check the news around the world with the single-minded purpose of tracking the course of the disease. Surely, the CDC would have a handle on it by now. The daily news spent an increasing amount of time devoted to the epidemic. The world had become infected and afraid. Curiously, one commercial insert in a news program touted the freshness of one company's fruits and vegetables over those of their competition.

Remembering the baggie with strawberry and grass leaves June had given him months before now in his freezer, he retrieved it. Feeling bored with another day of non-progress, he took it to the mini-lab in his home office. Placing a drop of immersion oil toward the left end a microscope slide, he used a single-edged razor blade to gently scrape off a tiny amount of superficial cells from the top layer of one of the strawberry leaves onto the drop of oil. He placed a coverslip over it and lightly tapped it down. Toward the right side of the slide, he repeated the process, using the scrapings from the bottom of the leaf. Then he placed the side-by-samples on the stage of the microscope and rotated the turret until the oil immersion lens clicked into place. Together with the 15x magnification of the eyepieces he was close to 1500x, having no expectations.

Within 60 seconds he had finished his work and leaned back. The boredom had been instantly replaced by yet another sick feeling. It wasn't only animals the virus attacked but green plants, as well. The virus was on the leaves.—another monster in their midst. He felt compelled to go public, to yell Fire. He repeated the scraping process with the grass leaves and could not escape the truth.

Jason leaned back in his chair and placed both hands over his forehead and eyes, gently massaging. He rubbed the back of his neck, made a decision and placed his cell phone camera up to the microscope eyepiece. Ensuring the image on the screen was proper, he took several pictures of what he saw. The next morning, drained from lack of sleep and depressed, he ambled into June's office and took a seat opposite her desk. She looked up from the papers before her and asked, "What'ya got there, boss?"

Jason pulled up a chair. He laid down the pictures he had taken on the desk. "These are photographs of the strawberry leaves you gave me. I think they're becoming infected where the carbon dioxide gets absorbed, mostly on the bottom of the leaves where there are more stomates. The virus is also present in my own lawn, as you had guessed. I'm thinking the rate of photosynthesis is increasing because of the infection. That's why the plants are growing faster."

June looked at the photos carefully, as a professional artist might critically examine the work of an upstart. The dark virus particles clearly stood out on the edges of the circular stomates, like flotsam on the outer edge of a whirlpool. She picked them up and held them at different arms' length. She looked up at her employer with a look he had never seen before. To him it was a look of fear. "Jason, the implications of this are horrendous. If this is real, then insects might also get infected. They absorb oxygen through their outer covering, metabolize it and release carbon dioxide. I know this because of art pieces I was hired to draw where I had to show the fine anatomy of their carapace, their outer shell."

Jason began to pace, unsure of how much more of this he could take. "Okay. Animals and now plants are ready targets for our space alien. It's not a killer and it's not a symbiont; in other words, it's not like a married couple sharing their lives. It doesn't provide solar protection in exchange for nutrients, or enter into any one of a countless mutually beneficial relationships that exist on our world. It's a parasite plain and simple. It takes what it wants in exchange for nothing. There's no purpose for it to kill that which supports its life. However, it is also a mutagenic agent, one that causes changes in the host, either by accident or for reasons of its own."

Jason pointed to the close-up of the two photographs. "I'm thinking the virus particles haven't been absorbed into the stomates yet, at least in these pictures. Stomates are where water vapor exits the plants along with the oxygen. Plants also take in carbon dioxide there, animals exhale it one way or another. It doesn't matter to this creature. It's all CO2. While stomates are present in other locations in plants, such as trunks, branches and flower parts, their highest concentration is in the leaves. They are most common in the underside, and that what we're seeing here."

Jason's degree in molecular ecology took charge of his mouth, now bringing forth his darkest thoughts. "I'll go one step further. If this virus spreads throughout the vegetative system of our planet like it's spreading through animal life, we can expect a lot more water vapor in our atmosphere. That's because of the increase in water vapor extruded from the now more rapidly grown green plants. We might want to invest in a company that makes dehumidifiers, because we're going to need them."

June tapped a red fingernail on the desk, thinking. "It's frightening, not knowing what kind of train is coming down the tunnel toward us; not that there's a lot we can do about it. It's kind of like the first inning of a ball game that is promising to have a limitless number of innings. Humans like to prepare. We're used to it. We've had the worst thrown at us and understand we might die from cancer or small-pox or the plague, but at least we know how we're going to die."

Jason responded darkly, "Dear God, I'm not too sure that's any better than knowing how we're going to live."

The next day Jason learned he was awarded a quarter-million dollar grant from the NIH for re-search into the New Flu based on their breakthrough research, as published in the medical literature. The new sequencer was paid for, local news stations interviewed him, while numerous scientific cir-cles confirmed his findings. None suspected a link between the spread of the epidemic and the rap-id growth of plants, in large part because few had thought to look for the fibers on the leaves although fruit produced by the more rapidly growing plants tasted a little bitter these days. Botanists surmised it must be due to a water issue because it contained the identical vitamin content as before the infection had spread to plant life.

Protesters held up signs and banners in front of hospitals and national research centers demanding honest answers to anything. Conspiracy theorists pointed out that officials who claimed to know noth-ing proved they knew everything. Rock stars and country-western singers wrote new songs about the disease. Every illness imaginable was ascribed to the New Flu. Attendance rose sharply when religious leaders concentrated their sermons on end-of-world scenarios. Stadiums and arenas became filled to capacity to hear their message. Donations didn't hurt to encourage the doomsayers.

At the lowest end of the spectrum, Jason found new ways to become frustrated. His team could make no headway in deciphering the alien codes, let alone finding a way to get it to disentangle from the host DNA. In terms of making further progress regarding the New Flu to satisfy the NIH, it wasn't happening despite the money awarded. He was driven toward directing his energy toward the making of products, yet Gottlieb had disappeared off the face of the Earth.

Early one evening, after another day of unproductive work, Linda called Jason at home. "Jace, I'd like to invite myself over."

Not certain how to respond, he offered, "Okay, can I have time to clean up all the liquor bottles and underwear the dancing girls left behind?"

Linda chuckled, "I needed a laugh. Is it okay if I come over?"

"Come on, babe, you don't need an invitation. It's your house, too."

Needing company, he made a quick call for Chinese food to be delivered and pulled out his electric razor. Shaving with one hand, he put away the latest Field and Stream and Guns and Ammo publications into the top drawer of his nightstand and worked his way to the shower where he finished shaving with a blade. Putting on clean sweats and an old Berkeley Tee-Shirt with its motto, Fiat lux, Let there be light, he slipped his feet into a pair of sandals and combed his hair. Twenty minutes later the doorbell rang. Jason opened the door. Linda stood there with a bag in her hand looking luscious. She wore a long warm black windbreaker dusted with snow over black slacks and white sneakers. Her cheeks were rosy, her hair layered perfectly, highlighted by white sparkles of snowflakes which were already beginning to melt in the warmth of the home.

"Oh, hi, what a coincidence meeting you here. Brought some Chinese." She held up the bag. Jason held the door open for her to enter as he swung his left arm outward in a gesture to enter. "Why, you shouldn't have. How thoughtful."

Smiling, yet remaining silent, she dusted off her coat at the entry, took it off, and hung it in the hall closet to expose a tight long sleeve cotton sweater she wore. She placed the large bag on the counter and began pulling out the containers while Jason set the table. Jason knew this woman. She had something on her mind.

As they dished out various contents from the containers, the doorbell rang again. He opened the door. His delivery had arrived. He paid the man and closed the door. "Thought you might like some Chinese," he beamed, setting down another heavy bag onto the counter.

Linda patted her stomach. "Just think, Jace, we're going to weigh this much more after we finish."

They laughed and feasted. After dinner Jason felt in a better mood as the couple relaxed side-by-side on the sofa, holding hands. A large jug of ice water stood on a coffee table in front of them to slake the inevitable Chinese Thirst, as they called it. Puccini's La Traviata played softly on the surround-sound speakers.

Pulled into the music, Linda thought, He's in a sensual mood. Good. She placed her hand on his upper thigh, moved it around gently, leaned into him and whispered in his ear, "Jace, will you marry me?"

Jason wondered how many ways there were for his world to come to an end. He immediately flushed, pulled away and looked at her. "Baby, I'm so self-absorbed with all this, well, stuff." He gave her an honest answer.

Well prepared for his reaction, as well as for other possible reactions, Linda confessed, "I know, Hon, it's all right. I'm having a hard time dealing with everything on my own. I want us to share the rest of our lives together. I love you. I don't want to be alone anymore. I want us to be good together."

Clearly puzzled by his non-answer and not knowing how to respond, Linda had a fleeting thought, one that brought the man's mental stability into question. She considered retracting her offer. In an instant, she reflected, not for the first time, about a serious problem they might have regarding the state of his home. The man was enthusiastic about life, yet his sterile home did not reflect that enthusiasm. There were a couple of mom and dad pictures in the hallway along with a few hunting and fishing pictures of himself with his father back in Virginia, but none were in the living room. At least in the bedroom stood a large bookcase neatly filled with hardcover books by classical poets and writers. On the wall there hung a Van Gogh lithograph of a man crossing a bridge and a couple of Japanese wall hangings that appealed to him. How would he react if she left a medical journal open on the floor next to an arm chair or on a countertop? She would need her own office.

With all of these reservations, Linda knew what she needed more than anything. Unquestionably, she sought companionship. They could work out the rest. Times were rough with no indication they would be getting better soon.

For Jason, other than to break her heart, he could find no way out. He couldn't do it. A man would be hard pressed to find a woman as good as the one sitting next to him who had just proposed. Their interests were common and her ability to put up with him placed her in a special category. Doubtless, it had been an ordeal for her to work up to this moment.

He wanted to tell her this required some thought until a very human emotion grabbed his heart. Tired of analyzing, he looked deeply into her eyes. Finally, putting both hands to her cheeks, Jason came out with what he first wanted to blurt out before his brief moment of prattle, "Yes, my dear, I'd love to marry you." If words could have a taste, these tasted like sweet desert after a salty dinner.

Two weeks later, on a late Sunday afternoon, the couple was married. Jason, Linda and Don agreed it would be a good idea to invite Gottlieb. Linda made the call to his office only to be informed he would be in Germany the day of the wedding.

Jason invited his parents to attend. The last time Jason's parents visited Lincoln was before he started his research center. After that, he would fly back to Virginia every couple of years for a visit. At the present time, they were on a Caribbean cruise and would not be able to get to the wedding. Sending their well wishes, they expressed their best congratulations to Jason. Their own previous investigations found Linda Beaufort to be a woman of lineage. The Beaufort family could be traced back to the 14th century British nobility, including a long line of counts, dukes and duchesses. Her education added a nice plus and she was fluent in French. In their eyes, she would make a suitable mate.

Jason's father did mention that everybody on the cruise ship had this cold or flu that was going around. He wondered if anybody in Jason's lab had the same thing. He also expressed, not for the first time, whether Jason was to be the last of their line of the Randolphs. Perhaps there might there a male child at some point in their future. Jason was tempted to say, "Almost, Dad. I don't think you or mom would have been pleased with the appearance of your grandchild." Instead, he told them his work was keeping him busy while the future looks very bright in terms of making serious money. Reading between the lines, his mother told him it was all right to have a secret. Everyone has a secret they don't feel like sharing for various reasons. You'll know when it's time to tell the secret and if that time never comes, that's all right, too.

They held a quiet ceremony conducted by the pastor of a church Jason occasionally attended. Afterward, the group met at one of the better restaurants in Lincoln located in an old mansion where they enjoyed pomegranate duck, lamb, veggie dishes and cherry lemonade. They spoke of silly things unrelated to work.

As an amateur magician belonging to the Omaha Chapter of The Society of American Magicians, Dustin's expertise fell in the realm of simple magic. He astounded the small audience with tricks he performed with the use of objects on each of their tables such as turning odd and even stacks of sugar packets into even and odd stacks and he rubbed a fork against a knife to have them link end to end.

Personally, Dustin was deeply troubled by the changing ecosystem. He had lost weight by refusing to eat produce not grown by himself. He was concerned that, because of its fast growth rate, it, too, had become contaminated. He compensated for this by cutting back on the amount he ate. He preferred fresh fish, not farmed, or avoided it altogether if he thought it might have mercury or lead. He also eschewed red meat, especially after seeing pictures of newborn cattle.

Tomás brought his wife and son to the wedding.

All three had the cough. Alice was a smaller version of Linda and the son a larger version of his father. Given his father's middle name of Angel (pronounced with a soft "g") for his first name, the son played as an offensive lineman for the Cornhuskers football team and was anything but an angel on the field, having been nicknamed "And Hell" setting school records for quarterback sacks. The entire team was faster and stronger than opposing teams from other states that had not yet caught the virus.

Jason took a lot of convincing by Linda to forget the lab for a while, and damn it, this was their time together. With Don and June overseeing operations, everything would be fine. A few days in the fresh air of a beach can heal a lot of wounds. And not to worry, the epidemic would still be raging when they returned.

The next morning the newlyweds flew to Puerto Vallarta, Mexico, for a ten-day honeymoon. Situated in a resort midway down the Mexican west coast on the Gulf of California, they spent days on the beach eating their weight in seafood and took a bus ride around the cove to the Bay of Banderas where they attended a Sunday bazaar and drank margaritas on the beach.

Jason's spool unwound by fishing, zip-lining over chasms, eating fantastic dinners, swimming, and making love. No emergency calls had been forthcoming, although their hotel hosts did warn about a new cold virus that was going around and a lot of the guests had it, as did the staff.

The couple returned from their honeymoon to good news. Gottlieb had called wanting to talk. He requested a meeting at his lawyer's office in Omaha. Jason's lawyer, whom he had known for years, helped him with both personal and business matters and had previously met Gottlieb's lawyer on other matters. In the end, Jason sold Gottlieb a twenty-five percent share without Jason having to do anything except to make more powder. This opened up an intense period of discussion between two attorneys, Gottlieb, Jason and Don.

Jason agreed to permit one of Gottlieb's engineers into his personal lab to watch the procedure of making the sandwiches and to work on improving the product. Jason affirmed that he would do his best to supply as much powder as Gottlieb wanted. After that, it would be out of Jason's hands. Gottlieb could make bridges or toothpicks as far as he and Don were concerned, although they preferred the former.

When the two men returned from the meeting, the others were ecstatic, with the exception of Rick. Money didn't excite him; love of family did. This included the people for whom he worked. Jason often wished to have Rick's simple perspective on life instead of the endless chase after elusive ghosts that didn't buy real happiness. Not long ago, he had what it took to be satisfied in life. If this crisis ever ended, he'd do his best to spend more time outdoors, preferably with his wife.

Because Jason's parents were multi-millionaires and shared their wealth, he never knew a time when money wasn't there for him. They raised him never to want and he faulted them for that. He had passed the college aptitude tests with high scores and could afford to attend the schools of his choice. He had never expressed it to his parents, but he had always wished for a minimum wage job, to struggle to make ends meet. This was unlike the next guy, who wished he could have Jason's wealth. Maybe he should have been a career politician, to know everything about everything and never have to work a real eight-to-five job, a necessary prerequisite for the position, in his view.

Jason reflected on how hard he was working to find cures for diseases, all the while, ironically, distributing a disease-causing agent affecting animal and plant life. He felt as though he were a drug dealer who had succumbed to his own product. He found himself driven to find a cure, as might a professional compared with an amateur, or a true scientist over a pretender.

Linda brought him out of his thoughts. "You haven't coughed for a few days, Hon. Now that I think of it, I haven't either."

"I haven't?" His throat didn't irritate him anymore. "You're right," he admitted.

"What do you think it means?" she asked.

"Let's wait and see if it comes back," he suggested. Mentally checking himself, he added, "I don't ache either; well, maybe a zero point five out of ten. Maybe it's settling in."

"Shifting into a higher gear?" Linda offered.

"That doesn't sound good. Departing is a better word."

Linda counted off on her fingers. "Let's calculate. You, Don, and June got it before me because you were the first exposed, but for all practical purposes, we were all exposed on the same day or the next day when it began to spread throughout the building. The aches started maybe two weeks after that. We're a couple of months ahead of the other infected places because we took our vacations after we were well into the project. The poor babies were born some twelve months after the parents' exposure, so it looks like we were at the very beginning of the virus' spread. What scares me most is the unpredictable. First it's the animals, then the birds; now it's the vegetation. What's left?"

Remembering June's words, he added, "Except for maybe insects, that about covers it." He did not feel all that confident in his statement.

June of Year 2

Don and June hosted the traditional party held on the last Friday of the month. The Jennings' lived on the far west side of the city on the shore of Oak Lake, somewhat farther west than did Linda and near I-80 leading to Omaha. After picking her up, Jason drove to their host's residence in a gated community. Originally 2200 square feet, the Jennings' added 500 square feet to the house. Christened The Me Room, it featured beige Nylon carpeting and a double-paned picture window looking directly onto the lake.

Don's half of the room included glass-enclosed cases of gem and mineral collections along with a small library of geology and astronomy books. The Jennings Meteorite sat ominously in a display case of its own. Jason resisted the temptation to give it a wide berth and approached the case to stare at the messenger from Mars, wondering what other surprises it held. June's portion of the room included her framed medical and anatomical drawings. Dozens of ornithology books stood side-by-side in oaken bookshelves.

The room had been aptly named. Numerous awards that had been presented to Don and June had been expensively framed or laminated and mounted. Two side-by-side arm chairs with a coffee table between them sat facing the lake to the north. A set of zoom photo-binoculars stood on the table ready to capture images of the variety of birds frequenting the lake and the nearby trees. Next to the binoculars lay a well-worn book on birding. Reportedly, the binoculars also captured occasional misadventures of somewhat inebriated fishermen, along with their wives and friends who might enjoy a little lakeside fun.

A door to the north led to a lawn, some fifty yards above the lake, where a six-burner barbecue and picnic table stood. Several people were casting lines into the water off a small pier in the distance with other boats slowly trolling the water.

The foursome relaxed in the open air, finishing the pasta salad June had prepared and they started on Jason's chicken Alfredo casserole. June rubbed her temple and said, "Donny, be a dear and get me an aspirin, would you please."

"Sure," Don replied and got up from the table. "Headache again?"

"Storm coming in," she said.

Don walked back into the home. Returning with the bottle, he handed it to his wife who shook out a tablet, thought for an instant, shook out a second tablet, and washed them down with a swallow of red wine to provide an enhanced effect. "I'm a mess," she confessed. "This weather sensitivity is getting worse and worse for me, I think."

Linda was concerned about her best friend. June never complained about anything physical. "It's my right shoulder that gets going and right now it hurts like hell. But the sky is clear. How does that work, Jace? Didn't you tell me that was one of your areas of interest?" Linda asked, not letting him in on the fact that one of the reasons she had invited him over was for probe his mind.

Jason looked at her, evaluating. After more than 18 months of ailments attributed to the virus, symptoms of the disease began to disappear. People felt better, in general. Having aching joints, together with constant headaches for that long, can be physically and mentally draining. Now June complained of something he thought to be unrelated.

"It once was, not now. I used to write a column in

the college newspaper called Your Health Forecast. In the column I told people what to expect with the upcoming weather of the day. I'd begun researching the topic in high school back in Virginia. The study of weather and health goes back thousands of years. I'm told the Scandinavians give that information as part of their regular weather report."

Jason had the attention of the others as he continued. "Weather sensitivity is greater in women than in men by a factor of three and it's more relevant as one ages. We're talking about aches and pains, headaches, mood swings, changes in hormone levels, just a lot of stuff that's related to cloudiness, wind, change in barometric pressure, rain, heat, you name it. If you have gout, a form of arthritis, those areas will hurt, too."

"Don't stop now," said June.

Jason had the green light to continue. "The pains are mostly felt where scar tissue accumulates in areas we injure over time, or in the joints as they get worn, including fingers and sprained thumbs. Pain in the lower back is common, along with pain in the knees and shoulders. What typically happens is that, when the barometric pressure drops when a storm front moves in, tissue fluid leaves the blood vessels to flow into injured areas which become swollen, putting pressure on nerve endings. Swelling also occurs in the meninges, the covering over the spinal column and the brain, hence the headaches. One thing we can't understand is that the symptoms can begin a day or two before the barometric pressure begins to drop. One theory has it that the interface of wind on ground creates positive ions which precede the storm front to cause many of the effects. How it does so is up to conjecture. By the way, the sharper the drop in pressure, the worse the pain."

Linda said, "Wind makes me crazy. Is that normal or is it just me?"

Jason smiled, "That's totally normal. There are a lot of things going on we don't understand. I mean, ask a teacher about her kids on those days, if you don't believe me."

Don was about to joke about his wife always being a headache, but thought better of it. He understood it took great effort on her part to admit to her pain. He made a mental note to rub her temples later and to put a couple of ice packs on his own knees. He could identify with what Jason said, because both his knees ached from years of trekking over rough terrain. Walking up flights of stairs used to be simple. These days he used the elevator or escalator whenever he could.

June said, "That's not very reassuring, Jason. You're telling me it's going to get worse before it gets better as I get older?"

"No, I'm telling you it's not going to get better and it will become more frequent and more intense, that is, if global weather patterns change for the worse. An increasing number of people will be affected, too," Jason concluded.

June complained, "Thanks, Jason. I feel so much better now that I know my career as an artist may be over."

Jason asked, "Do your fingers hurt at all when you get these headaches?"

June shook her head. "Never joints. Only headaches."

"Then your fingers should be fine. Not to worry," Jason reassured her.

June did not at all feel assured by what she had just learned about the future of her headaches or her artwork. According to him, her fingers would be fine and if they weren't, she'd find a way to manage. Drawing with any kind of headache was not possible.

"One last question, Jason," June said. "Do you get any of these problems if you're indoors?"

"Yes," Jason replied, "You get them all. If you want more time to do your artwork, I would suggest the hotter portions of Desert Southwest where there are less fluctuations in the yearly weather. "

June turned to her husband and, with a little mischievous glint in her eye, and a wink Jason didn't see, requested, "Donny, order up a couple of cases of wine and a large bottle of aspirin, would you please, just as a backup?"

"You shouldn't mix..." Jason began, and stopped instantly as Linda stepped lightly on her husband's toes under the table.

After a short pause in the conversation, Don said, "Jason, You should watch sports. They're quite entertaining these days. Pitchers are throwing fastballs more than 120 miles per hour. Instead of batters swinging at thin air they're hitting a lot more home runs. Apparently the ball is traveling up to five hundred feet. Bats are being shattered more than ever. The league is testing reinforced aluminum bats. And if you like fast action, try watching basketball. Personally, I can't wait for track and field season. We can expect no record to be safe."

"Those are humans. You should see Tom, our cat." June added, laughingly."What's Tom done now?" Jason asked.

June motioned with a hand upward, "Jumped onto the roof of our garage."

"From the ground? Ten feet?" exclaimed Jason in astonishment.

June only smiled. "By the way, I read in the paper that WG Corporation, founded by Wilbur Gottlieb, will soon announce a new line of products. These are expected to revolutionize the lifestyle of virtually every person."

"Finally," exclaimed Jason, gleefully. "Now, maybe we can get someplace."

Linda interrupted, "You aroused my curiosity, Don. Let's find some game to watch. Got any cricket or soccer matches on? I want to see what you're talking about."

"Honey, we're eating and having polite conversation. It's not a time for television," Jason objected.

June glared at him. "You know how to push buttons, don't you, Jason? Donny, turn on the goddamn television."

Don smiled and went indoors. The other followed

and took seats facing the entertainment center. A large unlit fireplace stood in a corner to the right.

Don picked up the remote to find a basketball game in progress. The four watched the team from Seattle run faster and out-rebound the one from Los Angeles. Clearly, the team from Los Angeles hadn't been hit with the most recent version of a cold.

As if the gods of coincidence were smiling upon them, the game went into half-time. A male reporter stood in front of a building with Seattle General carved in stone behind him. The scene flashed to a female reporter standing next to another sign that read Maternity. Six deformed babies of mixed races were depicted in the scene that were part of the weekly toll. The scene flashed to the similar one from London to another in New York City and another in Lincoln, Nebraska.

"Guess we can start adding cities," Don observed. "These births may soon be so commonplace TV may not show them anymore."

Linda turned up the volume. The male reporter presented a wrap-up. "Sources tell us there is speculation the Russians ore the Chinese are involved because no abnormal births have been reported from those countries."

Jason thought, That's only because the virus hasn't reached that far yet. No problems in Russia other than Chernobyl, and a much worse on that went unreported back in 1957. Can any secret be kept forever?

Two months later, WG Corp. launched. Jason's group completed the last remaining project related to cancer research and began to prepare a report on more discoveries they had made about the New Flu, without claiming it to be a virus.

Jason now found himself in the odd position of spending no time working on cancer and all of his time in the business of making large quantities of black powder. When a container of it was loaded onto an armored truck and transported to the WG Corp. facility for creation of a growing number of products, he could not remain detached during the transfer process. What started with a few particles of dust in a flask of liquid had been turned into the equivalent of bags of gold.

Watching the truck drive off, Don declared, "Capitalism at its finest."

"Only if we get paid for it," Jason stated. He turned to his friend. "We need better security. This morning I ordered construction of a chain-link razor-wire-topped fence complete with cameras, warning signs, and a guard shack for 24 hour protection. That should make everyone feel a little better."

It wasn't the outside physical security that concerned Jason as much as did his personal insecurity. Should he add security to his house only a hundred yards to the south? He'd fenced his entire property years before, a move meant to deter vagrants. Soon enough, if he looked out the master bedroom window of his home, he would see a tall chain link fence surrounding his beloved research playground. It would look like a prison on his own property in the heart of America—more like his personal Area 51.

Necessity demanded that he surround the lab which contained the traveler, no, the invader from outer space, not his home. For that, he ordered a simple top-of-the line security system.

PART TWO

January of Year 4

Gottlieb had visited millionaires and billionaires from Delhi to Singapore; from San Francisco to Cape Town, and made it work. RCR evolved into to a black powder production facility. The money rolled in as WG Corp. began to manufacture and sell a growing line of products. Jason ordered the construction of another wing to be added onto the building and the addition of several more combination fermenter-centrifuges for which he had initially planned. He struggled to build a wall around his emotions which filled a mental dam to capacity with few sluice gates for outlets. One sluice directed a flow toward production of product while another went toward his relationship with Linda. Trying to find a cure for the epidemic was no longer a priority. Despite the presence of new wealth, one basic problem remained. He couldn't hire new staff. They would quickly learn the virus had come from the institute because of their production of powder made from it. Furthermore, he now had to spend time meeting regularly with accountants.

Linda saw it in her man's eyes, heard it when he spoke. She had loved him for his eternal optimism. Now her husband was close to giving up his dream of reversing the march of the plague spreading throughout the globe.

June summed up all their feelings at the office one morning. "My problem is personal. I'm filthy rich with no time to spend any of it. What would I buy, a bigger TV? Or perhaps take a trip to see a mutated Europe, Asia, South America or Africa and listen to them all moan and complain. It's almost laughable."

She concluded with a final thought. "What's fascinating is the great new inventions coming forth thanks to everybody's IQ being bumped up a couple of notches. Babies are learning faster and dogs are training more easily. "Would you guess my art is actually showing some improvement?"

Jason thought he might be coming down with the influenza of old and left work early one afternoon. When Linda came home she found him sprawled on the sofa asleep with the TV on mute. A program on hunting in wetlands somewhere in the southeastern part of the country flickered from one colored scene to another. Camouflaged men hid in blinds, others lay in wait with rifles ready, as flocks of birds flew overhead or settled onto the water.

She sat on the floor next to her husband, put a cool compress on his forehead and gently stroked his head. He confessed, "Babe, I don't want to go back to the lab."

"You need to rest. You'll be fine, Jace. You'll change your mind," she consoled.

"We've got the equipment, but we don't have the people to keep up with demand. Gottlieb wants more powder and I can't tell him the truth," he complained.

"Maybe it's time you did," she prompted. "He's got the resources to provide what we need. As a rough guess, I'd say those resources include people who know how to keep their mouths shut."

Jason paused to think before asking, "Yeah? To what end?"

"Forward progress will be made and one less worry for you," she whispered in his ear.

"You're right," he sighed in reply. "I'll call him tomorrow. I'd kiss you, but I don't want you to catch what I've got." They both laughed until it hurt.

One week later, at 9:00 a.m., the guard at the shack called to report the presence of a man calling himself Wilbur Gottlieb who had shown up at the gate to see Dr. Randolph. Would he please come out to verify Mr. Gottlieb's identity?

Don and Jason walked the short distance in the light snowfall to meet a man standing next to the same black Audi luxury sedan they had parked next to at the restaurant. Dressed casually in designer jeans, white polo shirt and sneakers, Gottlieb wore a three-quarter length black leather coat. Reportedly, he had returned from another meeting with several heads of state, this time in Asia, only days before receiving the call from Jason.

The three men shook hands. Don spoke a few words to Gottlieb in German. Jason had no idea his friend understood the language. Apparently, Don had asked Gottlieb to drive in and park, because that's what the man did. Once indoors, Jason led their guest into the front office where he introduced June as their resident illustrator, general organizer and ornithologist. Dressed smartly in a beige skirt, floral blouse, and headscarf to match her red hair, June stood from behind her desk to reach over and give Gottlieb a firm handshake. "You have a bird expert working for you?" Gottlieb expressed curiosity.

"Doesn't everybody?" quipped June. She stood ten inches shorter than their guest. He looked at the seemingly three-dimensional framed colored drawings on the wall to the right of the desk, action drawings depicting muscular and skeletal structures of both running humans and flying birds.

One particular drawing caught his attention. He drew closer and inspected it. The 11" x 14" framed black-and-white work depicted an Olympic weightlifter, wearing The Olympic Rings occupied the backdrop. The exactitude the muscle cuts, the striations, the concentration on the face and the fire in the eyes was remarkable. Areas of the body were shaded for emphasis. A fine scrawl in the lower right corner read the signature of June Jennings. To him it were as though the blueprints for a new rocket engine had been placed in front of him for his perusal.

"Trust me when I say it's not my picture," stated a bemused Don, holding his hands palms out, as though establishing a barrier between himself and the drawing.

"I can get you a lithograph of that one, if you'd like," June offered.

"Are all of those yours?" the engineer asked her, with astonishment.

Don bragged, "The good ones are at home."

Gottlieb turned down his mouth to denote his appreciation. "Yes, of course, I would appreciate your gift. Thank you."

"Shall we?" Jason led the two men onward where they stopped at the entrance to Lab No. 1, his personal workspace where marble counters gleamed with cleanliness—at least with the lights on. "This one is mine," he declared. They moved on to the next lab where Dustin and Tomás were at work, each wearing a lab coat. A genetic sequencing machine sat on a central marble counter. They were comparing a pair of readouts, too intent in their tasks to give more than a brief nod or glance at the visitors. In another part of the lab a scintillation counter ticked as it counted radioactive particles tagged onto genetic codes while a printer spewed out data. Sparkling glassware in cabinets awaited their masters to put them to use.

The third lab belonged to Linda. A second sequencer stood on one of the marble counters; otherwise the equipment was nearly identical to that present in other two rooms. Equipment filled the fourth lab with nobody present.

After the fourth lab, they passed the bathrooms, followed by the breakroom, and the door leading downstairs to the animal facility. At last, they entered the new wing with the new fermenters. Two of them were in operation.

In the conference room Don and Jason took a seat while Gottlieb stared at the back wall. On it was a life-size painting of the state bird of Nebraska, the Sandhill Crane, in-flight. The long-legged bird measured 37 inches from beak to tail with a wingspan of six and a half-feet with another several inches of legs as they trailed behind the tail. Subtly done, the plumage was gray with brown on the back and the wings with bright red around its eyes and on its forehead. A light signature had been scrawled in the lower right portion of the artwork: June Jennings.

Other drawings were present on the walls of hummingbirds sipping nectar from the depth of flowers, scores of ducks taking off from a lake, all subtly drawn.

Gottlieb said, "Impressive."

"She likes to share," replied Don.

Gottlieb didn't trust himself to make a comment, so he merely smiled and nodded. A moment later, Linda joined them.

Jason related to Gottlieb their discovery of the virus in Don's meteorite as a result of their attempt to find nothing and their subsequent research on the alien, including their genetic findings. He told of their symptoms, the worldwide epidemic, and the mouse data.

Throughout the story Gottlieb raised an occasional eyebrow, but didn't say a word. He waited for Jason to finish and nodded. "Naturally, I had my experts look at the black powder and all they saw were what you call fibers. One of them is a very good microbiologist. He thought they might be some new kind of microbe, but he couldn't make them grow in the slightest. So we dropped that thinking. The spreading epidemic served as a distraction and I never gave a thought it might have come from you."

Gottlieb changed topics and stated flatly, "We will soon be a multi-billion dollar corporation. My people tell me in five years you and I will be owners of the wealthiest corporation in the world. So what? To better enjoy our poison?" He voiced all their sentiments.

Stretching back in his chair, Gottlieb folded his hands behind his head and exhaled. He stared at the table in front of him while Jason poured himself a glass of water, each person wrapped in their own thoughts. Whatever Gottlieb did or didn't do at this point would be fine with Jason. He didn't care too much either way.

At last Gottlieb spoke in German to Don, who later told them Gottlieb's words: "We're joined at the hip on this." He didn't ask a question, he stated a fact. Jason didn't have to know German to understand Don's response. "Yes, we are."

In his slight accent, Gottlieb mused, "How does the saying go? There is no sense rearranging deck chairs when the Titanic is sinking. I will provide you with the workers you need to make more powder. We must try to do some good. I am a human. I, too, have had my coughs and my headaches and two weeks ago my granddaughter gave birth to...twin girls." His voice trailed off as he struggled with the vision.

The rocket scientist turned businessman regained his composure. He continued in a stronger voice, "We will help with the production. I give you my promise. You can trust my people implicitly. In return, I want your promise to me that you will work hard and try to find a cure for this madness."

The room became completely silent. The three scientists looked into each other's eyes without speaking, mentally reviewing all they had done to this point, using the slightest of nods and frowns, sending vibes, reading facial tensions, sensing heat signals; communicating. They were beyond trying to make words work here. They had done their best, failed and had given up. What else was there to try? A rampaging dinosaur had gotten loose in the world in the shape of a microbe taking down everything it touched. Could anything be salvaged out this mess? The human race might be the single species that could be saved. It sounded like a good place to start.

Maybe there are other things we could do, Jason thought. He must think outside the box. He felt like laughing out loud at the sudden thought that the weight of the world rested on his shoulders. Or was it the fate of the world?

When had the virus from Mars gotten loose? Had

it happened when he first dusted the rock? No. If that were the case the creature would have invaded the planet when NASA, JPL and whoever else had looked for signs of life. Once again he came back to the conclusion he always came to: It must have been when he first un-stoppered the flask of liquid. Simply pulling off the top of a cotton plug from the flask of liquid opened Pandora's Box. But the plug had to be pulled sometime, didn't it? How else are you going to see what was inside? Standard procedure, right? Any scientist in the world would have done what he did.

In Greek mythology, a large jar, not a box, was given to Pandora. It contained all the evils in the world. Forbidden to open it, she did so out of curiosity, unleashing evils, leaving only Hope inside once she closed it again. Jason had looked it up months before: Pandora (noun): a process that generates many complicated problems as the result of unwise interference.

That described him all right. Was hope still there? But there is no power in hope, only in faith and belief coupled with action. Those are the forces connecting humans to the power of the universe. Hope is only a word in the same category as wishful thinking.

Somehow, the sensory powers of the three scientists lessened in their intensity and the three came to an unspoken agreement. At last Jason proclaimed, in as straightforward manner as he could, "Wilbur, all we can promise is that we will do our very best to find one."

After the Second World War, the pharmaceutical industry in East Germany began to as grow as the country rebuilt to eventually become a major industrial sector. Hans Gottlieb, Wilbur's father, served as a chemist with the industry in East Berlin in the 1960s and 1970s. Hans was native-born, as was his own father. Hans' specialty was the clandestine production of anabolic steroids for athletic performance enhancement.

The government paid him well and East German athletes won an increasing number of gold medals in successive Olympics Games. He understood the importance of speaking English in a Europe torn by the Cold War and saw a better future for his family in America as that nation continued to grow to become an economic power. He wanted to be part of that growth and to move west with his wife and young son.

Hans applied to several U.S. pharmaceutical companies and was offered a job with each of them. He accepted the position in Boston for a number of reasons. For one, it involved the international sales of steroids, a field with which he possessed intimate familiarity—this time, as applied to immune suppression in the emerging field of organ transplants. He was fluent in German, English, and French, was personable and good looking. In addition, he would be able to take Wilbur with him to teach him the ways of the business world and to teach him the art of making contacts he might need later as he developed into manhood.

Boston was also the home of The Massachusetts Institute of Technology, another factor in Hans' equation. It would take money to get the boy into school when he reached college age. The subject of immune suppression interested Hans for personal reasons in that it related to the early and expected death of himself and his son. Surreptitiously, Hans obtained three passports for the family and arranged passage to a German enclave in Boston to raise his son. He passed away at fifty-nine years of age to leave his wife to complete Wilbur's upbringing. Hans had prepared his son for the inevitable and, if the boy wanted to have a chance at a long life, he must pay attention to medical developments, as they unfolded over time.

Distraught at his father's passing, Wilbur Gottlieb swore to himself and his mother he would honor the memory of his father. Now, nearing sixty years of age, himself, Wilbur Gottlieb had his own demons and they had nothing to do with Jason Randolph or a contaminated planet. Business, world calamity, and personal tragedy are three separate entities. He preferred to dwell on business.

He liked to keep operations localized whenever possible, so with money from numerous investors, he purchased an old warehouse in Lincoln and had it converted into a manufacturing plant where he employed a large number of local people. Inside the warehouse were presses of the type Jason had used in his lab to make the squares, but much larger. Expensive air scrubbers and exhaust systems removed the toxic odors of melted plastics. With the warehouse were industrial-strength laser cutting machines, product designers, containment areas, loading docks, and everything needed to make the burgeoning business work.

Once Gottlieb demonstrated the utility and functionality of the samples Jason had provided, including copies of the analytical reports prepared by the chemistry and engineering departments at the University of Nebraska, American and international investors were not difficult to obtain.

He found an old airplane hangar not far from Omaha's Eppley Airfield and purchased it from a private owner. Converting the huge building into an additional facility and outfitting it to manufacture specialty items took ten another million dollars.

Gottlieb had his source of material, two manufacturing plants, a civilian airport and a military airport—the 385th Bomb Wing and home of the U.S. Strategic Command—all within an easy drive. Given good traffic flow, one could make the entire circuit from Lincoln to the hangar operation near the airfield, take care of business, eat a quick lunch, drive eight miles down to the military base, and return to Lincoln within a single workday.

Armor for vehicles, vests for police, clothing and structural materials, and numerous other items would soon roll off the production line in the hangar. Similar to the laser, a fun toy at one point, the uses of the powder promised to have scores of applications. He projected the technology would make many aspects of the U.S. military invincible.

Gottlieb had moved one of the strongest laser cutting tools ever developed into the hangar. Purchased at extreme cost, he expected it to quickly provide a return on investment one hundred-fold. The products spoke for themselves. They were ideal, malleable, adaptable, and virtually impenetrable to bullets, radiation from gamma ray protons, x-rays, and wavelengths which included light, sound, and radio waves.

Through his contacts at the local bomb wing and a small demonstration there, he and his equipment were able to travel on military transport to Aberdeen, Maryland, the site of the proving grounds appropriate for catering to his tests. Aside from the impressive demonstrations, the clincher for Gottlieb's sales pitches to the military generals and politicians was that the emerging technology couldn't be stolen. There were no secret codes, no computers to hack, nobody to pay off, and no plans to be surreptitiously stolen in the middle of the night.

The Department of Defense tapped into priority-status black-ops money for funding and Gottlieb signed a five billion dollar contract with the U.S. military for everything from armament to uniforms.

When he contacted Jason on the landline in his lab about the sale, expecting congratulations, he received an angry retort by an angry scientist.

"You sold to the military? Have you lost your mind? Why would you want to do that? I would never do that in a million years. What did you sell them, if it's okay to ask?" Jason roared, uncharacteristically.

This reprimand surprised Gottlieb, but didn't bother him. He'd stood next to his father when the man had gone ten rounds with businessmen on the international circuit. Since that time, he'd learned how to deal with angry retorts. The facts could not be argued with. Gottlieb became formal. "Doctor Randolph, remember our notarized agreement which states I control this aspect of the business? I ask, what is your intent to do with the products I manufacture? Is it to make drinking straws to sell at the local convenience store, or is it your intent to make pantyhose or cosmetic cases?"

Jason sat at his desk hunched over, left arm flung over the back of his neck with the phone to his right ear and flushed. "No, Wilbur, it is to construct dams that won't leak and buildings that are resistant to fire or fall and crush people in an earthquake, and radiation-proof spacecraft so our astronauts can go to the planets. It is not to facilitate murder and warfare."

Gottlieb remained calm, and chuckled audibly in order to further trigger Jason's rage before replying. "As far as the latter, our military will win the fights our politicians permit them to win with this new equipment and nobody will be able to copy it. My question to you is, what is your plan to raise the billions of dollars necessary to get these pets of yours off the ground; you know, go through the committees and the regulations and small testing phases and finally the big dams and buildings you dreamed of?

I should think thirty years to half-century working full-time should raise enough capital, given you do it right; about which I have serious doubts.

"So, unless you know something about business I don't, which may a possibility, my instinct is to show the military something so spectacular and foolproof they will quickly find a way to give us what we both want, which is enough money to do with as we please. Then, Doctor Randolph, there will be enough to begin funding whatever we damn well desire to create; unless, of course, you have another half-century to wait for a slow boat to get to its destination. Personally, I don't."

Jason remained frozen in his chair, elbows on the table, handset to his left hear until he heard a soft click on the other end of the line.

Gottlieb starred at the phone a moment after hanging up. He propped his elbows on the desk, put a fist in a hand and leaned his chin on the triangle, thinking. Other than himself, the only people who knew where this powder came from and how to make it were at RCR and he had them protected around the clock, a small fact he neglected to mention at their recent meeting. Not even he had an inkling of the secret formulation, so stealing the raw fibers would do no good. Hell, the best space-age minds anywhere couldn't make life grow out of the rock until Jason had stumbled onto the secret.

He liked and respected Jason's people. He'd had them well researched. They were a little too starry-eyed and altruistic to suit him, but it worked for them and they were doing fine until the misadventure with the meteorite added a little complexity to everyone's lives.

Gottlieb had to smile. His own wife, whom he loved dearly, possessed a disposition similar to Linda's. No, there were no clinkers in this crowd. He would be concerned if there were no eccentrics within the group of hard-core fanatical researchers; one with whom he now found himself intimately tied.

His real problem lay with himself and his own lineage. No male member of his family had lived beyond the age of 62, not his great-grandfather down to his father, nor his male cousins. Now that he was approaching 60, he found himself thinking all too frequently about his situation. It was a disease of the white blood cells in which the bone marrow suddenly shuts down its production of the crucial part of the immune system so the patient dies within three to six months from the first disease with which they come in contact. In a strange way he felt thankful for the twin girls born into his family; girls mutated by an alien thing, rather than mutated sons destined to die an early death from an immune disorder.

When had he last taken it upon himself to see a specialist or heard a word from anybody in the medical community regarding his problem? Was it three years? His reading could discern no breakthroughs in the field, no way to keep him from dying. Now it was an all-out sprint to the finish line; to see how much he could accomplish during his remaining time.

His visit to RCR had been helpful. The problem with the visit was that he had been hesitant to talk about his own personal issues in front of these people who were honest hard-working scientists. That problem can be remedied. In an astronomical sense, their staff were all geniuses, who had been compressed into a small space, which had, figuratively, given rise to the Big Bang. In this instance, the results had been a pandemic. The press dubbed the epidemic the New Flu. Experts strongly suspected it had nothing to do with the influenza virus, but the alliteration became two commonly used words in many of the world's languages.

Gottlieb's sense of curiosity would not be sated unless he found out more about this virus creature. There was only one place where he could do that. They had shared their secret with him. It was time to reverse the roles. He made a phone call to Jason's office and asked June to set up another appointment at their facility. At the least he'd get to see her again. That thought caused him to look up for the hundredth time to see the lithograph she had given him which was now framed and hanging from his wall.

After setting down the phone receiver, he felt pleased with himself, not for his success in the world of business, but because this visit was something very personal he needed to pursue, if he wanted to live.

February of Year 4

June slid over a sheet of paper. Trying to keep his eyes off her and his own fantasies at bay, Gottlieb studied it. He saw what could have been a black wooden two-by-four with rounded ends the length of which was five times its width. A second drawing on the page was of two of the structures side-by-side. A third drawing depicted four of them stacked two-by-two on top of one another.

June handed him another page. This one depicted a lengthy spiral staircase with chemical structures at each end of the rungs. She had presented it with a sense of parallax where it disappeared off into the distance like railroad tracks. A second picture of the staircase looked as though it had tied itself into a knot, continued on normally, then tied itself again. June pointed to each of the pictures. "Normal DNA versus the DNA from the Mars virus."

Tomás said, "There are probably a hundred times more viruses out there than there are life forms. That's a lot of viruses; none we know of look like ours. Each single virus, called a virion, has a protective shell around it, called a capsid. The capsid aids the entry of the viral genetic material into a cell. Typically, it's made of amino acids that are formed into a protein. Some viruses are long or filamentous, some are round and have little knobs on them like influenza; a lot of them are in-between. Some have attachments. For what it's worth, ours happens to be filamentous."

Jason interrupted, pleased that Tomás and Dustin

were enthusiastically exploring the genetics of the invading virus. "We have some evidence this one came from Mars, but any way you look at it, it came from outer space. It does not resemble anything we have ever found on this planet for a lot of reasons, including its large size. To us, it's a combination of a rattlesnake and a black widow spider. It is an extremely nasty looking virus; a life form that quickly transformed its nest within a glass flask into a larger nest called a life form, and then a much larger nest called our planet."

Tomás came back into the conversation. "The structure of a virus can be simplistic in some ways, but quite sophisticated in others. Some of them have ways of attaching themselves to the outside of a cell as an aid to injecting their contents into the cells like a syringe injecting a drug.

"To visualize DNA, picture a very long line of, say, two or three billion dancers in the case of humans, less with small creatures or plants. Each holds hands with a partner across from him or her. That partner is always the same. That's called a base pair. Not so with our virus. It's not only holding hands with somebody else's partner to the left or right across from it, it's also holding hands with the person standing next to it. Any decent scientist will tell you that's not supposed to happen."

Tomás could see Gottlieb was beginning to understand. "A normal virus will have a protein coat, sometimes with a lipid or fatty layer which it wraps around itself as it exits the membrane surrounding all cells; plant and animal. Not so ours. It has neither protein nor lipid nor carbohydrate. It has some kind of composition we're not familiar with. It doesn't reproduce within the cell or exit the cell like other viruses. In fact, we don't think it leaves the cell at all—ever. Dustin and I are starting to think the shell is composed of some form of chitin, similar to the composition of fish scales or the armor plating on some dinosaurs. But it's not chitin as we know it."

Dustin added, "We know it has both single and double stranded DNA. Trust me, we've done our share of analyses. We know it's warped inside its own capsid and we know where it goes once it enters a cell. We learned those things early on. It gets more warped when it attaches to any genetic material. We still don't know what happens to the capsid."

This time Linda picked up the verbal baton. "Tomás thinks ours attaches to plant or animal cells end-on, like pencil poking into a piece of paper, because he found what he thinks are attachment points at each of its ends. Once it attaches, it may create a pore through which it injects its genetic material."

Tomás resumed his explanation. "In addition to active viruses, there are also latent viruses. Herpes Simplex is one example where the DNA of the virus attaches to the host DNA, but it stays dormant unless activated by sunlight or chemical exposure or other environmental factors. There are also a number of latent cancer viruses. Our virus is a combination of both. We see it as entering through the respiratory tract, producing the cough. It targets the cells of the muscular system and the central nervous system, resulting in the headache. It's active in that it causes immediate changes, but can also be passed down from one generation of cells to another because it binds with the genes in male sperm and female eggs. Most importantly, unlike other viruses, it is not specific to anything or anyone. From where we sit it is a total game changer.

"Furthermore, unlike other viruses, it does not attack or limit itself to the mucous membrane that lines the respiratory tract, or just the nervous system or muscular system of a single target species. It attacks all DNA in everything it touches."

Dustin concluded, "Our problem is, we can't get it to disentangle itself, disengage if you will, from the host DNA."

Gottlieb sat in awe at what he had just been told. These people were no dummies. They had learned so very much. Could they do nothing with the information? It went against his intuition as an engineer. Surely, when you have enough parts you can construct a functional piece of equipment. What and where were the missing parts? What was the rest of the story? Would it ever be known?

Don slid actual photographs of the DNA depicted in June's drawings across the table to Gottlieb. "This is a high magnification x-ray photo of normal DNA versus the DNA with our friend attached."

"Nobody else has seen these viruses under the microscope?" Gottlieb asked, perplexed, looking around the table, one to another.

Jason said, "That is correct, except for one botanist who reported having seen them on the surfaces of some leaves of which he provided samples for examination. He didn't freeze them and, by the time they were examined, they had been absorbed. There was nothing to see. I found them almost by accident because June gave me a sample. Fortunately, I immediately put into the freezer. Otherwise, I wouldn't have found them, unless, of course, I had looked at the sample the moment she gave it to me."

"I thought you said they are in every living tissue," Gottlieb frowned, clearly puzzled.

Linda countered, "No, I said they infect every living tissue. Somehow the outer wall of the creature degrades while it's doing its dirty work, warping host genetic material in very specific locations on the double helix. It forces cells to do things they don't normally do. Our invader doesn't reproduce itself unless there is carbon dioxide present. The fact that it reproduces on its own defies our understanding of viruses. And microbial reproduction in free air is something none of us is familiar with. If it does happen, it sure as hell won't be anything like we've seen with this thing. If we discount that it only looks like a virus, we still don't understand how any life form can reproduce without nutrition. Let me amend that to say, at least what we think of as nutrition. This leads to the question of what we define as life."

"How do you know it has an effect on plants?" Gottlieb muttered, not trying to mask his astonishment at the breadth of their research. The magnitude of the infection astounded him. "I mean, plants and animals both?"

"And fish, bacteria, protozoa, insects, trees; whatever has genetic material," reiterated Linda.

Jason said, "In answer to your first question, we don't know a whole lot for certain about how it behaves or infects cells." He told his guest about the vegetation at his own home and news stories about the apparent faster rate of growth of a variety of plants from greenhouses, fruit trees, and grains in the field. Then he asked, "Have you ever heard of using algae as a biofuel?"

"Of course. It could be huge industry soon, obtaining oil from alga that are pond-cultivated. I almost got involved in it myself," Gottlieb answered.

Jason nodded. "Good thing you didn't. A friend of mine at the university is one of the chief microbiologists for one of the companies poised to make tens of billions from this. Based in the Middle East, they have hundreds of acres of ponds in Spain, Saudi Arabia, Israel, Mexico, and Arizona; anywhere where there is lot of sunlight. The ponds have to be watched carefully to ensure proper balance of nutrients and pH. Otherwise bacterial contamination takes over. When things are right, the algae are harvested to get oils for fuel, carotenoids for medications, proteins for food supplements, plus a variety of vitamins and amino acids. It's all legit. In this case, the ponds matured too rapidly leading to a rapid harvest; they couldn't get it all and lost a good part of their yield.

"They sent my friend some of the algae for analysis and he couldn't find a thing wrong microscopically with the single-celled species being used, with one exception. The individual cells were up to twenty-five percent larger. He sent me a sample to find out what I could. "I found that the DNA was warped. That just doesn't happen.""

Gottlieb's brows furrowed. He asked, "What did you tell him?"

"The truth. I thought it might be a bacterial or viral contaminant that stuck its own DNA in there. I also told him I didn't know how to get rid of it. I suggested they might want to look more closely at their pond water for unwanted bacterial or viral presence."

June looked aghast. "You mean the entire industry will be lost?"

Jason shook his head quickly. "Not necessarily. It suggests they might need to cut back the number of ponds by, say, fifty to seventy percent, and go into rush production mode for those that remain. Faster growth means more crop yields per cycle. In other words, get more out of less. It is not all to the good. If the algae are growing faster in the ponds and elsewhere, this includes toxic algae in the oceans and lakes. Shellfish may soon be completely inedible, along with all kinds of fresh and salt water sea creatures that eat them for nutrition, including many species of fish such as bass, perch, and sturgeon, along with whales.

"There's more. The particular strain of algae in

the ponds I'm telling you about is grown in 20 percent salt water. Its parent came from the Dead Sea. The virus from Mars grows in that very nicely."

Don asked, "What's the concentration of salt in a saline solution?"

"Saline is 0.9 percent," Jason responded.

Don shook his head. "And here I'd been gargling with salt water thinking it might help my cough."

Gottlieb's mechanical brain tried to tease out some clue about his own status, and all they were giving him were fascinating observational facts. "Do you think this thing really came from Mars? If it needs water and carbon dioxide at a certain level of acidity to become activated, I mean, Mars doesn't have water, does it?"

Don answered, "At the poles there is water ice mixed with frozen carbon dioxide. It also has water lakes beneath the surface. Millions of years ago we believe it flowed on the surface. In a word, we'll never know where this microbe came from. What I do know is this: Whenever man gets to the planets and the stars from now on, this virus will be going along with him."

Jason's mind reeled by the impact of Don's words. This virus will be going along with him. Could it be that's what happened to Mars long ago? After this thing landed on a viable world, it worked its magic over time and turned the world into dust? How many worlds had it been to? Now it's here. Are we next?

Gottlieb's mind swam with facts. He managed to

ask, "We talked about this last time. What are you doing in your research to find a cure?"

"We've tried different chemicals to see if we can get it to release from the DNA," Jason replied. "After that, we tried maybe half-a-hundred of the most common medications that are prescribed today here in the States and in Europe. The hardest part about it was obtaining them because of restrictions put on the people who have access to the drugs. Believe me, I owe favors."

Gottlieb asked, "What makes you think what you are doing works or not? You can't x-ray everything."

Linda replied, "We don't. We grow up some E. coli in flask. Its DNA automatically gets infected and we add our reagent. Then we rupture the cells and check the DNA with a combination of stain and electric charge to see if there are one or two DNAs. So far, there is only one. In addition, the flask begins to glow regardless of what we add to it. Therefore, it always grows because it always glows."

"What will you do once you find out it doesn't grow?" Gottlieb asked, smiling at her little rhyme.

"We'll look at the host DNA to see if its's back to normal. After that, we don't have the slightest idea about how to conduct clinical trials for this kind of a situation," Linda admitted.

"What about non-chemicals?" Gottlieb offered.

Jason expected the question. "Sonication won't work. We haven't tried a variety of light waves."

The gears of Gottlieb's mind were meshing and turning. He was back to his roots. "Let me offer some suggestions."

Linda gave a brief shrug. "Wilbur, if what you are going to suggest actually does work, what do you think will be the next step?"

The engineer repeated the phrase of the day. "I haven't got the slightest idea."

Gottlieb stayed until after lunch to watch research unfold. He expressed interest in the fermenters and asked numerous technical questions about their operation. After pizza and Runza had been ordered for lunch, Jason stuck with the pizza. The Czech food Runza, a popular pocket bread with a filling consisting of beef, cabbage or sauerkraut, onions, and seasonings was an acquired taste.

Jason didn't feel very confident in the direction Gottlieb wanted to take the work. At the least his engineers would be running experiments at his facility. There would be different walls to stumble into by different people. Not his problem, anymore. He did insist that the formulation remain under his control, otherwise no deal. Gottlieb consented.

Over the next year Gottlieb's engineers reported making no progress at all in trying to disengage the viral and host DNAs.

3 February of Year 5

RCR's share of earnings approximated a quarter-million dollars a day. Within eighteen months it reached five million a day. If a pendulum swung two ways, the extremely rapid spread of the virus was emotionally counterbalanced by the acquisition of products that provided a wave of functional necessities, as well as scientific advancements.

WG Corp. brought in hundreds of billions of dollars, most of which went to Jason's group as they owned the three-quarters of the company. Meanwhile, Gottlieb counted the days until his demise, as he had done every day of his entire life since his father had disclosed the truth about the fatal affliction the day he graduated high school. Impending death can be a great motivator and he was so very tired of thinking about it.

Something rankled him. What were they missing? If people were getting stronger and smarter, changes were also occurring in the brain. Jason might be the wrong one to ask about the brain, but as a biochemist, he must know about physiological or hormonal differences. Had he looked at them?

Gottlieb tried to remember. At RCR nobody had ever discussed their animal studies with him in any detail. It was time to pay yet another visit to the scientists. And so he returned to meet with Jason, Linda, and Rick McIntyre, keeper of the mice. All wore their white lab coats as they stood among the scores of mouse cages situated on three tiers of racks in the large basement of the institute. Numerous bags of zeolite volcanic ash successfully absorbed the odors of the mice. Cheap and rechargeable by the warmth of the sunlight, the bags supplemented the fresh air and exhaust system in the building. A single small bag could remove the odor of an entire pastrami inside a refrigerator within a day's time.

After introductions were made, Jason asked Rick to tell the good doctor about what had captured their attention from his perspective.

Although not privy to the studies on intelligence, Rick dutifully related his rueful tale as the others stood by. He showed before and after photographs of normal mice. He told of the rounding of the shoulders over a period of several months, of their increased speed on the wheel, of the deformed offspring, and acceptance by the parents of their young.

Wait a minute, Jason thought. If the control mice have rounded shoulders, why don't I? We're all infected. He mentally ran the numbers. Six months to a mouse is 25 years to a human. That's why your shoulders are tight. Only some of your symptoms are gone, not all of them. Get used to it. That's not tension, it's the virus settling in for long haul.

After Rick completed his story, he returned to his glass-enclosed office complete with armchair, TV, radio and small fridge while the others went back to the conference room. Gottlieb broke the silence, "You have a lot of deformed mice. They look as though they were an unidentified species you caught from deep in a jungle somewhere."

"That's exactly what I thought when I first saw them," Jason replied somberly. "It could probably legitimately be classified as such." The mice did not present a pretty picture; hunched, thick-legged, with deformed faces, unbelievably fast and highly intelligent.

"I don't see any normal mice. Why don't you have them?" Gottlieb asked.

Jason answered, "Our supplier went out of business so we couldn't check on any other mice they'd sold."

"Why was that?" Gottlieb asked.

"Why did they go out of business? All their offspring turned into mutants. Nobody wanted them," Jason responded.

Gottlieb's eyes flitted around the conference room, processing data. "Why are they faster?" he asked.

The group explained the histological findings which described the denser muscle fiber and the buildup of collagen in the connecting structures of the shoulders and knees. Gottlieb was clearly confused. "But why are the eyes and ears offset? It's crazy," he uttered. "It makes no sense."

This time, Dustin, the mutations expert, went to the whiteboard. With a red marker he drew a line two feet long. After several inches he placed a knob in the line with a black marker until several knobs were drawn. "Here's what we think is happening. Like our familiar life forms, humans have what is called bilateral symmetry. Split us down the middle lengthwise and each half looks like the other half. The symmetry is not perfect, but it's close enough."

He continued, "This alignment, this organization of symmetry, occurs early on in the gestation of a species, early in the embryonic stage, when cells are first dividing to create a life form. Enter our friendly virus who ties up the alignment genes." He pointed to a black ball in the line. "But it only ties up those genes that affect the face."

Gottlieb asked, "If that were the case, wouldn't it make all genes misalign?"

"No," Dustin continued. "We didn't know this before, but there are alignment genes for the face, arms and legs. It lands on the genes for the face. It's not doing it on purpose, that's just what happens. For adults, there is no change because we have already been aligned. Our eyes and ears are set in place. But it also attaches to the genes that affect the structural development and cell repair that is ongoing all the time in the adult, so we have other symptoms." Here he pointed to another black knot in the line.

Linda said, "Just a second, Dustin. Let's back up." She looked at Gottlieb. "Wilbur, did you ever hear of epigenetics?"

"Not at all," Gottlieb confessed.

Linda gave a brief nod of understanding. Not many people had heard of the term. "Epigenetics is an emerging field of genetics. 'Epi' means onto or upon. In a word, there is another layer of something that is also a factor in inheritance, not only DNA. Here's what we know: There are areas of the genome in each type of tissue that is susceptible to environmental change and has a memory. This memory can be passed down through the generations. As a simple example, if you are an athlete or a concert pianist, there is a strong likelihood your child or children will have a similar ability, and it's not all due to growing up in an athletic or musical household. When children are removed from the influence of their parents who have a talent, the children will still have those or similar talents. That's due to the experience of one or more parent and the memory of that particular tissue, whether it be an aspect of the brain or muscle."

Linda continued, "Here's another example. If one or both parents go through a period of famine, their offspring, down to grandchildren and beyond, may develop symptoms of malnutrition. It is fair to say that the medical community has been mystified by occurrences such as these. In the past we believed the genes defined everything, the Holy Grail. Now we're finding out there is literally a frosting on the cake. While it may be true you are what you eat, it is also true you are what your grandparents ate. It may be the basis for instinct itself. It is the role of epigenetics to turn on and off certain switches that regulate the genes.

"In addition, we think early bone marrow cells are affected by the virus." Linda paused when she saw Gottlieb was about to speak.

"Bone marrow is where white blood cells are produced. I know that much." added Gottlieb, dumbfounded by another revelation.

"Correct," she affirmed.

Gottlieb sat up straight and leaned forward, moving to the edge of his chair. "Does that mean more white blood cells will also be produced?"

Jason answered for Linda. "Yes, a variety of immune-related white blood cells will be produced in abundance. We see that happening across the board. The immune system is enhanced."

"What if the white blood cell production is genetically programmed to shut down at a certain age?" the engineer asked, almost stammering.

"It won't happen," Jason declared. "We've tried to shut it down. Every time we try, the program is overridden by the DNA of the virus. We think it might be due to the action of epigenetics. Whatever you want to call it, the off-switch doesn't flip. It stays open."

Gottlieb's jaw didn't drop; however, it did slacken enough for his mouth to open. He sat back in his chair, took a deep breath, and shared his family secret. The others were taken aback at the revelation. The great Dr. Wilbur Gottlieb was human after all with very human issues who now had a piece of driftwood to grab onto.

Jason had lost too much inner strength through following the progress of the virus' advance to encourage others to hold onto theirs. To him, they were all in a prison of their own making and could only look out through the bars as the disease advanced across the world. "Wilbur, come on, we can't say we have positive proof. Let it go. If you make it to 63, you'll have the answer. But what do I know?"

Gottlieb remained silent. It took time to digest a large meal.

Linda explained, "Wilbur, when we sent in tissue samples for analysis, we also made samples from different parts of the brains of our mice. We found the virus in almost every cell with a high density of warped DNA in the frontal lobe of the parents and the offspring. The frontal lobe is responsible for problem solving, decision making, reasoning, and other important attributes. These factors are a big part of what makes us human."

"Do you think it targeted that area specifically? Why aren't we dumber and not smarter?" Gottlieb asked.

Linda replied, "That's a fair question; one we've asked ourselves. The answer is that we don't know. Again, we think it is serendipitous circumstance, blind attachment, if you will. It could have attacked the brain stem. If that were the case we might want to sleep all the time or be awake all the time, or it could have been some other area that affected our coordination, or sexual drive, or some area that affects common sense judgments. If that were the case, we'd be asking the identical question—why is it in this or these locations?"

"Or it could have killed every person or thing it touched like smallpox virus and not give a damn about it," Jason added. And may yet do that, he thought, visualizing the planet Mars.

April of Year 5

It was one of Gottlieb's personally-appointed technicians who went to the press to report he had discovered the cause of the disease. He worked in the large room of the new addition that housed the fermenters waiting weeks to make his move. He and his partner took lunch breaks into town on alternate days, when they chose to do so. He also knew that Rick, their animal caretaker, went out to eat with his daughter every Friday. The day arrived when he had the fermenter room to himself for an hour.

He opened his lunch pail, removed a small screw-top flask and withdrew a small amount of liquid from the sampling port on the fermenter in which a culture of virus was reproducing. Putting the closed flask back in his lunch pail, he quietly exited the swinging door to fermenter room and walked down a hallway to the basement. Opening the door, he noticed the lights were on, and descended the stairs.

He saw a roomful of cages containing mutated mice, white hunched mammals with off-kilter faces. One was running on a mouse wheel moving unbelievably fast. The image might stick with him for days or weeks or forever. Within seconds he had returned to the upstairs fermenter room, feeling so sick he decided to leave for the day. Once his partner returned from lunch, he'd report his illness, but not what had caused it. They couldn't pay him enough for this.

Once out the building, he drove directly to Omaha and dropped off the flask at an independent laboratory for analysis. They were expecting him. One week later he received the lab report in the mail. It noted the presence of various basic elements in the liquid and listed the concentration of each and the pH of the solution. The solution also contained an abundance of ultra-thin fibers. Gottlieb's man understood that the ingredients for the WG Corp. line of products were coming from this lab. The reason was obvious. He and his partner were making pounds of mash which came from a flask he was given to pour into the fermenter. There could only be one thing growing in there. The independent lab called them fibers. He called them disease germs.

The technician didn't need money or notoriety. Gottlieb paid well. It was about principle. To him, the fibers caused the New Flu. The mice proved it. He had seen the same births and news stories, as had everyone else. There was too much coincidence floating around to suit him. This facility grew and shipped fibers to WG Corp. It caused the creation of mutants, maybe the New Flu. Didn't the authorities say they were connected?

When his wife returned from her department store sales job, he told her his suspicions. She asked, "Did you tell Doctor Gottlieb what you think?"

"Yes," her husband responded, simply. "I didn't tell him about the sample I took to the lab in Omaha; only that I had my suspicions and thought he should know."

"What did he say?"

"Doctor Gottlieb sat there and listened like he always does. When I finished he laughed and said I had a good imagination. He'd heard the story many times."

"Well, then?" she shrugged.

"I know the two are tied together," he insisted.

"You can't move without proof," she admonished.

"No, but somebody else can," he countered. "I mean, if I go the press..."

"If you do that, you'll lose your job whether you're right or wrong. Furthermore, if you're wrong we'll be ostracized," she said.

"There's one other point," he added.

"Yes?"

"I didn't like his dismissive attitude, so I didn't tell him the rest."

"The rest of what?" she inquired.

"A couple of months ago, when I was leaving the bathroom, I saw one of the workers come up from the basement. He was holding a mouse, but it wasn't a mouse. It was strange, like what is being born these days. I started to think they were running experiments, like maybe they knew something nobody else did," her husband asserted.

His wife's ears perked up. "Now that is interesting. You mean they are growing bad mice on purpose? That's terrible." She gave a shudder.

He grudgingly told her about what he had seen that very day in the basement, almost shaking by the time he'd finished the short tale.

"We need to stop this," she declared. "They're probably breeding them and setting them loose. What monsters." She recalled a movie she had seen once in which almost the same thing had happened. In the movie, bad dogs were bred that would go out and bite other dogs which would bite humans until there were no good dogs left.

"I really should report it," he offered, in a manner suggesting her input would be helpful.

"It's your decision; follow your conscience," was her reply. Her meaning was clear.

Two days later, the Lincoln Sentinel quoted reliable sources who claimed the New Flu originated from Randolph Cancer Research and that the place is raising diseased mice to spread the infection. As noted in the article, June Jennings, spokeswoman for the organization, denied absolutely any of those claims and said they are so ridiculously laughable they border on being sick. The company is registered as a cancer research institute and they, like everyone else, are dismayed to find their own research mice are giving birth to diseased babies. Their progress in cancer research, as funded by the NIH and backed by the U.S. Government, is trying to overcome a major setback in their research because of the disease.

She, June, had personally spoken with the owner of RCR, Dr. Randolph himself, who said they tried to get a disease out of the blood of the mice to see if it could be transferred to others and couldn't make it work. Not only that, but they couldn't find any disease in the blood of the mice. Can you imagine? I mean, this is what they do, but couldn't find a thing in the blood. He feels sick about the whole epidemic, more so than most people. Dr. Randolph stated that probably every lab in the country had infected mice and is sorry for the mice and other animals, too.

The spokeswoman concluded by suggesting that further questions regarding this issue be addressed to the institute's attorney, who will be preparing a lawsuit against the unnamed source, once he or she is identified.

Two days later June got a call from Gottlieb's personal secretary. She reported that a new man would be sent over to work the fermenters to replace the one who had left. She provided the new man's badge and ID numbers for her to give the guard at the gate.

"What happened to the other guy?" June asked the secretary.

"Oh, sometime after his wife went to work, I guess he slipped in the shower and hit his head. Died right there in the shower. He might have been drinking. We can send you the funeral notice, if you'd like us to."

"Thank you, that would be nice of you," June returned, graciously, and softly hung up the phone. She turned on the radio for soft rock. Instead, she got an announcement that on the Andy Watt's show, the day after tomorrow, the host will lead a discussion on the causes of the New Flu. She quickly called Jason to inform him.

Jason slid out of bed at 2:10 a.m. letting his wife sleep. A niggling thought refused to depart. He needed quiet time alone to think. He knew a fair amount about ecosystems, if a Master's Degree in Molecular

Ecology counted. Could he predict what might be happening? He sat at the kitchen counter, pondering, penciling notes in shorthand with bullet points, highlighting words, and arrows. In a worst case scenario, where might the Earth be headed in terms of life with the Martians on the loose?

What if the Earth itself and all of its myriad life forms change as the fibers made their sweep over the planet? If so, their spread might reach from the top of the mountains to the bottom of the seas, stretching above and beneath the soils. Changes would accelerate as species within all life's ecosystems struggled to compete and survive. The one constant to life and to death was DNA.

With 10 million species of life on land and water with the potential to be infected, the human race represented only one them. Online and on television, as he followed fishing and hunting reports, he read about fishermen in Nebraska and in the Seattle area around Puget Sound. They were pulling up salmon, trout, walleye, bass, catfish and other species with sideways faces, as his research group called them, a term also coined by the media. Now more difficult to catch, they were fished from local rivers, streams, and larger waterways. This included a 400-mile stretch of the Missouri River that ran through eastern Nebraska. Many fish caught were egg-filled females and fish farms were rife with mutants.

Other local fishermen reported fish to be seemingly wary of standard bait; they were forced to use more specialized and expensive types. Jason could understand how that could happen. With eyes on either side of the head, fish normally lack depth perception. In order to properly judge bait, they have to face it head-on where there is a small area of binocular vision. This would be completely lacking now because they would have two different views of a prospective source of food. They would also have two angles to view predators above them. The fish-farming companies in Seattle reported the disease had affected all of their fish. Similarly, hunters related tales about prey being faster and more adept at escaping.

What about insects? June's research found photographic evidence of genetic defects in many of the 500 or so species of insects found in Lincoln and Omaha alone. Such reports, presented by expert entomologists at the university, highlighted honeybees, flies, butterflies, ants, mites, ticks, cockroaches and spiders. The common denominator was that, whatever they were known for, they were doing it faster, including crawling and running. Flying insects could also hover longer or fly backwards faster, similar to birds. The changes were attributed to realignment of the legs and wings of the progeny. For some unexplained reason, the eyes were somewhat askew; faces not quite symmetrical.

What about plant life? If photosynthesis were to increase throughout the planet, it would suggest the Brazilian rain forest and other smaller rain forests in Central and South America, along with those in Asia, might reclaim by over-production of trees what man's rapine had taken from them. If the forests became choked with undergrowth, deer and other hunted animals would be forced outward. Smaller species would adapt to a life within the forest to find more food and shelter; yet with more undergrowth and a denser thicket of trees, fires might become more devastating, like many of the many fires incurred in the Pacific Northwest.

Farmed or not, vast areas of the oceans and seacoast could be expected to see algal blooms beyond anything comprehensible, similar to a poorly maintained swimming pool or pond that would turn green almost overnight because of rapid reproduction of algae which would stink when washed ashore. Because death of the blooms occurs both chemically and through action of microorganisms, the surge in the microbial population in the water will use up the dissolved oxygen and cause the death of fish to further contribute to the smell.

Warmer waters around the world will give rise to micro-algae known as phytoplankton and zooplankton which are fed upon by invisible sea creatures known as copepods. Because copepods carry the cholera bacterium, outbreaks of the deadly disease might occur, not only in traditional poverty-ridden hotspots such Haiti, India, and North Africa, but virtually anywhere.

The phytoplankton and zooplankton are also fed upon by Baleen Whales and Right Whales which are immune to the cholera bacterium. Because there would be more food available, the whale population would increase, yet toxic algal blooms might kill them off through lack of oxygen.

If the virus were to combine with the DNA within the cholera bacterium itself, would that mean the toxin would be more potent or less potent? How would it change the behavior of Salmonella or the E. coli bacteria prominent in the human gut?

In the case of eutrophication, where fertilizer runoff affects algal growth due to excess of nitrogen and phosphorus, growth of aquatic life is known to become further enhanced, leading to additional depletion of dissolved oxygen. And so would warming waters, which would cause more rapid reproduction of aqueous life, with or without fertilizer, to use up dissolved oxygen and result in more death of life in the seas.

Jason had recently learned that the polar ice caps hosted algae growing in crevices in the ice, as well as in large pools of water on the ice sheets. The algae would spread to result in the absorption of more sunlight, hastening the melting of both ice caps. Captured nutrients present in the ice would be released, further feeding the chlorophyll-containing plants and phytoplankton, thus boosting the vast food chain, each member feeding upon another. Melting ice caps would open the poles for exploration of untapped oil resources as coastal flooding occurred. People and animals could be displaced or killed.

What might happen to the amount of oxygen in the atmosphere? An increase in photosynthesis would cause the atmosphere's oxygen content to rise. Above its normal 19 percent, which might cause an increase in oxidation and the formation of more free radicals.

More atmospheric oxygen would mean more fires. More oxygen would also lead to larger insects because the size of many is dependent on available oxygen.

Jason drew two circles with an arrow going from left to right at the top of one page. Above each, he wrote the words Earth; at the bottom, he labeled one Blue and the other Green. Finally, setting down his pencil, he put his head in his hands, closed his eyes, and slowly rubbed them with his palms. If he didn't quit writing now, he would be writing a terror novel.

Gentle hands began massaging his neck and shoulders. A voice behind him spoke softly, "Don't forget that the growth rate of corn, rice, wheat and other agricultural products will increase dramatically to help offset the inland migration of people due to coastal flooding. There's always a trade-off. We'll have to adapt to it like every other creature in Earth's ecosystems. We're only one of millions. Aren't humans supposed to be the intelligent species and aren't we supposed to be getting smarter all the time?"

At that moment, Jason didn't feel very intelligent or very smart. This feeling carried over into the next day. The noon hour approached and his lab-line rang. Jason picked up.

June said, "There's a Doctor Shenero here to see you."

Shit, Shenero. Jason's heart went cold. Trapped. "Tell him I'll be out in a couple of minutes." This was the end. The man would see it all because he'd want to see it all. What if he did? Would he understand? Would he want to put himself in the limelight by reporting what he saw, what he learned? Despite that, beneath the personal prejudices and life styles and personality differences, weren't both of them just basic grunt scientists?

When there is no way out, the only way to go is deeper into the maw. He made a quick call down to Rick in the basement asking him to start cleaning the cages immediately.

Rick answered, "I just cleaned them three days ago, Doctor."

"Just start. I have my reasons," Jason insisted.

Jason walked out to the office and greeted the scientist. June sat at her desk while their visitor, was looking at her art.

"Jeff, what a pleasant surprise. What brings you here?"

"I gave a lecture at the college of medicine and events were moving so fast I didn't have chance to call. Please let me know if this is an intrusion and we can visit some other time," Shenero grinned, sheepishly. Surprise visits were not always good for either party.

Jason showed his teeth in a broad smile and checked the clock on the wall. Twelve noon. "Do you want to start with the fermenters and go on our tour after that? Then we can go out for lunch."

"Sounds like a plan," the Oklahoman returned.

Jason led his guest past the four laboratories to the fermenter facility where they greeted two of Gottlieb's men who had just finished weighing a batch of black fibers they had removed.

"A little over four point three pounds" said one of them, looking at Jason. "We'll get this over to Dr. Gottlieb this afternoon, as soon as we dry it, sir."

That's interesting. Almost the exact weight as the meteorite Don found. Why did the guy have to mention Gottlieb? "Good work," he said to the workman, smiling. What else could he tell him?

"Who's Gottlieb?" Shenero asked.

Jason jerked his shoulders up and down. "No big deal. I'll tell you at lunch. Let's see the rest of the building."

"You have animals, right?" asked Shenero.

"I'll show them to you later. Rick, our animal man, is cleaning cages at the moment."

Jason felt more at ease after he and Shenero had completed a lengthy luncheon at an Italian restaurant. Wealth or success in any field did not define a person's ethical standards, but somehow Jason had good feelings about his new friend. This was, in part, based on what he'd read of the scientist's adventures and awards. It was also based on the personal relationship they had developed. If a relationship cannot be built upon a foundation of trust, then there is no relationship. So he told him the entire story from the beginning. He included Gottlieb in the tale and, while doing so, inwardly explored his own emotional wreckage, hoping it didn't show through during his presentation. Shenero listened attentively, not casting judgment, understanding, perhaps casting himself in Jason's shoes.

To Jason's surprise, the great scientist was only superficially aware of the new world epidemic, engrossed was he in his own little microcosm. The man had isolated himself so completely, it was as though Jason's input of information had given good eyesight to a person who wore thick glasses.

"Let it go, Jason," Shenero advised.

"Let it go?" Jason thought he understood. He wanted to verify.

Shenero again advised, "Let it go. In another life, I worked my way through college. One of the jobs I had was changing tires for a big bus company after they rolled into the service center in downtown Oklahoma City. I'd get into the cab, make sure the brakes were set, crawl beneath the thing, jack up the area next to the flat, unscrew the lug nuts using a thirty pound pneumatic wrench hooked to an air pressure hose, pull off the big tire, and roll it back to the shop. Those tires weighed maybe 150 pounds or more, with the rim on. If the tire got loose from the roll and started to swirl, you let it go—you let it spin like a top until it settled on its own. If you tried to catch it while it was spinning, you got hurt. What did the old timers advise me to do? You relax and let it go."

Jason felt a moment of great weakness and needed to confess to that weakness. "How do I deal with it if the public learns the disease came from my lab?"

"You think about the tire," Shenero responded.

Jason nodded, trying to integrate the story and his present state of affairs in terms of some kind of Zen relationship with a damned rolling tire. The time had come to move on. "I think Rick must be finished with the cages now. If you have time, I'll show you our animal facility. By the way, when are you going back home?"

The mycologist answered, "Well, I didn't know how long I was going to be here so I've got an open ticket. Why?"

Jason said, "Because you're family now and I'd like you to attend our conference tomorrow after a radio program I'd like you to hear. I'll tell you about it later. My wife, Linda, and I will treat you to dinner. You can stay at our house tonight and go home tomorrow after lunch. What do you say?"

"Only if we can get in some fishing," Shenero negotiated.

"Sure, if you don't care what the fish look like," Jason warned. He saw the expression on the other man's face. "We'll catch some trout in the lake across the street and I'll pan fry them for dinner. I've got clothes that will fit you, too. No guarantee on the shoes."

"How far away do you live?" inquired Shenero.

"Behind this building," Jason said.

By 10:00 a.m., introductions had been made. In the conference room, the radio was set to the syndicated Andy Watts program as they waited for the long promised truth behind the cause and spread of the New Flu. Despite what the Oklahoman had advised him the day before, Jason felt great apprehension about what Watts might say.

Watts' promoters called his program the scandal magazine of the air, which was precisely why nearly 100 stations across the nation ran his program, with over two million listeners. Each year, he collected a small fortune from sponsors while commercially selling Andy Watts Coffee Mugs, Tee-shirts, baseball caps, and an assortment of other products to the public. He covered such topics as the Martin Luther King, Jr. and Kennedy Assassinations, the moon landings, possible mercury in vaccines and pesticides in foods. Watts took advantage of the concerns and fears of the nation and used the abnormal births of humans and animals to promote his own agenda, which turned out to be surprisingly accurate at times.

After the theme music, Watts began speaking in his recognizable gravelly voice, "Welcome to the Andy Watts show Fact or Fiction. After we take a close look at what we know about how the New Flu began, we'll give you, the listener, a chance to give us your thoughts and theories right after our commercial break."

Nobody in the conference room said a word, as they suffered through five agonizingly long minutes of commercials.

Watts came back on the air, identified himself,

reiterated what he had said before, and began with his famous monologue.

"Folks, you know my wife, Sandra and I, have a spread right here outside Atlanta. We're animal lovers and we've got a lot of them. Well, I will tell you both of us are scared witless, just like a lot of you are. This New Flu doesn't care what kind of pet you have, it's going after the newborn. It's not just here, it's everywhere. It's in Indochina, Peru, Hawaii, freaking Egypt, no less, and it's in your hometown, too, like it or not.

"Now, the Centers for Disease Control or CDC is located right here in Atlanta and I know a lot of very good people there and they know me and we have lunch together. They tell me in private what they tell everybody: Nobody has a clue where this thing came from. Computer models show it will blanket the entire Earth very soon and no animal may be safe. The really bad news is that this includes all kinds of animals and fish, and bugs, and yes, human babies, too.

"You know you're going to get it when you start with the headache and cough that I had that won't go away for a long time. Nothing helps either one of those. Besides, I don't think I could have found an aspirin, if I wanted to. People are afraid of each other anymore as if riots and killings are going to make it right. We need ideas and I'll tell you what folks, you and I are in this together and I want to hear about what you think. Maybe somebody out there has some information that will help us.

"When we go back a few years, what we saw

were hotspots where the disease first appeared. Now, we all have our doubts about the government, but here is some official health department information. Listen up. These hotspots were Lincoln, Nebraska; Seattle, Washington; Richmond, Virginia; London, England; and Mexico City.

"From Lincoln, the New Flu radiated outward to Omaha, Council Bluffs, Kansas City, Oklahoma City, Norman, Denver and Des Moines.

"From Seattle, it moved down to Portland, Sacramento and San Francisco. Northward it moved into western Canada including Vancouver.

"Remember, we're not just talking about people, we're talking about fish and wildlife. We're thinking salmon may be carrying it from Puget Sound up to Alaska where cases are starting to show up. The fish farms off Seattle are totally changed .Try going into a market or fish store anymore and buying a normal fish. Won't happen.

"From London, it traveled, and is still traveling to Paris, Berlin, Madrid and up into Scandinavia. From Mexico City, it is moving downward into Central America and spotty areas in South America. From our standpoint, that's how we see it folks. Right after our next break we will take calls from concerned citizens who demand the truth."

Another five minutes passed, Watts came back on the air and reiterated his previous statements and began to take callers. There was the typical eight second delay between the caller and the host, a break instituted by the station itself that the caller didn't know about. This delay served as an assist in screening out calls for a variety of reasons. These would include those with foul mouths, threats to the station that might be heard on air, and people would were incoherent for various reasons.

"Now it's your turn to talk Fact or Fiction on the Andy Watts program. First caller of the day: Wilma from Atlanta."

Wilma came on the air. "If it started in one person, why would he or she from any one of those cities have a reason to go to the other cities? What does somebody in business in some small place like Lincoln, Nebraska or Norman, Oklahoma, have to do with all those different places?"

Watts answered, "Great point, Wilma. My team of top investigators couldn't come up with an answer. Maybe a group of people from say, Seattle, had it before they got on a lot of planes and headed out to the others places. Let's hear from Jim up in Montreal."

"That's the point I was going to make," replied Jim. "Maybe it's not the people, maybe it's the plane. The bug got on the plane somehow; maybe a vial of the stuff broke because some guy was sneaking it around."

Watts was upbeat. "Another great point, Jim. The problem with that is different planes are used. Typically, local flights involve small to medium-size regional jets, cattle cars we like to call them. They're much more fuel efficient and get around the airports a lot more easily that the bigger planes, kind of like driving a small car compared with a large truck. Longer flights use the big boys, the 747s on up. They hold more passengers and luggage and give a smoother ride with more comfort for the long haul, such as to Mexico City and London. So, Jim, for now, planes are out. Thank you for calling.

"Billy, from Amarillo, Texas, you're on the Andy Watts program."

"How about the food, Andy? Do you think there is a single supplier that served those areas?" asked Billy, with enough of a drawl to distinguish it from Oklahoma- speak.

"We can't rule it out, but that would be highly unlikely, if we take in the wide variety of locations. Nonetheless, the idea has some merit. Consider a batch of lettuce from Mexico that comes up to areas of the Southwestern United States and this lettuce has E. coli on it. Or a batch of moldy peanuts that gets shipped out. This does happen. But that stock doesn't go to our five locations only. Why would Seattle get the same lettuce or peanuts that London gets?

"Emily from Tulsa, Oklahoma, you're on the Fact or Fiction program with Andy Watts. What say you?"

A concerned Emily contributed, "I'm thinking a bunch of people from different places were together, like on vacation in one of those cities, and got it from some animal and when they went home they took it with them."

On the air Watts could be heard speaking to his

production manager, "Johnny, hold Emily on the line after we're finished and send her a copy of my book."

Watts returned to his caller. "Emily, that's a pretty good idea. It's something my CDC friends and I have knocked around. It does tweak my interest again. I'll put my team on it and see what they can come up with."

The next several calls related to either American or foreign government conspiracies or military experiments gone wrong. Jason turned off the radio. There was silence in the conference room for several moments when Dustin offered, "There's both good along with far out ideas there."

Tomás said, "My parents back in Mexico think the Guatemalans or Hondurans brought it with them when they snuck across the southern border. They're always sick with something down there."

Jason didn't feel as cavalier as he tried to sound. "The theory Watts latched onto was pretty good. They'll never get anywhere with it and so what if they did? What's done is done."

And a cooked goose can't be uncooked. The broadcast triggered a serious round of paranoia in Jason. He asked his guest from Oklahoma, "Jeff, so far it's strong conjecture, but if a legitimate link were made between New Flu symptoms and the effects on the animals, how would you approach the problem? That is, if you were an epidemiologist charged with finding the source of the disease?"

Heads turned toward the man with shaved head

and the scar in the forehead over his left eye. Shenero remained silent for a moment, deep in thought, then answered, "From what you told me yesterday and from I'm hearing on the radio, everything matches. The first reported cases of animal birth mutations occurred here and then in Omaha, thanks to Don's travels. As an investigator, I'd start with the zoo in Omaha as a common meeting place for a mixture of visitors. There are many confirmed instances of humans catching diseases from animals or insects. Didn't AIDs first start with humans eating contaminated monkey meat when the blood entered the person through a cut or a wound? How about rabies, malaria, and good old fashion Salmonella food poisoning. So the disease gets in your skin, or the animal bites you, the flea bites you, or you eat the bad food.

"Next, I'd have the zoo check the animals that are accessible to the public, or in any way, shape or form, might transmit the disease, or animals that might be ill themselves. Of course, you won't find anything after spending a lot of money anesthetizing these animals or checking their vital signs, so you go to Plan B, which is to go next door to Lincoln, the original hot spot.

"I'd reason that all diseases have an incubation period. If you're going to eat egg salad with mayo or a gravy that's been sitting out in the sun at a church picnic, you've got maybe six hours or less before it hits you, as opposed to maybe 20 years of incubation period for leprosy. With smallpox, you look and feel healthy between 7-14 days after contracting the disease and you're not communicable during that period.

"When typical influenza or a cold hits, it can strike hard and fast and a person will get symptoms 2-4 days after exposure, on average, and be infectious before and after that. With the Mars virus, it sounds like incubation is at two weeks. At least, that is when your symptoms first started appearing.

"As an epidemiologist, my investigation will lead me to people who undergo procedures which involve genetic testing. For example, people who want to have their ancestry checked and who submit a saliva sample find out that no data can be obtained. Why? The DNA can't be read.

"What do I do now? Do I look for a time period when people started buying cough drops during cold season in Lincoln and trace it back a couple of weeks for starters? Then what? Do I look for flights from Lincoln to Omaha to the other cities that are involved and find out what all the thousands of passengers have in common? Good luck with that. Dead end. Or is it? Can it be correlated by a good computer programmer? Maybe. Do the authorities care anymore? Probably not. They could say it originated from a pig or a monkey. It doesn't change a thing. Nothing will. If it came from the Chinese, retribution coupled with an increase in military spending wouldn't change reality.

"At some point, any government has to run out of money to fund this inquiry. This is especially true when international accusations and finger pointing are occurring as we speak."

"Except for Andy Watts," Jason said. "He's a very angry man who has a lot of money, goes after what he wants, and a man who depends on the government, but dislikes its intervention." A man, who Jason sourly reflected, was all too similar to himself.

June spoke, "What the pundits don't know is what we know. The virus hangs on to people on airplanes. It grows in the air. It's probably infecting a hundred billion birds belonging to 10,000 species, many of which travel their migratory flyways thousands of miles in length. There are 400 million pigeons alone in the United States and these are in the thickets of human population centers. An equal number of fish are also migrating."

"Sorry, what's a flyway?" asked Tomás. He gave a slight shrug. Neither he nor Dustin seemed to be at all concerned about what they had heard. To Dustin, it was another day at the firehouse.

June answered his question, "Birds around the world move from one place to another to seek warmth, a place to give birth, to follow insects or reptiles and rodents for food, and to look for shelter. In our country, there are four main routes that birds follow to go south or come north as the seasons change. This happens all over the world. In general, it's twice a year. Heck, insects travel such routes for thousands of miles. As only one example, swarms of Monarch butterflies migrate some 5,000 miles from the northern United States and Canada far down into

Mexico. Numerous species of birds migrate into and through your home country going south or heading north. Many of them travel over water so you can't always see them. Recently, we tracked a single bird that travelled from South Africa to Mongolia, some 7500 miles. It flew for months to get there.

"So far, what used to be anecdotal reports about the New Flu originating in Russia, China and the Far East including India, are wrong. Those distant areas were the last to get hit. Without their knowing it, birds are probably the primary line of attack ahead of people carrying the virus with them on airplanes." She glanced at Jason, who smiled briefly. There was no point arguing the issue.

June resumed her explanation. "I mentioned fish. Lest we forget, all life in the rivers, bays, seas, and oceans may soon be completely subjugated by the fibers."

Jason interjected. "Here's my take. Plant life is the other side of the coin. Similar to high density human populations, high density plant populations, such as forests, jungles, fields of grass, clusters of fruit and nut-bearing trees, as well as croplands, should all exhibit rapid changes sooner than others. Croplands would include corn, wheat, sorghum, rye and rice, in particular the western and mid-western portion of our country; which means us."

"And strawberries grown at home," Linda said, looking at June.

"And gut bacteria," inserted Tomás.

"But apparently not viruses," argued Dustin.

Without waiting for a reply, he continued, "The other day I read a paper in the New England Journal of Medicine submitted by researchers at Johns Hopkins University. The usual viruses normally infecting their diseased mice could no longer cause infection. Their genetic material was inactivated."

"That's damn fascinating," entered Jason. "Could most viruses be inactivated? I mean a virus attacking a virus?"

"I guess, as long as the host has some genetic material, why not?" Dustin conjectured.

Tomás answered, "If that happened, it would include cold, flu, herpes, chickenpox, mumps, measles, HIV, and some that are associated with cancer. Those diseases may disappear. If both viral and host DNA are warped, I can't see how infection could occur. But what do I know?" He'd picked up this last phrase from Jason.

"That's in humans," proclaimed June. "What about avian influenza, distemper and rabies?"

"Viruses infect everything living—elephants, bacteria, algae, fungi, plants, animals, birds, fish, insects; it's what they do," said Tomás

Jason stepped up to the white board next to June. "We think it attaches to all DNA. Just because some viruses have RNA and not DNA, it's close enough. We also know it prefers some cells more than others."

He wrote as he spoke: "Frontal lobe of the brain, musculature, ligaments, tendons, and the production of white blood cells. Effects: faster, stronger, more analytical, enhanced immune system. We have to see how other bodily tissues respond. Some may do so quite subtly. We may see radical personality changes or more aggression or passivity. There could be a long list of emotional changes."

June offered, "If we're so smart, why can't all these wonderful minds solve this problem?"

Jason scratched his head, thinking. "Maybe we're out-thinking ourselves. This means we're still inside the box of chemicals and vibrations. Maybe we can make this work to our benefit. I'm wondering if that glowing chemical is a metabolic waste product. So far, the only positive finding we received from Gottlieb's engineers, as far as separating the two DNAs, is the use of ultra-high-frequency sound on the atomic level of vibration. They say this matches the frequency of the proton shift of the hydrogen atom during hydrogen bond formation. I don't see any future in that."

"What the hell does that mean?" June asked.

"Say that three times real fast," offered Dustin.

"Don't short yourself, Jason," Linda chided. She turned to Jeff Shenero. "As you probably know, the DNA in most cells is too small to see with the light microscope. If we stain cells with ethedium bromide, the DNA will give off an orange fluorescence which we can see with a good laboratory microscope. If we see two dots, supposedly we have separated our friend from normal DNA. We don't have to use the electron microscope or x-ray anymore to check on that."

"Does the method work?" asked the guest.

"The stain works fine. The problem is, no matter what we do, we still have one orange dot," Linda replied.

"It's helpful, but it's not progress," Jason groaned, clearly frustrated. Treading water made him almost as crazy as elbows on the table or people talking with food in their mouths or using cell phones while dining or sticking pens in their ear.

He turned to Don. "What happened on Mars millions of years ago?"

"No much," replied the geologist, smiling cutely.

Everybody snickered.

Jason gave a flash of a smile waiting patiently for Don to go on, which he did. "It's more than millions. About four billion years ago some cataclysmic event occurred, not long after the planets themselves were formed. A lot of us think the reason may have been one or more strikes by big meteors. At that time period, a lot of them were flying around, as you can imagine. Look at our own moon. It was formed during the same time epoch. If the meteors hadn't hit the moon, they would have hit Earth. Some of them did and more will in time. There is fairly strong geologic evidence pointing to the fact that Mars once had an oxygen-rich atmosphere with liquid water on the surface.

"Also, the eruption of Olympus Mons volcano occurred over the years; most recently, some 25 million years ago. Before that the earliest eruption would be 200 million years ago. I think the Jennings

Meteorite came from one of those two eruptions, but it could have come from the Kuiper belt or beyond."

"That's a long time to be flying around in outer space," mumbled Shenero.

"Sorry sir, I'm not up on astronomy," stated Tomás.

"The Kuiper Belt is a theoretical icy belt outside the orbit of Neptune. It may contain trillions of rocks of varying sizes. Some think there may be planet size objects out there," contributed Don, whose interest in rock hunting brought him to the world of astronomy years before.

"What do you think?" asked Dustin.

"I think it came from Mars," Don replied.

"That's it for cataclysmic events on Mars?" Jason asked.

"Pretty much," Don stated.

"I don't get the carbon dioxide part," June interjected.

Don replied, "Nobody else gets it either. The gas is frozen at the poles along with oxygen at close to 200 degrees below zero Fahrenheit. The problem is, we can't figure out why there is so much of it in the atmosphere. The elements we found in solid land don't contain that much carbon."

Linda raised her hand as if asking for permission to speak. "Excuse me, nobody is talking about oxygen. Carbonates have lots of oxygen and so do the lungs. For Pete's sake, green plants produce it, not to mention it makes up a high percentage of our atmosphere."

"She's right," said Don. "That makes sense. We have 200 times the oxygen compared with Mars. Maybe its activity is triggered by the oxygen in the air."

"And?" queried Jason.

"And I don't know," Don responded.

"Words, words, words," sighed June.

Jason ignored her. "We now have a couple of major problems. If we can get it to release its grip from the host genetic material, the body's own defense mechanisms should make short work of it. Remember, it doesn't have its outer shell anymore; it's naked DNA. The body will recognize it as foreign."

Don asked, "Why didn't the body go after it in the first place?"

Shenero answered Don's question. "The body takes time to respond to an invasion. Sometimes it takes seconds, sometimes a week or more in the case of first exposure to a new antigen, such as getting a sudden burst of pollen up our nose. In our case, it probably did respond. Remember the headaches? Remember the body aches and cough? I think those were our defenses reacting. The attackers moved faster than the defenders could establish themselves."

Don said, "Okay, but how do we keep it from re-infecting the host, even if we can get it to disengage?"

Jason answered, "I don't think we have to worry about that, Don. Once the internal defenses are established, any further attacks will be instantly repelled."

Suddenly Linda broke out in laughter. "How ironic if the world were informed that we, of all people, had found a cure for the New Flu."

Shenero said, "Don't give up hope. If I can help in any way, let me know. I'm thinking about your growth cycle in the fermenter. Jason, if you don't mind, I'd like you to take me through your data once again before I leave for home. I have an idea."

As Jason and Jeff entered the fermenter room, one of the workers was holding a flask of red liquid up to the light. Seeing Jason and said, "This one's ready, sir."

"Okay, go ahead," Jason directed.

The two workers began to spin out the contents of the fermenter by switching to the centrifuge mode. Shenero led Jason out into the quiet of the hallway and said, "I'm sure you know most of this, but indulge me while I think out loud. All life, whether bacterial, or plant or animal, follows a basic pattern of growth. So far, your virus seems to be following the rules. You start with a small number of seeds or bacteria or elk, fish, or weeks in a lot, and you put them into a larger environment that is similar to the one you grew them in. It takes time to adapt to the new environment, sometimes minutes, sometimes days or much longer. Let's call this an adaptation phase."

Jason nodded. He wasn't about to interrupt this man during a teaching session.

Shenero continued, "Once that phase is over,

they enter into a lag growth phase and begin to re-produce. The flat line starts to rise a little. This is followed by an exponential growth phase where our life forms are using available resources to reproduce as fast as possible. If you put in on paper, the graph would show a sharp increase. Incidentally, what is your rate of reproduction, as far as you can tell?"

Jason though for a moment and replied, "We think it's about 10-15 minutes."

Shenero's eyes widened. "Doubling in number that quickly? That's faster than the rate of reproduction for E. coli. It's worse in your case."

Jason didn't understand. "How so?"

"I'll get to that. So, once the nutrients run out, things start to slow down and they enter a lag phase. We see the graph start to level out. People generally harvest their cells at the peak of the growth phase to get the maximum amount of cells and whatever product they're after. That's what you're doing here: maximum glow equals maximum number of cells or virus particles. Okay, so far?"

Jason nodded, as Shenero continued, "Therein lies your problem. Once the population runs out of food, it begins to poison itself with whatever it ex-cretes. It begins to die. This is the death phase. This is where I suggest you harvest your cells—well into the death phase. That's when cells degrade, the cell walls disintegrate, the cell membrane decomposes and the guts leak out. If you do that, you may have more play toys."

Jason mentally slapped himself. It was so simple.

He had never imagined death would ever occur to this virus. "Jeff, I don't get the part about the rate of reproduction being worse in my case."

"Because, my friend, everything I just described is in a closed container, a closed ecosystem. Give it lots of carbon dioxide or maybe oxygen, as Linda suggested, and the Mars virus can reproduce in free air. From what you told me when we were fishing yesterday, it should be in hog's heaven in the exhaust of vehicles or airplanes or wherever there is an ample amount of gas it needs. In our case, no closed container exists other than the planet itself. It can happily reproduce with nothing to stop it. At that rate, its numbers may exceed the number of stars in the known universe in a short period of time."

Gottlieb needed more product. He tried to talk Jason into allowing the powder to be produced in his other manufacturing plants around the world. Jason adamantly insisted he maintain control.

"Jace, give him the formula already," Linda implored, wiping her hands on a dish towel.

"Absolutely not," was his angry response. Shenero had understood. Fine. Jeff could easily give advice when he didn't have to face shame in the eyes of humanity. Jason did not need the entire world finding out he was the source of the virus.

"But why?" Linda insisted. "Nobody cares anymore where it came from. Nobody can do squat about it. They need products to help people survive. You're doing that. If anything happens to the lab here it's all over. Honey, you're stuck in a deep rut."

She finished the dinner dishes by hand. Wiping her hands on a dishtowel she turned to face him and said, "Don said he was talking with Gottlieb about this reluctance on your part to give the up the growth formula and Gottlieb came up with this: Suppose everything Gottlieb makes comes from, say, crystals, for example. The crystals need various nutrients in various concentrations to grow. Suppose there are three different groups within a single building that make three parts of the growth medium and nobody knows what the other is making. He said this happens all the time in the business world. They all send their batch to a central area of the building where they are mixed and put into the fermenter. Your secret is safe and Gottlieb gets what he wants."

Jason scratched his head. He had to admit she had a point. He was still considering what Shenero had told him about the growth cycle. All he had to do would be to not harvest at the point of maximum glow. He would instruct the men not to worry about the glow at all to let the culture run for another—what, week?

The tornado sirens made the decision for him. The staff at the institute headed down to the animal facility for protection just as a power surge occurred when the tornado touched down. It hit in close proximity to the Les Rokeby Power Generating Station, seven miles to the east. Nearing the end of the growth phase, the last fermenter in operation blew out a motor. The emergency lights went on in the building until power was restored. Several days passed before the manufacturer could ship down a new motor. In no great hurry, Jason had Gottlieb's people install it, ensure that it worked, and asked them to turn it off at that point.

Curious about the four days of down-time for the fermenter that should have been harvested at the peak of the growth cycle, Jason drew off a sample into a flask. As he held the flask up the light, he and the two assistants saw an extremely intense glow. It wasn't the normal type that resembled Imitation Strawberry Soda; this was blood-red. Through it, he could see a murky black instead of a pitch black, with globules suspended in the solution.

Feeling a surge of excitement, he gave the men instructions to use differential centrifugation—spin at low to moderate speed, drain the tank and transfer contents to another empty fermenter. Transfer the remains from the first unit into Nalgene jars. Centrifuge the second batch at high speed and make another transfer. Save the glowing liquid in large containers. Put everything in the walk-in freezer after labeling and dating everything. Save a small sample of each for Jason to analyze.

That evening at home he went to the small desk that held the microscope in his office. Linda peddled on the bike in the next room. With a small sharp pointed metal pick, he removed a tiny sample of the first sediment that had formed. It appeared black. No surprise there. He placed the sample onto a drop of stain on a microscope slide and gently placed a coverslip over it.

"What are you doing?" Linda asked, as she entered the room, wiping her forehead with a sweat rag.

Jason didn't say a word. "There you are, my little darlings," he spoke almost lovingly, in a sing-song voice adjusting the fine focus of the microscope. "What's this?" He twisted the turret to a higher magnification. Is it my imagination or are the fibers split?"

He got up and said, "This is the overripe batch from the fermenter. Take a look."

Linda adjusted the eyepieces closer together to accommodate the width of her eyes, peering at what had caught Jason's attention. "The little buggers are definitely split, all right. That's new. They look like pea pods split down the middle lengthwise."

"Let's see if we can find the peas," he offered, and repeated the process; this time working with the gray sludge that had once been free-floating globules. He added a drop of stain. The entire sample turned orange. Jason knitted his eyebrows. He got up and Linda slid in after him.

A short moment later they stared at each other in realization of what had happened. The culture had become old and the fibers self-destructed. Shenero had been right. The virus particles had reached conditions of overpopulation and under-nourishment. They went the way of all living things under such conditions as they entered a death phase. The shell had split releasing its DNA and its glowing contents. The black shells constituted the black sludge, the DNA constituted the gray sludge. In outer space, inside the rock, they weren't trying to live, only to survive. They were in a resting state, resistant to environmental pressures; a feature common to spore forming bacteria, many fungi, and common in the plant world. Once they began to reproduce, they became subject to the laws of nature.

Jason got up and paced, three steps one way, turned, three the other way, turned. "The globules must be made up of free viral DNA intertwining with itself."

He repeated the test with the clear sample and found neither shells nor DNA.

"We have three new toys to work with," Linda smiled. Both understood hard research. For every year of hard labor, there would be a single teasing instant of happiness. One always waited for the big breakthrough, as false leads paved the way. Now it appeared an actual breakthrough had been achieved, ironically by accident again.

Jason commented, "Gottlieb will be happy if these shells work better than what we've been providing him. We have thinner logs taking up the spaces, therefore, thinner sheets of whatever Gottlieb wants to do with them. Not only that, but we have two different antigens we can use to make antibodies; the shell and the glow. We also have pure viral DNA. We also have a high concentration of glow we can purify. Call Dustin and Tomás and let them know. We'll put them on it tomorrow."

Linda pulled out her phone and made the calls without asking her husband why she had to make the call now rather than talking to the men the next day. When Jason made up his mind, he would take action immediately, if at all possible. When the money's in the slot machine, why wait to pull the handle?

How long had it been since her husband had been out shooting or camping or on his boat? How long had it been since she had gone with him. Before this new discovery, she had resolved to offer him her companionship for a week-long outing, if only as a palliative for him. It wasn't attractive to her, but she'd do it for him. The sound of thunder made her pause as she was about to call Don. Would it ever stop raining?

She recalled the notes her husband had made in the middle of the night about changing ecosystems. Normal climate change couldn't happen so quickly, could it? After only a few years? Maybe this is one of those odd years. Does this follow the normal eleven-year sunspot cycle or is it something else. June and Don keep records of events and would have a better idea of worldwide changes.

The next morning she went in to see June. This day the redhead had dressed Western with high brown George Strait leather boots, and a turquoise lace dress.

"You look happy today," Linda said.

June turned smiling. "I try to wake up happy and go to bed happy each day. Whatever happens between is not my fault."

Linda laughed. "I know you and Don keep closer track of world events than we do. Just because we finally got a TV doesn't mean we watch it. The commercials make us crazy."

June chuckled. "Really? I'll be sure to report it. What's on your mind today, my dear?"

Linda said, "Help me with something. This whole epidemic thing has been going on for what, five years? I was wondering how that tied in with any weather changes. I mean, it is raining a lot more here this year."

At that moment, Don walked in. "Perfect," Linda said. "Just the person I wanted to see."

Don stopped. "Works for me. I heard you ask something about rain."

Linda nodded and asked the question again. Don walked to a small coat closet and pulled out a laminated world map that had been rolled and tied with a rubber band, which he slid off. He opened the map and spread it over the surface of desk and placed a paper weight at each end to hold it down.

"It's not just the rain here," Don began, pointing as he spoke. "Over the past several years, vast changes have been occurring throughout the world. For example, many of Europe's busiest seaports, which are located in the Netherlands, Belgium, and Germany, are becoming more and more handicapped because of flooding along major waterways and high water in the ports. Changing weather patterns are bringing about brought more rainfall, hurricanes, and tornadoes to areas that had never had them before, including the areas I mentioned. Once those seaports go down, over a billion tons of cargo will not be shipped out or brought in each year. The Coriolis effect is different now than it used to be."

Don saw that Linda didn't understand. "As the earth rotates, it causes the air to rotate with it. Each hemisphere rotates in a different direction, if you look at them end on—counter-clockwise for us here in the northern hemisphere. In general, the direction that hurricanes spin in each hemisphere is due to this rotation. Now add moisture and warmth. The rotation of the earth didn't change. The amount of moisture and heat did. In today's world, hurricanes are frequent and more powerful in both hemispheres. So are tornadoes because they follow low pressure systems."

Linda thanked Don for telling her more than she needed to hear. There seemed to be a lot of negativity going around.

July of Year 5

Linda understood her husband's work held more importance to him than did money. He remained hog-tied to the lab. She knew that would be the case going into the marriage and she was okay with it because she got what she wanted—to enhance her sense of security and share life with a partner. To make life easier, she'd learned to keep her reading material off the floor or the counters. Besides, she mused, she had gotten more than even with him by completely taking over the master bathroom with her cosmetic supplies.

At last, the four scientists hovered over the gas chromatograph. The glow-factor had been concentrated shot it into the injection port of the machine. A few moments later the printout began to scroll. They watched the baseline for a few moments and suddenly a sharp single peak formed. Jason and Dustin shouted, "Yes," and Linda screamed. Tomás exclaimed, "Yeah, man. That's what I'm talking about."

"Get the stain," Jason directed to no one in particular. Using edge of a microscope slide, Jason scraped skin cells from an area of his forearm. Tomás handed him the bottle of stain and Jason applied a small drop of the liquid he'd injected into the machine. Adding the tiny drop of it to the skin cells, he hooked up the microscope to the projector for everyone to watch. Placing a coverslip over the preparation. He slid the slide into the brackets on the stage of the microscope and turned the turret to the highest magnification, adjusted the fine focus and looked up at the screen. They all held their breaths.

What they saw that day was a single orange dot slowly separate into two orange dots. The two DNAs were untangling, the ropes were separating.

Tomás was puzzled. "Makes no sense, doctor. Why would the virus produce a product that would undue its own attachment to the species it's attacking."

Jason thought for a moment before replying,

"The glow chemical must be a byproduct of normal metabolism. It's a waste product. That's why it's being excreted."

"By jove, Doctor Randolph, I do believe you are spot on," Linda declared, in the best British accent she could muster.

"Maybe it's making the glow chemical to repel attackers," Dustin threw in.

"Of which there are none. That is very encouraging," Jason concluded, thinking that if both he and Linda could be cured, a normal baby might be born.

January of Year 6

The animal studies had been completed. Only Sider mice could be used because normal mice were not available. After a single injection of the glowing compound into the mice, no noticeable changes occurred; however, their offspring were normal white furred mice. After weight adjustments had been calculated as to dosage for humans, trials would be completed within the year.

"Do you want to tell Gottlieb?" Don asked, and Jason answered, "I'm not sure. Honestly, I don't know why I should. The contract is very specific in that we produce powder and he makes products. It says nothing about what else comes out of this lab."

"True. On the other hand, he does have the distribution mechanism," Don noted.

"So does the CDC, the World Health Organization, the French, and a number of other agencies. Besides, the man might want to want to sell it. This is a gift," snapped Jason, suddenly understanding another ironic statement coming out his mouth.

Don shook his head. "You don't know if he'll want to sell it. He may have some good ideas about distribution. Just call him. What's the big deal? It's a good move to make."

Remembering Don's earlier suggestion years before about telling the world about the virus and his reluctance to do so, Jason did call. Gottlieb offered to handle the distribution of the new vaccine for no fee as long as WG Corp. got the publicity. As a compromise, Jason's people would get the credit. Jason consented.

Toward the end of the year, no harm had come to humans and normal babies had been born to volunteers who had been well compensated. Desperate for a cure and seeing no other option, national health agencies authorized the distribution of the Randolph Vaccine. Permission was given to RCR to mass-produce the vaccine to be distributed by WG Corp.

Linda and Jason were excited by the news. Perhaps the time had come try for another child. As scientists, they saw the evidence pointing to a normal birth; as humans, the trepidation remained.

Gottlieb still remained healthy and refused to try the cure lest his own immune system return to its deadly status. The engineer had become at ease with himself. After learning his immune system had been restored, the daily emotional weight of impending death had been lifted.

January of Year 7

A full seven years had passed since Jason first saw the glowing flask in his lab. He stood before the cameras announcing their discovery of a cure for the New Flu. He spoke of the tireless efforts of so many researchers in so many countries to find a cure until his group tried a new approach. He would not reveal the nature of the approach.

Jason worked his way to the hard part, something he had given up years before; lecturing. He felt as though he were reading his audience a story from H.P Lovecraft or Tales from the Crypt while heavy Bach organ music might be playing in the background. "We will have a generation of humans who will be different, if not several generations. We can't force people to take the cure or give it to their pets to prevent them from giving birth to abnormal babies.

"We can't do anything about other plant or animal life. Those lives may be changed forever and will continue to change as the real effects of the New Flu take hold. We are alone now, as though we are humans freshly landed on an alien world who must survive, to tolerate the absurdity of what befell us. I have no doubt we will not only survive; we will become successful in many ways, while we learn to progress as a single race."

The office phone rang at 1:37 p.m. and June picked up.

"RCR" she answered.

"Yes, good afternoon. This is Russell Merrick, an

investigator with the Andy Watts radio program. Do you know who we are?"

June's heart stopped. She had to think fast. "I know what radio is. I don't know who you are," she replied in her cutesy fashion.

Merrick said, "Our research leads us to believe that the New Flu came from your laboratory. You do genetic research there. Is that correct?"

"I don't do genetic research," she said. "I just answer the phone."

Accustomed to uncooperative people, Merrick continued. "Is there a Doctor Randolph present there with whom I can speak?"

"Yes, there is," June replied. "I'll see if he's available." She put Merrick on hold and called Jason.

Jason's mind calculated, "Tell him I'm in the middle of an experiment and can't talk now. Get his number and tell him I'll be happy to call him back later."

June gave the message to Merrick and hung up the phone while Jason scratched his chin. He could just hear Andy Watts on the air with the story of viral movement they all knew had taken place, including Watts. The tire had stopped swirling. It was time to pick it up. He mulled over his strategy for an hour, then he called Don and Linda to join him in the front office.

He asked June return to Merricks's call and to put the phone on speaker.

"Russell Merrick," came the reply.

"Mister Merrick, this is Jason Randolph returning your call. How can I help you today? I'm afraid were in the middle of collecting data points, so let's make this brief."

"Sir, I'm with the Andy Watts radio program. Do you know who we are?" "No," Jason responded, curtly.

"We run a syndicated daily program that reaches millions of listeners and we do investigative research," Merrick continued.

"And you're either looking for sponsors or you want to sponsor us. Is that right? Great, we can use the money," Jason said, as he look around at the others in the office.

June sat at her desk and smiled as did Linda who stood next to Don. Don's lips were tight. He still wanted Jason to use the opportunity to tell the truth about how the virus got loose.

"Not really," said Merrick. "We have evidence..."

Jason cut him off. "Just to let you know, Mister Merrick, all our phone conversations are automatically recorded for later reference, if necessary. You can't believe the number of nut jobs who call a cancer research center for all kinds of things."

Merrick paused, then replied, "To get to the point, our research indicates that the New Flu may have originated in your lab. The flu appeared in a number of cities at the time your people were there."

"And?" Jason demanded.

"We like to give people a heads up that they're going to have their story told on the radio," Merrick said, bluntly. "It's the right thing to do."

"The right thing for whom. Doubtless to minimize the chances of a major well-publicized lawsuit for false accusations against reputable and respected agencies," Jason stated, just as bluntly.

"Sir…"

Jason cut him off again. "Mister Merrick, in answer to your statement, my people were fine when they left this lab to go on vacation to these cities. When they returned, they had the flu." (Which wasn't accurate because their symptoms occurred two weeks after exposure and their vacations occurred three months after exposure—let Merrick work out the math because the man has to be clueless about the incubation period.)

"But the time frame indicates the flu began after they got there." Merrick persisted.

"Mister Merrick, I'm not going to nitpick with you about your theories. If you're so certain we caused this New Flu epidemic, go ahead and run your story. Doubtless you had a cough at some point. Those are the first symptoms. As a suggestion, you might want to take care of yourself and your own family before you worry about others. We all caught it here, too. Welcome to the club."

Jason set down the phone and let out a deep breath. He gave one big nod downward as if to say, "And that's that," and returned to his lab to collect data points.

It started out as a rare perfect November day in Nebraska. Wisps of high-altitude cirrus clouds hung at 40,000 feet. They were crisscrossed by an occasional lower altitude jet contrails. Winds aloft pushed at them, spreading them out. Conspiracy theorists argued that the spreading contrails were proof of poisonous gases being released into the atmosphere by the planes. In one sense they were, as the exhausted carbon dioxide supported an explosion in the rate of viral reproduction in the upper atmosphere, as did any concentrated source of the gas.

The foursome sat at the picnic table in Jason's back yard. The fish was baked, the baby back ribs were nearly ready to remove from the grill and several bug zappers maintained a syncopated rhythm. Fortunately, Jason had purchased his before the store supplies ran out.

"Your grass needs cutting. Especially around the fence line," June said.

"Yep," Jason replied.

"Where'd you get the salmon?" asked Don.

"Alaska," Jason stated. "It's the Silver variety I ordered. All they had was what I call sideways stuff, so it will be a little tougher than we're used to. Same with the ribs."

The doorbell rang. Linda got up to answer it. Moments later she arrived with Wilbur Gottlieb and his wife, Isabelle, a tall stately light-skinned woman dressed in a flower-patterned Sioux Indian designer blouse and matching dress. She carried a bottle of expensive white wine.

Introductions were made and Isabelle presented the bottle of wine to Jason. To Linda, she possessed a core of strength and awareness in her dark brown eyes along with a French accent which Linda immediately pounced upon. The women began to speak in French, Isabelle's first language and Linda's second.

Ignoring their banter, Gottlieb reported, "The vaccine is in forty-two countries, soon to be sixty."

Jason made a motion to the chairs on the lawn. "What about clothing and shelter?"

"We're moving them into new countries on a regular basis," said Gottlieb. "Military-related materials have decreased to twenty countries."

"How are you feeling?" Don inquired.

Gottlieb replied, grinning. "Fine. I did have a cough a few years ago; something that was going around."

June asked, "What now, Wilbur?"

Gottlieb paused in thought, then said, "Now? Now we forget about the past," as he slapped at a large mosquito settling onto his neck. In the distance, a red-tailed hawk, riding the circle of an air bubble, broke out of its circuit and quickly dove. An instant later it rose again, carrying a feral cat in its claws.

June's face became somber as she asked, "I know Don has, but have you others paid attention to the Sandhill Cranes' coloration lately?"

Gottlieb shook his head quickly, then paused, remembering her drawing on the wall in the conference room. The others wondered where she was going with this.

June explained, "Depending on the year, we get half-a-million to a million here every spring coming into the Platte River basin. They fly down the Central Flyway from Northeastern Canada, Alaska, and Siberia. Well, they usually display red around the eyes, but this year their entire heads are quite reddish."

"That's an interesting factoid," chuckled Linda.

"It's more than that," said Don. "We've been watching them for years. The coloration of a bird depends on several factors that affect the pigments in their skin and feathers. One of those factors is what they eat. Birds with more coloration tend to eat more carotenoids such as those present in certain vegetables, fruits and berries, and also in algae. In many cases, you'll see the pigments in their colorful droppings. Another example is salmon. The reason salmon are red or pink is because they eat a diet rich in shrimp that have carotenoids in their shell."

June summarized, "What Don is getting at is this: We believe the cranes are eating fewer insects, but they're eating more berries and other foods with carotenoids. If insects have suddenly become less palatable to these cranes or to birds in general, it could mean that a major factor in reducing the insect population will be eliminated. In other words, there could be more insects."

Don said, "Add warblers, jays, wrens, finches, and many other smaller species to the list of birds that eat insects or, at least, may be more selective in the insects they do eat."

"On the other hand," June threw out, "There are reports that some rain forests have demonstrated a decline in the number of crawling and flying bugs, lizards and frogs by a five-to-ten-fold amount over the past three decades. It's being blamed on global warming, but I'm not too sure about that."

Isabelle, seated next to Linda, continued to swipe at her feet and ankles above the low-cut boots she wore, and asked, "What's going to eat the insects, if the birds don't?"

Linda leaned over and whispered, "Isabelle, let me grab you some lotion for those bites. Hang on." She quickly got up and went into the house and returned moments later with a tube of antihistamine-combination bug repellent in her hand. She handed the tube to Isabelle who squeezed out a good portion of cream and rubbed it over her lower and upper ankles.

June scrunched her mouth. "That's a little out of my area. I would think there would be some bird species and dragonflies that would find them palatable. Bigger and stronger insects might relish eating the smaller ones more. At the moment, it's only conjecture."

Jason said, "Another catastrophe. Can you imagine a world with an uncontrolled insect population? On the plus side, don't more insects like locusts or crickets give us inspiration to eat them as sources of protein and vitamins without going to cattle and pork? I mean, an overabundance of insects could be catastrophic or could be a blessing for the hungry, especially if we set up insect farms or develop insect-capture techniques."

A sudden gust of wind caught the group by surprise. They all looked up to see black thunderheads moving quickly down from the north. "Let's get inside," Jason directed.

Don helped Jason with the food on the grill and the condiments and within only a couple of minutes the group had relocated and had taken seats in the living room. Jason put the food in the warmer.

Drawing from his early education, Jason picked up where they had left off. "You may know this, but the word catastrophe comes from the Greek word meaning overturn and is usually related to the end of a tragic play. It is similar to the word cataclysm, a sudden upheaval in the natural world. What happened to the Dinosaurs in a short period of time was cataclysmic when a meteor struck in the Yucatan Peninsula and led to the darkening of the skies. The sudden event resulted in the death of most life on Earth."

"Let's include tsunamis and other natural phenomena, along with the eruption of Mount Vesuvius and the destruction of the city of Pompeii in A.D. 79," Linda added.

Don contributed, "Geologically speaking, let's not forget the eruption of Mount Tambora on one of the islands of Indonesia in 1815. It's in a volcanic ring of fire around Sumatra. The eruption changed the climate of the world for the next several years. That led to the development of the opium trade in Asia, because the regular crops grown in one region of China were washed out from the heavy rainfall, but opium could do well under those conditions. So it was imported and flourished. Thus, it became a popular worldwide commodity."

Linda felt compelled to add, "I know climate change caused by the eruption of Mount Tambora served as a backdrop for Mary Shelley's Frankenstein novel, as England was besieged with record cold and snow while eastern India was hit with hurricanes, again, thanks to that eruption. The area that is now Bangladesh was nearly wiped off the map for the same reason."

"Here's another one," Jason offered, "The Black Plaque that swept across Europe and Asia, in only a two or three-year period in the mid-1300s, can be included. With a world population of only about 300 million at the time, it killed a third of Europe's population; in some townships, over 90 percent.

"In more recent times, the flu pandemic of 1918 afflicted some 500 million of the world's population of only 1.8 billion and claimed a death toll of five to ten percent. Which brings us to modern times when a new virus from outside our world rapidly sweeps across the planet and affects virtually all life."

Linda glared at her husband. He wasn't going to give it up. It wasn't the truth of his statement, it was the way he said it. He was pouring guilty fuel onto his own fire.

Gottlieb said, "In all honesty, I've been occupied with running a business over the past few decades and I'm embarrassed to confess ignorance of a lot of events outside my financial empire. Of course, I

see more than most from my position as a manufacturer and promoter of goods and have had more than
my share of bumps and bruises traveling by plane. I
just don't understand why the world is changing so
rapidly."

Jason said, "This seems to be a good time to find
out. So, Don, you're the old meteorologist and have
been tracking this; what happened to life?"

Linda looked sharply at him and a flash of anger
surged through her. Nobody else picked it up. They
were all looking at Don waiting for him to speak. To
Linda, only a small part of her husband's question
related to scientific curiosity. The bulk of it related
to himself, wanting to know exactly in every detail
what misery he alone, Jason Randolph, had wrought
to the human race, to life on the planet, so he could
wallow in it. Jason caught her quick down-turned
mouth, the flash of her eyes. He looked down.

The geologist inhaled for an instant, gathered
himself, puffed out his cheeks, blew out air and
scratched his head. "Jeez, it's not just life. It's what
we don't understand about how the universe works.
I've been to Antarctica three times and slept in tents
out there, so I have to pay attention to what's happening on that continent, which leads to an effort to
follow what's happening globally. I've read about
experts forecasting a rise in sea level from a fraction
of an inch to over a hundred feet. From my standpoint, here's what I think happened:

"First: Over the past ten years, half of Antarctica's ice melted, accounting for much less than one-

tenth percent the volume of the oceans. That started well before the New Flu hit.

"Second, in terms of sea level rise, when icebergs broke off, they displaced water by only a small amount; like a chip of ice in a glass of water.

"Third, the oceans expanded and are still expanding in terms of both area and volume for a number of reasons. One reason is that there is less ice. Another is due to the expansion of water when it gets warm. When warm water expands, it takes up a larger volume and encroaches on any land at sea level. It also expands when it freezes, but that's not the issue here.

"Let's take a brief look at our current situation, no pun intended. Simplistically, fresh water is less dense than saltwater, so, with the melting of polar ice, which is fresh water, its influx overlays the ocean surface. This changes the rate of vertical mixing and influences the conveyer belt of ocean currents that surround the globe which has its own effect on climate. The point here is that the increased volume adds to the amount of moisture in the atmosphere, which, as you can imagine, causes a global climate changes. Additional rainfall is another factor adding to our atmospheric moisture and hence, leads to flooding, which I'll get to in a minute."

Jason asked, "That was destined to happen, anyway, wasn't it? We were burning fossil fuels as fast as we could, we were creating heat islands out of our cities and generating more electricity each year. All this equates to heat. Our own records go back a hundred years to prove it."

Don shook his head. "Yes and no. Maybe it would over a long period of time. Not like this. One of many global events that happened was when temperatures rose faster than predicted. In my view, we can trace that back to our friend from Mars. I'm trying to tell you why."

Jason felt chastened. Don continued. "By definition, change relates to occurrences over time. To me, this entire slow shifting of ecosystems and climate differences due to global warming may or may not have started with man, but the incredible speed of the change can be totally blamed on the virus. Once it got loose, well, what is happening was inevitable, because that's the role of the virus. I feel like Dustin should be saying this. It acts like an enzyme, a catalyst, if you will. In some cases it caused a deceleration of the heating effect by absorbing more CO2 through a faster rate of photosynthesis in plants. It also accelerated it in terms of increasing the rate of ice melt because of algal growth, expansion of the oceans, and exposure of the permafrost to microbial action. The heating won out and the end result is a heat gain of five degrees Fahrenheit. That so far and it's a huge number destined to become larger. It's nothing we predicted. Where it stops nobody knows.

"When the permafrost began to melt, it exposed a trillion tons of vegetation that had been frozen for eons. This was and is attacked by bacteria, fungi and other microbial life forms. Thus, an enormous amount of methane gas was and is being released. This, in turn, caused a further increase in overall global temperatures. So, both relative and absolute humidity increased in the presence of warmer water. That gets added upon by the rapid growth of plants for the reason that they release water vapor through transpiration."

Gottlieb addressed Don formally, in appreciation for the man's knowledge. "That's a heck of a story, Doctor Jennings. It sounds like a chain reaction."

Don replied, "At first it was. At this point events have become randomized, all leading to a worsening situation. With all of that going on, there was a change in the jet stream and the ocean currents. Storms are more massive and hurricanes are becoming commonplace. The storm surge from the higher winds and more rainfall from the increase in strength of tropical storms is causing the coastal regions around the world to flood. This adds to the already rising waters and more evaporation.

"I mentioned the jet stream. It moves from west to east following the rotation of the earth at 35,000 feet and controls the daily weather. If you watch your news reports, you'll see them show how it flows up and down to give us low pressure in some areas and high pressure in others. This up and down motion can fluctuate greatly when there is too much heat, which will lead to flooding in some areas and drought in others.

"Furthermore, some astronomers and geologists, including myself, believe the wobble of the Earth may be affected thanks to our visitor. Not only can this affect our seasons, it will affect our astronomy.

See, there was a loss of ice mass at the poles, especially at the North Pole which once was designated as the refrigerator for the planet. The Greenland ice sheet is almost gone. While ice reflects the rays of the sun, water absorbs them.

"Furthermore, we've lost and will continue to lose hundreds of cities including all of Scandinavia thanks to their low sea level location. There is no reversing this effect. Islands have disappeared or will soon disappear, low-lying countries like Australia are contracting in size."

Don took of sip from a bottle of water he had at his feet. The classroom was attentive. No person spoke a word, waiting for the next chapter of the story. Linda had a sudden urge to take notes. How could anybody remember all of that? She had known Don almost as long as Jason had and they were learning new things about him as time went on—he spoke German and had this intimate relationship with the evolution of planets, especially their own. She felt shallow in his presence, a woman who kept herself in confinement, reading, with no outside interests when there was so much out there to learn. Her husband, with all his flaws, sought new adventures from his love of the outdoors to creating vaccines to the production of God knows what with Gottlieb and the damnable virus. What was her list of accomplishments? Not a whole lot when you came down to it. Don had touched something latent inside her; a spark that needed oxygen, something she had to prove to herself.

Don continued, as if he were a man on a mission to spill it all. "As we know from local occurrences, major waterways overflowed their banks to an unheard of extent. Of particular interest to us here is when that started happening to the Missouri. In Omaha, it took out Eppley Airfield, our acclaimed Henry Doorly Zoo and Aquarium, the Old Market, and the courts, together with thousands of businesses and residences. Boys Town was far enough away to escape. On the other side of the river, Council Bluffs, Iowa, was devastated.

"One reason for this local flooding is that each year for the last five or six, Montana and Colorado received new record amounts of snowfall. I expect this trend to continue. The melt first enters the upper end of the Missouri in Montana where the river originates. As people fleeing the river can attest, the banks have widened considerably due to greater water flow velocity and erosion. "

In her heavy French accent, Isabelle interrupted. "Excuse me, Donald, have you ever been to Paris?"

"Not for many years," he confessed.

Isabelle continued, "I grew up there. The rainy season in Paris in December-January and May-June, but it can rain anytime. The weather is unpredictable. The Seine River begins in northern France and winds like a snake through Paris. When I grew up, it would flood over once every few years, sometimes up to 20 feet above its normal level. Now it floods twice a year and is 25 to 30 feet higher than normal because there are heavier rains that happen more often. Many cities and towns along the river are washed out. Instead of a couple of thousand people displaced, now there are up to fifty thousand displaced in Paris alone. Almost quarter million art pieces in the L'Ouvre had to be moved to the upper floors. Many places in Europe are like that." Tears came to her eyes. Linda quietly said something to her in French and touched her hand.

After a moment of silence, Don went on with his tale. "In Africa, some 10,000 miles of flooding occurred along the banks of its major rivers. Tens of millions in Mumbai, India; Shanghai, China; New York City, Miami; and Cape Town, South Africa, were forced to rethink their present residences and workplaces. Venice, Italy, is gone.

"Worldwide, three billion people, 200 billion birds and billions of animals have been displaced as mass migration forced all water-based life inland and upland. This did not count insects and reptiles.

"Wars and skirmishes took another 500 million lives, add another 300 million due to Cholera and a variety of mosquito borne diseases."

"The oceans, which made up 70 percent of the Earth's surface prior to the time of the calamity, now comprise closer to 75 percent. The fact that coastal areas and islands went underwater added to the total.

"I could go on about dust storms in the Middle East and here in the States, and dry areas becoming dryer. If you recall, we'd gotten fairly good at weather forecasting. Now it's a joke," said the former meteorologist.

Like everyone else there, Gottlieb had picked up bits and pieces of this information. Now to hear it in such a context was overwhelming. He'd been through a lot of bad weather; yet he couldn't wrap his mind around the rapidity of the transformations occurring over the planet; or even that they were occurring at all. He looked around. Jason sat with his head hanging down. Isabelle and Linda sat stone-faced looking at nothing and June gazed into space, probably conjuring a picture to draw.

A long rumble of thunder could be heard in the distance. June summarized her husband's monologue and said, "What I hear is: lots of heat, humidity, free water, vegetation, and bad weather. It would be quite intriguing to live another thousand years to see what happens to our world and its occupants."

"We must plan for the future. Yes?" Gottlieb said at last, scratching at his last mosquito bite.

Don held up a hand, to get everybody's attention at almost exactly the same time as a heavy downpour began outdoors. "In summary, you can start just about anywhere you want in this circle of dominoes, push one over, and they all fall down, with increasing heat as the granddaddy of them all. Now let's eat."

"Yes," agreed Jason, happy to change the subject, not successful in coming out of his latest episode of self-loathing. "For entertainment later, I've got a taped track meet and a basketball game. We can watch a few minutes of each to give us something to talk about."

Year 12

Early in its distribution program, WG Corp. incurred a major setback. A class action suit had been filed against them. Their water-proof clothing was so resistant to penetration of any kind that moisture could not evaporate from the skin. This created a layer of moist air between the skin and the shirts, pants, and shoes. The presence of high humidity in many parts of the world caused ringworm fungus to rapidly spread over the body and feet when the clothing was left on for an extended period of time—a practice all too common in the wet new world where migration had become a way of life.

The highly contagious disease caused uncontrollable itching. Topical ointments were of little use. There was no cure except to move to an area of dry heat. Desert areas included the Gobi in China, the Arabian in the Middle East, the Kalahari in Southern Africa, the entire Southwestern United States, the Patagonia along the western coasts of Argentina and Chile, the Great Sandy in Australia, among a limited number of others. Now hotter and dryer than ever, these areas had few resources to deal with an influx of people who sought a cure for the fungus.

WG Corp. advised against throwing the clothing into the landfills in that it was not biodegradable or burnable. Articles should not be given to another person to wear because the ringworm spores and mycelium would be imbedded in them.

Experts in the field suggested placing the unwanted articles into a sealed plastic bag until further information about its disposal would be forthcoming. Branches of the US military were particularly miffed that they were having to pay exorbitant prices for their new camos only to see many of their troops become infected with ringworm. WG Corp. was in the process of developing new laser technology to create fine holes in the clothing to enable the skin to breathe. This would affect the insulating ability of the clothing, but not its durability or longevity. When Jason heard about the problem from Gottlieb, he immediately called Jeff Shenero in Norman.

"Jeff, it's Jason."

"Jason who?"

"How quickly they forget," Jason said flatly, then added, "The one who showed you how to use the right bait for the fish you're trying to catch."

Laughter on the other end of the line. "Congrats on the cure, by the way."

"It's your deal, not mine. Thanks for the tip on the growth phases. Sometimes death can be a good thing for the living," Jason said, philosophically. He explained the circumstances surrounding the uniforms and the clothing to his colleague.

"Jason, the antibiotic I told you about is meant for deep fungal infections. It is very successful for that. However, we've never tried it topically. We'd need to run clinical trials first. Normally, ringworm fungi attack the areas between the toes, toe nails, the groin and scalp. It can also grow on spotty areas of the skin and is transferred from one place on the body to another through scratching. An infection over the entire body is rare, especially with so many people. It could work, though. Got any volunteers?"

"Oh, say a few million, more or less," Jason answered.

There was a pause on the line. Shenero requested, "Line up a hundred or so. A thousand would be better. We'll need lots of data. It'll take time, but if it works we should be able to mass produce it within a year."

"That long?" Jason asked. He knew the question to be ridiculous and wanted to take it back. The mycologist would need fermenters to grow the mold to produce the antibiotics and the toxin separately, purify and crystalize them, and prepare them in a salve or a spray for application. This aspect alone would take months.

Jason didn't wait for Shenero to tell him it was a dumb question and continued, "Tell you what, Jeff. Order what you need to make it work, no matter the cost. Money is no object. Send me the bills as they come in and I'll make sure you get paid within 30 days. Bill me for your labor charges on a rush job. Can you do it?"

"That's a lot of work..." Shenero paused, then said, "Wait. I can order the antibiotic from a commercial firm, so all we'd need to make is the mycotoxin. That'll cut the time to less than half."

Jason had hoped his friend would agree to help him. "I'll have my people send you a bank draft for a quarter-million to get you started. You'll have it by this afternoon. When that runs out, bill me for whatever. Will that work?"

"That part will work," replied the scientist, surprised at the large amount of cash Jason had at his disposal. "No guarantees on the workability of the product."

"Understood. Take care. I'll connect you with June who will get your bank routing number and we'll take care of the rest. And thanks."

Nobody was certain when the term Sider came into common usage. Similar occurrences tend to give rise to similar terminologies. Some, like Jason, gave them the name because of their facial appearance, which he ascribed to any creature born with the New Flu. Others thought it might be for the reason they were outside the norms of human appearance. After the first human abnormal births occurred, one newspaper humorist wrote, "Their eyes are so of offset you'd think they were born on a Wednesday looking both way for Sunday." He later retracted that statement when his wife gave birth to a Sider son.

Out of some four million human births in the U.S. each year, Sider births accounted for 200,000 the first year. During that period of time, out of 130 million human births worldwide, Sider births accounted for only a few million. By the third year the number had increased to almost all births in the U.S. and 40 million worldwide. By the fifth year, virtually every child born on the planet was a Sider, with the exception of isolated outposts.

After introduction of the Randolph Vaccine, the number of human Sider births dropped dramatically. Not all of the decrease could be ascribed to the cure. There were many who were reluctant to have sideways children. Approximately 700 million human Siders were born among a surviving population of 5 billion humans with no accurate figures available. Nearly three billion people had lost their lives since the outbreak of the New Flu for a variety of reasons. Most of the deaths were climate-related and included flooding and meteorological phenomena accompanied by subsequent collapse of buildings and destruction of infrastructure. Disease and pestilence followed at a close second; wars and local skirmishes were third.

Seven years after the New Flu began, the citizens of Lincoln, Nebraska, found themselves in a relatively safe environment, if one discounted hard, long, windy winters, a sharp increase in tornadic activity and flooding of the Midwestern croplands semiannually. In short, virtually all cropland in the United States had all but disappeared. What crops remained grew faster. Cattle and chicken still served as mainstays for meat, in addition to the presence of abundant wildlife. For local residents, food was not difficult to obtain when compared to other areas of the country.

The security of homes and offices were paramount in the lives of the citizens and intruders were dealt with accordingly. Law enforcement had more to do than to follow-up on the death of a stranger trying to cross through somebody's property only to get shot as a consequence.

Locals were extremely protective of their treasures, including the headquarters of WG Corp. and RCR. Everybody knew about the relationship between the two. RCR had not only found a cure for the New Flu, but also supplied W.G. Corp and the world with crystals to make products. You don't mess with either company.

After years of working for Jason, Tomás quit RCR. He joined Gottlieb who trained him for a year and sent him, his wife, and son, down to Mexico City with unlimited money to open a product manufacturing plant there, while the family still maintained their home in Lincoln. Gottlieb made their lives easier by providing with one of his private jets for the flight both ways. In the meantime, the family stayed in Mexico City for two months initially, then the men returned every other weekend. Finally, Tomás and Angel visited Mexico monthly to ensure the plant operated smoothly. To Tomás' great benefit, Gottlieb had already made the necessary business contacts to speed the setup and operation of the plant.

Dustin dated a women whom he met on-line and they were soon married. He remained at the lab, his happy spot, as he called it.

Another plant opened in Berlin, Germany. Hamburg, the second largest city in Germany, had applied to be a site until the overflow from the Mediterranean broke the banks of the River Elbe and its tributaries, causing to the city to completely flood. Like Paris, France, virtually its entire population relocated.

Once with a population of 13 million, now down to seven million, Moscow vied for a plant. This request was denied and brought amusement to those who reviewed the applications. It made no sense. The Moskva River ran through the central portion of the city and overflowed worse each succeeding year. The overflow would then freeze during their brutal eight month-long winters to provide ice sheets that covered the roadways.

China's application for Beijing was accepted to receive a plant because of its population held steady at 22 million and the fact that it had incurred no floods. Delhi was also selected for a plant site thanks to the presence of over a billion densely-packed people in a land mass 40 percent that of the United States. Their extensive network of buses, trains, roads, and a mail delivery system that reached the smallest villages gave it a big plus sign in the eyes of the decision makers. The fact that their east coast, from Madras to Calcutta to Bangladesh were pummeled yearly with devastating hurricanes did not affect the selection process.

Religious and ethnic groups promoting large families tended to back off their promotions after the birth of their first Sider child while others proclaimed them to be God's children and propagated more. Meanwhile, the average man and woman got faster and stronger, while new neural synapses were being formed in the brain to make them smarter. The children of Sider parents proved to be surprisingly adaptive, and creative. They held their focus well and parents who expected the worst found themselves with children who took their advanced condition in stride in a surprising number of cases. Experts believe the Siders accepted their plight objectively. Linda believed the traits were associated with specific infected areas of the brain. As she was to learn the hard way, there might be wide variations from the norm.

May of Year 12

The oldest of the children were twelve years of age. They could be found concentrated in the initial primary sites of the infection, change of residence notwithstanding. Since the inception of the epidemic, a total of 48 Siders had been born in Lincoln with a total of 10 at the oldest ages. Linda wanted to meet them. Jason didn't. The more she thought about it, the more she believed in a personal cause—a way to satisfy her yearning for something undefinable that suddenly could be defined—helping children.

"Don't you want to meet your children, Jace?" she asked over dinner one evening, as he mulled over what to do with a quarter-pound of alien DNA stored in the freezer at work.

"Hey, you don't need to say it like that," he said, sharply.

"Like it or not, I'm going to call for a meeting

to be held for parents who want to bring their Sider children," she declared.

"For what? To promote some new Sider agenda?" Jason's ire flared.

"The answer is yes. They don't have any trouble with the name, do you? I've heard you use it more than once like it's some racial epithet," she answered sharply.

"I'll ask it again. For what?" he demanded.

"Because I want to found an organization devoted to the development and expression of their talents. That's for what."

"What about your lab work?" Jason implored, switching tack, saying it almost beseechingly.

"It's time to do something else in life," she stated forcibly, then backed off. "Honey, I really need you."

"What if I said I really need you with me?" he retorted.

Linda looked at her husband somberly, and said, "Well, I guess that would mean we'd have one less common interest. "

Then her voice changed to a deeper timber and stared hard at him. "Hello, Jace, I need you." She gave a sign with her knuckles striking hard on something impenetrable.

As she spoke those words, a pang of guilt swept over her. She realized that, for an instant, through her prodding and poking, she had joined him in being responsible for the fate of the world. She might be blaming herself and sought recompense by starting this project. A psychiatrist might have fun dissecting either one of them.

Jason relented. He saw that Linda was about to break into tears. "All right, babe. Talk to me. What do you have in mind for a project?"

Linda brightened, as she saw what appeared to be his genuine interest for her work. "It'll take six months to a year to get off the ground, but I want to buy or build a school for Siders. I've already got my sites on a piece of land. There are 152 acres with nothing on them but range grass and a creek just east of Highway 77 and south of Saltillo. There's a nice creek that runs through the property."

She paused to check if he was still following her and hadn't lapsed into cleaning his fingernails, so she continued explaining her plan. "To get my idea started, when the time is right, I'm going to put a little ad in the Sunday Lincoln Sentinel; keep it local. I talked to the high school about using their auditorium for the meeting place. They needed to run the proposal by the school board. If the board gives us permission, we'll be able to use their auditorium on a Monday through Thursday."

"Why wouldn't they okay it? If you can remember, we give them enough money each year," Jason threw in as he returned to his bad mood like a petulant child.

Linda was over her instant of kindness. "No, Jace, I'd completely forgotten about it. Thanks for the reminder. I can always count of you to keep the door revolving to nowhere."

Finally, she'd had enough and jumped on him, "Hey, you're the one who's always complaining about today's lousy public education and soft courses that are only fit for a politician's child. What I'm trying to do is create a setting to bring about the most educated group of human children on the planet and you can be part of that setting, so stop whining and listen to somebody else for a change. Here's what I have in mind..."

Eight months later, Linda's ad in the Sentinel read: Siders ages 4 and above are invited with their parents to attend a meeting at Lincoln High School auditorium this Wednesday. The meeting will focus on the training of Siders to be the best they can be. A new affiliation is proposed.

Ten days after the announcement had been made, a little before 6:45 p.m., Linda was so engrossed in detailing her notes she lost track of time. When she realized the lateness of the hour she grabbed her purse and, rushing out the door, yelled, "We're late."

Jason reluctantly turned off the TV, glanced at the clock and followed his wife. He had been watching a game he'd recorded between the Chicago Blackhawks and the Boston Bruins. Since purchasing the television, Jason found himself becoming engrossed in the world of sports. The announcer commented on how the rapidity of the game made his job more difficult, describing how today's top puck speed of 130 miles an hour contrasted with that of 100 miles an hour a few short years ago, while the speed of the skaters had also increased, along with the severity of collisions.

When Linda and Jason pulled into the parking lot of the school, they found it to be crowded and had to stop in a fire zone. Excitedly, June met them at the door. "Where were you? Omaha people are here. And the press. We have maybe fifty Sider kids of all ages and a hundred parents. Go on in, I'll take care of the car," and reached out her hand to take they keys from Linda.

"I was hoping for a good turnout, though I must confess this certainly not what I expected," Linda admitted, pleased with what she saw.

June handed each of them a six-page color brochure and the couple entered the school auditorium that had a capacity of six hundred. Television crews had established themselves early and had strung their cables down the outside of the aisles preparing to telecast live.

Jason saw Don in the front row tagged with RE-SERVED on each seat and sat next to him. At first, Jason wanted his wife to fend for herself, but soon got out of his funk. He was there to provide support and protection. If you don't take care of what's yours, it won't be yours anymore. His mood swings had been a concern to him and getting worse. He knew why, too. The virus had progressed through his brain from one lobe to another and it scared the crap out of him. Shouldn't it be the same for everybody?

Linda gathered herself and walked to the podium. June walked back in and joined the men in the front row. The clock read 7:10. She took a moment to survey the audience. The auditorium went completely silent.

Sider children of all ages were dotted amongst their parents, mostly concentrated in the front portion of the auditorium. A Sider girl, about five years of age, looked at her with head tilted slightly to the right. She wore a pink dress with a pink bow in her shoulder-length light brown hair. Her legs were short, her shoulders, thighs and calves strong, as though she had been a student of gymnastics. The most impressive quality about the child was her intense focus on Linda.

Linda took her time. This show belonged to her. Nobody here lacked for intelligence. If they lacked it once, they didn't anymore. Another child, a tall Sider boy, who might have been taller in other circumstances, sat at an end seat to Linda's left, ten rows behind Jason, Don and June, head also canted slightly to the right. He had a slight smile on his lips, watching, waiting, evaluating.

Linda had planned to start the school program with only a dozen older children, all local, and build the school slowly. The school would be free of charge—no tuition whatsoever. She didn't care about money or the time she spent on reorganizing her life. She and Jason made huge donations each year to local and state charities. Life goes on, doesn't it?

If the program flopped, she'd turn over their entire new building to their church or to one of the local colleges and she'd be forced to think twice about going back to lab work. She quickly came to love charitable work. Life had more to offer than to being holed up in a lab for decades.

"My name is Linda Randolph. As you undoubtedly know, my husband is Jason Randolph of Randolph Cancer Research. I am here on my own to propose a new program designed exclusively for the training of Siders of all ages. The purpose is to enable each of them to reach their full potential in skills they may possess, whether they be mental or physical. No expense will be spared in the new training facility that has just been completed."

Linda spent some time describing the facility and the teaching staff, the scientific, artistic, and athletic facilities. Counseling would also be provided for both parents and their children.

She completed her presentation by saying, "You are all holding a brochure titled: InSiders School. This brochure describes the location of the facility here in Lincoln and the dates and times of the classes. Our goal is to provide the best education possible. This will be administered by our best local teachers. There is no charge to you. As parents you may wait in the lounge at the school, but you are not part of the classes. They are for your children. We do ask you to become part of this program by encouraging your child to study and work hard. We will have a full-time registered nurse present for the needs of both parents and students who may incur a problem while at the school. I will now answer questions."

To Jason, it seemed the appellation of Siders had come into such common usage that Linda was able to use it freely during her presentation. There were no objections. Nobody had come up with a better designation. Mutant children wouldn't work. They were just kids, like those of any ethnicity. Well, almost. Most of the questions asked were related to maximum size of classes, various agreements that might need to be signed.

The boy in the aisle seat ambled to the microphone at the front near where Jason, Don, and June sat. He waited his turn and stepped to the microphone. His speech pattern sounded mushy, which was attributed to the left-sided downcast of his mouth.

"Missus Randolph; Doctor, isn't it? I'm somewhat leery of the motivations behind your benevolence. What makes you think any of us Siders, as we are called, need assistance or need you, for that matter? A simple answer will suffice."

Prepared for the question, Linda was surprised it hadn't come earlier. Here it came from a boy almost old enough to be the child she had aborted. She kept her answer simple, as requested. "I lost a child and I love children, especially ones who are intelligent and want to learn. They have a gift like you do. Does that help?"

"Yes, somewhat," said the boy. "Again, what makes you think we want anything?"

Linda became enamored with this boy who challenged her. Ignoring the audience, she replied, "First, I didn't say anybody should want this. It's an offering. Second, there are always people who want to learn, especially in this changing world of ours. Maybe you're not one of them. There will be others. What's your name?"

"Jason Whitmore, named after my grandfather. Not so pleased with the name of Jason because it's the name of your husband, my stepmother calls me Jay, the name I prefer. Obviously, she did not like my father's name choice."

"Why not? There must be a reason for that," she responded, curious and surprised by the boy's candor.

Jay stood his ground. "There are rumors about your activities that cast doubt as to your well wishes."

Linda stood her own ground, in turn, in the face of grumblings from the audience. She discerned that they were angry at him for bringing the sanctity of the Randolphs into question. "To assuage your feelings, maybe you should visit us where we do our work, or attend some of the classes at the school," she challenged. "They say that education helps give a person a better perspective."

"Maybe," responded the boy. Turning to walk back to his seat, he glanced at Jason without emotion.

While Linda answered more questions, Jason tried to shake off what had just happened. The boy puzzled him. Rumors and suspicions are part of human nature. Still, the only person within RCR who had ever started trouble had died in the shower at home years ago. The broadcaster, Andy Watts, still promoted theories about the origin of the disease, but never ran his purported exposé about them. Plus, there was the fact that Siders were notoriously easy-going and not reputed to challenge authority. That is, except for a few cases.

Opening the fold-out color brochure June had given everyone, Jason read. InSiders School taught a variety of subjects including chemistry and other sciences, literature, art, and mathematics. The school included a sports facility. The last two pages listed the numerous citizens skilled in major disciplines who would be teaching. Don's name was listed as a teacher of two basic courses: Geology of Earth and Mars, and Climatology. June's name appeared next to Don's as a teacher of art and ornithology. She also served as Executive Secretary of the school.

Jason saw his name under chemistry. He showed the brochure to June, his finger on his name. She smiled and nodded. He turned to the left and showed it to Don who smiled politely. Finally, he looked up at Linda sharply and she caught his glare. She smiled and knew what he was thinking. It sure would be nice if somebody consulted with me first about things that involve me.

The meeting lasted another hour. A number of instructors who were listed in the brochure spoke briefly about their subject and how it would be taught. These included Don and June. Jason hadn't expected to say anything and when he saw he might have to speak before a live audience, he began to shake. There was no way to escape without making a fool of himself.

When called upon, he walked to the podium with eyes focused on the brochure, spoke for a single minute into the microphone, then walked back to his seat, hoping the sweat on his brow and pale face weren't evident.

Jason remained silent on the drive home while Linda became chatty. Once in the house, he turned on the TV. Linda took the remote from him and turned it off. "All right, talk," she ordered.

He flopped onto an armchair and explained his problem to his wife who took a seat on the sofa, stern lipped, facing him. He began, "You need me to help. I need you at the lab. There is too much we didn't know about the virus. Before this thing started a dozen years ago, there were people on staff. I was making plans to expand to ten or fifteen. Now, only two people are doing hard research, me and Dustin. It's going in the wrong direction."

Linda shook her head slowly. "We've been talking about this for a long time. You're the one who doesn't want to let anybody in. You don't need to make new discoveries this second, do you? Let Dustin work alone. "

Jason frowned and was about speak when Linda suggested, "Do something else for a while besides hard research and making powder. No matter how much money a person has, they can still drown in their own woes. Money comes and money goes.

Time only goes. The Siders are not theoretical. There are millions of them. They're here and they need your help."

A feeling of rage surged through Jason. Damn her truthfulness and triple-damn her practicality. He was by far the wealthiest man on the planet. For those willing to sell, he could buy whatever he wanted, including whole countries. He'd pumped billions into space exploration and spacecraft to the moon and Mars, low cost health care, medical centers and shelters. He helped rebuild Lincoln and Omaha, as well as areas of the east coast on both sides of the Potomac River. He also funded amateur and professional sports because people needed diversion. Hell, he wasn't only wired into the system, he was the system.

To his great regret, he couldn't buy the top scientists in the world, which is what he needed. Growing the crystals, as the press called them, was all right for manufacturing purposes. But hiring scientists to work on genetics would be the end of him once simple observations were made. He felt as though he were trapped in a maze. Every time he seemingly found an opening, he would run into another wall without a clear path to the exit.

"Keep going. There's more in there," she demanded. "What's going through your mind?"

"You want to know? All right, here it is. My institute is ruined. So is every other research facility on the planet that has to do with DNA, skin cells, muscle cells, cures for diseases, genetics. I have precious little time for personal research. Instead, I get to spend time getting briefed on finances. I don't know any presidents or meet with any worthwhile people anywhere. I don't travel because I feel like an ostrich with its head in the sand. The three things in life really important to me are my research establishment, which is destroyed, my camping, which I have no time for, and you, whom I don't see anymore. How's that for starters?" Jason scowled.

Linda couldn't resist and replied, "So what's your point?"

Before he could say another word, she added, "You forgot something."

"What?"

"You found a cure for the New Flu."

"Not for everybody or everything," he grumbled.

"Jace, live with it. The ship's not sinking, the captain is. Do you remember the lecture you gave me when we first met? You said that in order to become successful and great you first have to yearn, burn, then learn. You said life is a hard teacher. First you get the test, then you get the lesson. Well, you haven't learned yet. All you wallow in is the burning and you won't move past it to learn."

She'd had enough of his whining. Linda had issues of her own and now that she had an exciting new direction, she wasn't going to let a complaining husband destroy her passion. She continued, "Furthermore, there were three others in on this deal and we all found the bottle on the beach together. We opened the bottle and found a message inside for everybody in the world to read. So, stop making it all about you. For all we know, the meteorite could have landed in somebody's backyard instead of in Antarctica—a yard that had a lot of carbonates and moisture to trigger the virus' release."

"So maybe I'm depressed," he confessed, sheepishly.

"No shit. That's not going to cut it, mister."

Jason had never known her to be so worked up and expressive. Intimidating would be a better word. She must have been saving those thoughts for a long time. He tried to remain neutral under the assault. The alternatives were to block her out, wallow in his own filth, or admit to the truth she told.

"I'm not finished with you yet, bud. Let's go one step further with the blame game. Try wearing this cloak: We all know you destroyed the world. You couldn't just settle for little animals, you had to destroy the human race along with all the vegetation, microbial life, civilization, and, guess what, even the climate and geology of an entire planet. In my book, that makes you by far the worst person who ever lived. You set a new record for murderers. Everyone knows you're demented with no redeeming qualities and we all wish you'd drive off a cliff somewhere. Maybe we'll all luck out and somebody will do you in. So, choose one: No blame, shared blame, or all the blame; and all the blame is not an option."

Slam, bam, thank you, ma'am. Damn her honesty. Or is she the one who is doing the confessing? Jason thought, deciding against expressing his thoughts verbally. Trying to recover from the onslaught, the volcano continued to vent.

"How dare you make this all about you when we have been right there by your side every step of the way? How dare you completely disregard, our, my efforts to reconcile the parts we've all played while you hide in your self-pity year after year. Let's put it in a nutshell. I want you to doubt your doubts until you see a new reality. I'm here for my community that needs hands-on help, not just money. The question now becomes, is my husband going to help me or not?"

Linda softened, "Honey, it's not forever, just help me get this off the ground, will you?"

Jason had never been told off like that before. Excoriated would be the right word. His youth had been filled with love, guidance and gentle suggestions for improvements, not how much of a total loser he turned out to be. He understood her sarcasm and its mockery of his attitudes as they came across to others. It didn't make him feel any better; in fact, it made him feel worse in that she had to resort to such means in order to penetrate his defenses.

He had no choice. For the time being, Jason consented to teach at the InSiders School. Research would have to wait while he performed a mental tune-up. The trouble light was flashing. Diagnostics indicated major repair work required immediate attention in order to avoid complete engine failure. Heart attack or stroke could not be ruled out. He needed a new philosophy on life.

When Linda Beaufort was first interviewed by Jason, she found him intriguing. He understood himself and had his priorities set. She also saw potential there for growth of his company, if she could get over his eccentricities and his insufferable exactitude. The job description in the medical journal she read drew her toward him. She'd searched for more than a year and there it was, the opportunity to lock herself in a laboratory without feeling as though she were part of an assembly line of researchers.

Despite herself she became attracted to him, to his honest principles and dedication. That counted for a lot. Jason had a penchant for being impersonal by being relaxed, friendly and demanding with his staff. Within the year they began occasional dating. He remained aloof and that was all right with her. He could not be read like an open book. She knew little about his past except for what she had learned from other workers and had gleaned over the Internet. Rumors of past relationships with other women abounded with no record of a previous marriage. This suggested he was not gay or a eunuch, simply a cold objective scientist. Good. No complications.

She remembered one Friday, after she had been working with him for the better part of a year, Jason invited her over for dinner and she accepted. After work, the pair walked the short distance to his home. As they entered the front door, the smell of baking fish had tickled her nose. Were there lemon slices on the fish? She smiled to herself. He knew she would say yes to the dinner, had probably put the fish in the oven frozen in the morning or slipped out during lunch and had set the oven on a timer. She found the home to be simple, well-appointed and immaculate, certainly neater than her home where medical journals were stacked in several locations. When she walked into his large garage, she saw the boat and gun safe and other outdoor equipment. Now she saw Jason Randolph in a new light. They talked more intimately that evening and she ended up spending the night. With that, they both understood they had a similar mindset and found great relief knowing their working relationship would not be changed.

Now she felt sick about having to yell and scream and rip into her husband. This was a first for her, but the man was pig-headed or bull-headed or whatever they called it here. Furthermore, he possessed this intractable philosophy and a set of rules he'd established for himself about dedication and overcoming obstacles. She'd tried everything else to kick him out of the ditch; hopefully this would work.

PART THREE

The Humans First organization promoted itself as an overtly-aggressive KKK type group with tentacles throughout the world. Within the United States, they had located one of their largest branches in Omaha, until the great Missouri River flood took out their building along with a greater portion of the city and Council Bluffs on the other side.

Five years after the New Flu began, the local group moved their base of operations to Lincoln and went underground. The fanatics attracted the malcontent and depressed, the frustrated and the bigoted, successfully recruiting under some twisted guise related to patriotism. Although the bulk of their members were above college age, all members expressed frustration with the trend toward treating the mutants, as they commonly called them, as equals; if not special, in some cases.

Angered by the unwillingness of local governments to round up the Siders and send them somewhere, the movement promoted an anti-Sider campaign in public speeches and on-line. Their philosophy revolved around the simple concept that if the government couldn't fix the problem, Humans First could and would regulate the growing number of human Siders. They infused themselves in governing bodies throughout the world. Murder and terrorism was their reputation; internment camps were an acceptable solution.

The federal government labeled Humans First a terrorist organization, despite the presence of their advocates within the House of Representatives and the Senate. With the opening of the new Linda's InSider facility, they saw a great opportunity. The local chapter sent out messages to leaders of other branches throughout the nation that a meeting of a select few would be held in an old barn owned by one of their members situated outside the Czech town of Crete, a few miles south of Lincoln. The plan called for a full-daylight attack with destruction of the building and the death of everyone inside it during school hours. Casualties would include close to two hundred Sider children, parents, teachers and support staff. Once the destruction of the school made the news, worldwide recruitment would grow enormously.

Gottlieb thought of the Randolphs as family. Their research efforts had saved his life and the lives of future sons born to his family. The Randolphs' efforts to assist Sider children made him pay attention to the Humans First movement. His own local and national security personnel consisted primarily of mercenaries and military men who kept him apprised of the Humans First activities and learned of the meeting.

Once Linda had made the public announcement

regarding the school opening, Gottlieb ordered the security team to attempt an infiltration of the movement. A man purporting to be a college student made the effort and was rejected for his perceived lack of commitment to their cause. A second person, an angry housewife past middle-age with Real American Roots, also made the attempt. She put on the best performance of the two and got invited into the group. Thoroughly vetted by the movement, she was found to be all she said she was—a divorcee who claimed she had aborted a Sider child and who hated the government and the Siders. She would stop at nothing to eliminate them, along with her ex-boyfriend, if she could ever find him. If Human's First didn't have the wherewithal to do it, she'd find her own way to kill as many as possible. She wanted a weapon but was told she'd have to wait and prove her loyalty first before they granted that wish. Her response was that she didn't need them to give her a gun or their permission to get one, she'd borrow one from a neighbor or go to a gun store.

Several weeks later, prior to leaving for the midnight meeting the night before the planned attack, the woman switched her phone to vibrate only, but kept it on so that her GPS position could be followed. Thirty people attended the meeting. Topics included the method of attack, escape routes, and instructions to members about what to say and how act once the school had been destroyed the next day.

Gottlieb contacted one of his supervisors who had gained skill as a recreational drone flier and who was expecting such a call. The drone overflew the GPS coordinates provided by the phone's location. Its infrared sensors detected a number of vehicles outside the barn. With Gottlieb's team following the drone's images, the female infiltrator received a series of vibrations on her phone which served as a signal to her—time to escape. She had only a half-hour.

Gottlieb closely followed the situation and his mind wandered. He wanted to make a call of his own up the chain of command, and to provide the proper ID and security codes to pull it off. He already possessed top secret security clearance. Subsequently, instructions would then be sent to the 385th Bomb Wing, home of the U.S. Strategic Command south of Omaha. Less than 30 minutes later, a Bell AH-1 Cobra helicopter gunship would rise into the air to cover the 50-mile distance between the air force base and the Humans First meeting in Crete. This gunship was the type that had been used to test his new lightweight armor made from the new "crystalline" material. At that time, the gunship used 20 mm rounds fired from Gattling type electric canons. Residents of the community would believe the thousands of rounds fired to be the rumbling of distant thunder. His fantasy brought him around to reality. He didn't want the place vaporized. He wanted to capture documents and identifications and take out the local movement. Ideally, the national organization would be seriously hurt.

The military did respond to the meeting of national terrorists, not with Gattling guns, but with troops. Twelve members of the movement were killed and seventeen captured in the shootout with no military casualties, thanks to their protective body armor and shields. Two weeks later, based on captured Intel, and information received after the interrogations, the entire nationwide movement of Human's First was dealt a crippling blow, only to recover and gain strength again over time, as is the nature of human resilience.

Jason and Linda agreed on the new school's primary platform. Learning should be hands-on, fun, and challenging. Jason's personal belief was that the five Rs should predominate: readin', writin', 'rithmatic, respect, and responsibility. For him and his wife, the best laboratory equipment could not substitute for imagination and drive. Yet, both would be incorporated into the educational program. In a sense, he felt like an abused child returning to his abuser. In another sense, he felt a weight slowly lifting from his shoulders. Recovering from a beating tends to provide one with a different viewpoint on life, and Linda had given him a very bad one.

Twenty-three Siders attended the first day of school. A backup list included parents in Kansas, Oklahoma, and beyond who were tired of being ostracized; they sought an intense and accelerated educational program for their children.

Linda wondered about the boy, Jay, who had asked the question: What makes you think any of us Siders, as we are called, need assistance or need you? He didn't attend the first couple of weeks; her recollection of him soon became a fading memory.

The third week after the school opened, Linda sat at her desk before classes began. Working on enrollment numbers, she saw a motion and looked up. Jay stood in the doorway wearing a rain-soaked poncho. These days it rained more than it did a half-dozen years before. The great flood of 2019 in the Midwest had become almost an annual event. The number of tornadoes in the Midwest and South had nearly doubled to two thousand yearly with every indication they would increase in intensity, if not in number.

"I'd like to start taking classes," Jay said, dropping his poncho on the floor of the hallway. Linda motioned toward a chair and he took it. The window behind her displayed the city of Lincoln in the distance, a view somewhat obscured by water running down the windows.

"It's nice to see you again," she admitted, albeit with some reluctance. "May I call you Jay?"

"Yes," he replied. "I had to talk my parents into it. They're suspicious of people trying to help Siders; even the Randolphs. They opted to stay home, so I came alone."

"You walked in the rain?" she asked.

Jay didn't answer. After some time he spoke. "I want to study biochemistry and molecular biology."

"I'm sorry, Jay, that's too advanced. We don't teach it here. Maybe someday," she told him.

"I'd like to investigate the attributes and deleterious consequences of my disease," he said.

"Nobody understands much about it," Linda responded, wondering where he was going with this.

"You and your husband do. I'd venture to say you know more about it than anyone," Jay proclaimed. "If you don't teach it here, then teach me at your institute."

Linda moved her head slowly from side-to-side. "It won't be with me. I'm busy running this school. I can ask my husband. RCR belongs to him."

"Fine," said Jay, folding his hands in his lap.

"I'll be back," Linda said, after she gave a quick thought about telling Jason something he didn't want to hear. She returned after a considerable period of time had passed and took her seat again. "All right, Jay. What can you tell me to help me make that decision?"

Jay shrugged. "We'll start easy with the Kreb's Cycle or fatty acid synthesis beginning with ingested cholesterol, or the synthesis of nucleic acids. We'll include their base pair coupling within genetic material. You tell me."

"All of them," she answered. The boy wants to play, so let's play, she thought.

For an hour Jay recited in correct order the names of each chemical present within each of the cycles as it branched into the next, its physical appearance, and the energy required for each step to occur. "Not bad for starters," she conceded. "You left off one or two details about double bond formation, but we'll let that go for the moment. Any lab experience?"

"None whatsoever, ma'am," Jay said.

"Where did you learn this?" she asked.

"Memorizing information from books is easy. Once I read something, the information becomes imprinted. Finding real life experience is tough for anyone my age, especially for a Sider."

"When are you available?" she asked.

"All day, any day," he responded. "It's not like I have a busy social schedule."

"We'll see you at the gates of RCR tomorrow morning at 8:30 a.m. I'll tell the guard to expect you. Wait a minute. I'll arrange for a car to take you home now." She picked up the land-line.

When Jason had received the call from Linda, he turned over the basic chemistry lab teaching duties to his assistant and stepped outside. He listened for a few moments and turned red with anger. She knew his lab was sacred, yet she attempted to get him to accept an unqualified juvenile to take part in what he considered to be a top-secret research facility. He felt he had been disrespected and felt embarrassment by his naysaying at her request for help. She had already reamed him out once. He didn't need another beating.

Watching a flight of migrating birds, he wished to join them; to go anywhere from here. Sider or not, he didn't want any kid in his lab. To Jason, the boy was an OutSider.

For her part, Linda sat dazed for a long time after the boy's departure. Did she handle this right? What was she supposed to do? During the phone call, Jason had urged her to turn him down. He didn't need this.

Linda thought the opposite. She thought they both needed it. She patiently voiced those words to her husband and made him feel badly enough to accept the boy on a trial basis, disturbed that she had to pile more guilt onto the man to make it work.

Jay learned fast; others in the lab explained to him that research involves precision. Without precision, no meaningful discovery can be made. They failed to mention the importance of serendipitous occurrences such as stumbling across a visitor from outer space. Glassware must be soaked in a solution of chromic acid and sulfuric acid and washed with triple distilled water; endless calculations have to be made by hand and checked and rechecked. You stand less chance of making a basic math mistake that way compared with use of a calculator. Instruments have to be serviced to ensure their proper operation, counters have to be wiped down, notes have to be kept in proper notebooks with carbon paper which has to be removed occasionally and kept in a separate location; and experiments must be conducted in an exact sequence of events. Occasionally, there is blessed downtime between routines or waiting for results that might take hours to present themselves.

The enthusiasm of both Linda, and later Jason, increased over time as they assisted Dustin in teaching Jay whenever they could break away from work at the school. Soon, they looked forward to their visit with him and tried to do so as often as possible.

Jay never asked about the fermenters or the ship-
ments of powder, nothing deviating from the lesson
of the day. The animal facility was off-limits. Each
day a driver picked up the boy from his home and
returned him at the end of the workday. After three
months, Jason put him on a minimum-wage salary.

Jason's mood improved as he also spent what
time he could with the boy. Jay was a person with
whom he could share his skills, an intelligent young
man who showed great promise in terms of becoming a very good scientist. Yet, another layer of conflict had been added to Jason's concerns. He found
the InSider school exciting; everything he envisioned education should be, but he couldn't let himself enjoy it with total abandon. He grieved that his
beloved cancer research was gone forever.

They were doomed from the start. How did he fit
into the big picture? The question repeatedly asked
by his over-analytical mind was: Why had the universe singled him out to do its bidding? He had always enjoyed being by himself. Now he understood
the terrible consequences of true isolation and he
knew where the deep and terrible feeling came from.

He had always been ahead of his class. When
he was 10 years old and starting junior high school
there was a lunch wagon on the school grounds
where they served tamales. He bought one for a
dollar and that night he had a psychedelic dream in
which he floated in space, in free fall, the only thing
alive among the stars. He was terrified during and
after the dream and its memory brought him back to

the same feeling of terror. He continued to have the dream sporadically over the next several months and thought he was losing his mind. Out of desperation, he reasoned that the dream might be related to the one food he occasionally ate at the food wagon at lunch. He realized a chemical was the problem—an additive or a flavor enhancer.

The memory never left him. The chemical would not be allowed for use in today's world. Back then it had sparked his interest in chemistry. Today's reality had thrown him back into the dream—one that would live on forever with no waking up permitted. It had been a precognitive foretelling of the future.

At the beginning of the fourth month of work, Jay mentioned that his parents were moving. His father had managed Hanson's Clothing and his mother worked as a seamstress there until the business closed. They were moving to Oklahoma City where his father had landed a job.

Jason found both parents good positions with WG Corp. and the boy stayed. Dustin gave him his own experiments to design, run, and analyze data. Then he was tasked with writing a report and after discussion, he would be assigned another task.

One day, while Linda worked with Jay in Jason's lab, she made a casual remark. "Jay, your knowledge is terrific. Your technique needs work. I know it's because of your eyes are a little off..." She never got to finish her sentence.

"You think I don't know that," snapped Jay, angrily, his voice rising. "Let's see, there is a strengthening of the ligaments, tendons and musculature of the shoulders and legs, and, yes, my facial features are offset. Do you want to know details?"

Jay's voice carried. Dustin and Tomás entered from the adjoining lab. Exclamations borne out of making a discovery are permitted in a laboratory. This was not one of those occasions. "Yes, tell me," she said gently after several seconds, ignoring the entry of the two men.

Jay chanted, "My muscle mass is denser and my synapses are firing faster so they must be closer together or are more numerous, thus my ability to learn and think through problems is superior to yours. Also, my shoulders are hunched and my legs are shorter than they should be. Ah, I almost forgot, I've got an enhanced immune system."

Linda looked over at the three men, who stood watching, several feet away.

Had he read the lab report from histology? Jason wondered. No, the boy was living it.

Dustin said, "Hey, man, look at the bright side. You think you fell off a cliff until you look down. You find out you're only on a ledge and the bottom is so far down you can't see it."

"You guys are really starting to get to me," Jay said, angrily. "You think you know about this?"

The others looked at each other. The time had come. Jason replied, angrily, "If you think you're finished, you're not. Come with me." He pushed a button on his desk phone to let Rick know they were coming, then turned to Jay. "I want you to think long and hard about what Dustin communicated to you about the difference between a ledge and a bottomless pit."

Jason led the boy down the stairs into the basement. Once at the bottom among the cages, Jay's eyes fixated on what he saw as Rick placed fresh water bottles into each cage. Jason introduced his animal keeper of many years to the boy and said, "Rick, please explain to our friend what you have observed with our mice over the years and take as much time as you need. Start with the photo albums and then go to the live mice. I'll go back upstairs."

Rick led Jay into his office and pulled out several albums from a shelf and laid them on his desk. The other three departed to return to work. An hour later, the buzzer on Jason's desk went off and he pushed the intercom button.

"He's on his way up," Rick reported. "He had a lot of questions I couldn't answer. Go easy on him."

The twelve year old, soon to be thirteen, returned. He tried his best to wear a straight face, but they knew he had to be reeling inside. "All the generations are the same. There was no cure except for the last generation. These mice are normal. Will it always be that way? Somehow they shot from one end of the cage to the other. And their faces-—they're not from this earth," Jay said.

"That much we do know," Linda said.

Jay frowned and looked at her.

"You just had part one of today's lesson. Better

have a seat. Here comes part two," Jason warned. He had no intention of telling Jay that the disease originated from his lab. Instead, he proffered a modified version of the truth. "The reason the vaccine came out of this facility is because we are the only people who have found a way to make it."

"Why didn't you tell other people how to make it?" Jay asked pointedly.

The question didn't surprise Jason, who stated flatly, "Two reasons: First, it's proprietary information; second, we don't need to. We can make it all right here and distribute it anywhere on the planet." The boy would appreciate the straightforward approach.

Jason asked, "Do you want to talk details about distribution or do you want to know about your disease? That was your stated purpose in being here, was it not?"

Leaving out the part about how they discovered the virus, Jason related information regarding tissue findings and mutations in plants and animals, how all life may be affected, and the new evolution of life on the planet. Jay was familiar with the animal part. "What I want know is: Are you a member of the team or not?" asked Jason.

"Uh, I'm a member of the team," Jay stammered.

"If that is the case, understand something. What is said or done here stays here," Jason proclaimed.

"Yes, sir, Doctor Randolph." Jay replied, a too little smugly to suit Linda. She was starting to have a bad feeling about this. The boy was a little too convenient, from his sudden appearance to his effort to become part of their operation. He still had a ways to go before earning her complete trust.

For his part, Jay had heard about the Randolphs all his life and when Linda opened InSider it became a dream come true. Something funny was going on in that research facility and he wanted to have a look at the guts of the place. First he had to meet the headmistress.

"All right. Let's shake on it," Jason stuck out his hand.

Shake hands with a real human? Jay stuck out a sweaty palm. Linda shook and reluctantly gave him a hug, trying not to muss his neatly combed head of dark brown hair.

Jason offered, "Linda will plan your education. You will spend a portion of your time teaching general chemistry at the InSider school. The remainder of your time will be spent with us researching this disease. Another small part you need to know about is this: We're the ones who supply WG Corp. with the core of everything they make."

Jay's eyes flitted around as he processed data. Why was Jason telling my something everybody already knew? Playing dumb, he replied, "That's a lot, sir."

Jason paused a moment to let that sink in and prompted, "Dustin, please explain to our partner about how the products are made."

"Doctor Randolph, I'd be happy to explain to our new employee the ways of the world," Dustin began, as he put an arm around his shoulder. "Come with me, my friend. We're going to have a close look at Doctor Randolph's space-time machines."

Jay had seen enough. His mother had been right. Could it be her first husband hadn't died of an accident in the shower? He had seen flasks that were growing something. The flasks were being poured into the fermenter vats to produce pounds of fibers. The Randolph bunch may be trying to find a cure, but they had become extremely wealthy people thanks to a little problem they caused.

Thanks to them, he had been born a Sider.

Daily InSider on-line news blog from the InSider News Agency:

Bowlegs Oklahoma: According to his statement, Richard Oglethorpe, a government employee, found a dropped rifle bullet on the ground at the local shooting range. He wanted to see if the round was live so he placed it in a vise in his workshop at home. He held a nail up to its end which he tapped with a hammer. The round went off, traveled through the wall of the shed into his home to kill both his wife and his Sider son.

Authorities arrested Oglethorpe for negligent homicide. He and is being sued by the Sider Defense League, a well-funded organization backed by WG Corp.

Oglethorpe stated: "I must have hit the nail too hard."

Paris, France: Francine Dubois is collecting money to undergo surgery to convert herself into a Sider, although she is having difficulty in finding a surgeon who will take on the job. Her mother declared, "You can't fix stupid."

Lincoln, Nebraska: The first InSider school has expanded to include 250 students. Numerous other branches of the school are opening throughout the world. Contact us for a complete list of cities.

Lincoln, Nebraska: In last week's news, we reported that 13-year-old Jay Whitmore, part time worker at Randolph Cancer Research, had scheduled a news conference to reveal what he has learned about the origin of the worldwide epidemic. He made the announcement from his home and did not go to work that day, claiming illness.

According to his driver and a passenger, when they arrived at the Whitcomb residence, they found the door ajar and nobody inside. There was no evidence of foul play. Abduction of all three family members is suspected. The parents, who worked for WG Corp., never arrived at the job site that day and their car was still in the garage. Suspicion is cast on foreign intervention, although the reason for this is unknown.

Because Mr. and Mrs. Whitcomb worked for him, Wilbur Gottlieb is personally offering one million dollars for information leading to information regarding the whereabouts of the beloved family.

About the disappearance of the Whitcomb's boy, Jason Randolph stated, "His kidnapping is a terrible tragedy; a loss for everyone. We knew the boy had personal problems and we did our best to work with him. He had become a valuable resource. We considered him to be a member of our team and he will be sorely missed.

"Personally, I don't see why discovering the origin of the New Flu was so important to him. Knowing that won't change what happened. In my opinion, the world has bigger problems today."

PART FOUR
Ten Years after Jay's Disappearance

Jason and Linda had trusted Jay, and the young man's traitorous act had was devastated them. He had been instructed not to talk about lab matters outside of work and had engendered their trust while planning to divulge information they considered classified. He had played them and caused them to become emotionally involved with him.

After arguments and fights and compromises, the two decided to divide their time between pure research, managing the growing number of InSider schools, and hunting and fishing, rare good days of weather permitting.

Finally, Linda steadfastly refused to spend more than 20 hours a week running the schools and turned over many of the administrative duties to Don and June. They, in turn, hired Siders to run the programs.

Years before, Jason had accepted the fact that there was nothing more he could do to change the course of the epidemic's spread. In general, his compassion for the human condition had increased. He relegated his guilt to a deeply recessed area of his mind he rarely frequented.

Compelled to fill in missing pieces to the puzzle, Jason acquired tissue samples from the brains of dead humans, both affected and non-affected by the disease. Histological reports confirmed the presence of an excessive amount of human DNA-virus interactions in the parietal portion of the brain of all those tested, as Linda had noted years before. What she hadn't found at the time was their concentrated presence in the anterior insular cortex, the portion of the brain controlling empathy and compassion in humans. Mice did have that portion of the brain, but directives given to the team doing the histological work requested general sections of the brain be analyzed, not its sub-sections.

As Linda had explained to Gottlieb, it could have had the opposite effect had it affected another part of the brain. It might have increased anger or hormonal output or turned everyone into blithering idiots. Most likely blind luck dictated it landed where it did.

The effect of this interaction in that portion of the frontal cortex could be seen over the years. As the virus spread, humans waged continuous warfare against one another for territory and basic survival. Global changes in weather killed billions. Survivors were squeezed into smaller spaces due to the unheard of flooding. Whole coastlines and countries were lost. In time, the strife lessened, as the brain became more infected and empathy replaced anger.

Emotions aside, Jason wondered whether attitudes would become similar to what they were in the Old West of the 18th and 19th. Europeans, along with tens of thousands of Chinese, were paid to assist with the gold mining activities in Tombstone, Arizona and in Sutter's Mill, California. Thus, an intermingling of many ethnic groups was commonplace. In short, finding enough food to feed the family, fighting very pissed off Indians, and keeping a wary eye out for a lot of bad guys running around overrode evaluation of another's character, regardless of their ethnicity.

Ultimately, other than commonplace prejudices that dictated social cliques, ethic differences had been minimalized. Jason reflected on something else. The feelings of guilt that developed from his role in the release of the virus had been enhanced and prolonged. The virus slowly took charge as moved into its little niches of the brain—an incubation settling-in period. Eventually, his mood swings became more moderate and provided him with a sense of tranquility.

The fears that had engulfed Jason in the early years after his discovery were nightmarish and horrific at times. He fully understood the dreams were based on reality, yet their magnitude surprised him such that he had nearly reached the point of no return. He had slid into depression as smoothly as oil slicks onto ice. It had taken Linda to knock him out of it, whenever she caught him heading for a collision with a brick wall. Today's tranquility wasn't total; not nearly enough to turn him into a zombie, but enough to grant him a great sense of peace compared with what he had lived through.

Jason and Linda sat in their living room with Don

and June and Wilbur Gottlieb, whose wife, Isabelle, had passed away from natural causes only recently. Her courage was noted as the woman who had infiltrated the Human's First organization and had brought about the demise of many of their leaders that day in the barn. Gottlieb would soon reveal to them that, when he had first met her, Isabelle's her early work with the French Government was related to counter-terrorism in her employment by the Central Directorate of Interior Intelligence. More importantly, she successfully operated W.G. Corp. during his frequent trips abroad.

The blended smells of dinner cooking filled the air of the home. The sky threatened heavy rain. Linda said, "Hon, you should have invited your fishing buddy, Jeff Shenero, to join us again."

Jason gave a brief shrug and a smile. "I did. When I called, he was wearing hip waders fishing for King Salmon in Alaska and couldn't make it."

At that moment the doorbell rang. "The maid will get it, "Linda announced.A few moments later, a muscular Sider man dressed in the standard clothing of the day stood in front of them. He wore a loose-fitting light brown short-sleeve pullover shirt, matching cargo pants and sneakers. Each article of clothing carried the WG Corp. logo. His appearance was not unusual. Human and Sider visitors were often entertained at the Randolph residence, although typically, they did not arrive uninvited.

"We're going to eat soon. You're welcome to join us," Jason offered.

"We won't take no for an answer," added June.

The stranger appeared confused. In a strong British accent he said, "You don't know...look, I came to apologize. You may or may not remember me. My name is Jay."

With the exception of Gottlieb, a moment of hot anger surged through the others. "Of course we remember you, Jay," Jason was the first to speak, with more than a hint of bitterness in his words. Compassion only went so far and had reached its boundaries when Jay decided to go to the press to break the sanctity of trust.

Linda stated bluntly, "You must realize that you helped change the course of history, and possibly not for the better."

Jay's offset eyes widened in surprise at her harsh words. Without glancing at the others, Linda went after him. "After you betrayed us, we realized we couldn't trust anyone. We resigned ourselves to being alone in our research and to being alone as a family. We didn't put our heart and soul into our work anymore. You came into our house and deceived us. You lost our trust. Trust can be lost in an instant. Regaining it will never occur." Something inside her refused to say anymore to this almost son whom she had lost years before. In her heart she had lost two children. Bad energy filled the air.

Struggling with his own emotions, Jay he tried to remain objective. "But you started the whole thing."

Accustomed to hard talk after a half-century in the business world, Gottlieb watched the unfolding drama with interest, emotionless, as though he held a secret.

Jason said, "Not really. I used to think the same thing. Now, at least to some of us, it's called life in the universe. It's a way of terraforming, similar to what we are doing on Mars now. Life goes from one place to another and things change. It's natural evolution.

"Maybe we need to rethink the time scales in which we believe changes might occur on other planets. Instead of thinking in terms of eons, perhaps we need to think in terms of a few years. We're a grain of sand on a beach. What do we know about the ocean of space? We always knew that ecosystems could change overnight, small ones and large ones. Our change was a large one. "

Don added, "There's a trade-off. We have much less land to live on and the population density is getting worse in many areas of the world. On that land we face terrible weather conditions. Those conditions will not change for a very long time. Perhaps a hundred million people die each year. On the other hand, many terrible viral and bacterial diseases are gone. It's back and forth. It's life reorganizing itself."

"So you shipped me off to England," Jay interjected curtly to no one in particular, as if he had been waiting to make that statement and Don's words went unheard.

Gottlieb chuckled and the group looked at him. "You weren't doing a hell of a lot of good around here, were you, young man? You had it all and you threw it away." Gottlieb held up a tight fist, then opened it in an instant.

"You sent him to England?" Linda gasped in surprise.

Gottlieb gave a short laugh and answered, "Sure. England was one of the first hotbeds of Sider births, as you will recall. People there were familiar with their non-symmetrical appearance. I could have flown him to India or Russia or China, but I don't think things would have gone well for him there. Besides, he was too damn smart to waste."

Despite herself, Linda inquired, "Where did you live in England? Remember, England's my home."

Jay scratched his neck in a slight show of discomfort. "Doctor Gottlieb arranged for my parents and me to occupy a flat near Cambridge and he had somebody introduce me to the staff at the university."

"Cambridge? I graduated from there," Linda stared hard at a grinning Gottlieb.

Now is was Jay's turn to smile, somewhat embarrassed. "Yes, ma'am. I guess my mentioning your name and the fact I trained under you and your husband helped me get a job at the school. Somehow, my folks found jobs and after I worked my way up and proved my worth, I got admitted and earned advanced degrees in chemistry and engineering. Rumor had it a lot of scholarship money came into the school around the time I got there." He glanced at Gottlieb, who sat stone-faced.

"My mother was both right and wrong. She was right about your lab being infected, but she was wrong in believing you were deliberately sending it out into the world. I should have taken things at face value when you both accepted me. Therefore, I ask you to forgive me."

"Dinner is served," announced the maid from behind them. "Will the guest be staying for dinner?"

"I'll think about forgiving you, if you eat with us," Jason addressed Jay. He wasn't about to speak for his wife.

"Yes, he will. Please prepare another place setting."

Jason said, "Understandably, you focused on your own plight and that of other Siders. Welcome to the human race. Look out there. We've got people who range in color from pitch black to ebony to off-white to albino. There are thousands of languages, different religions and differing governing systems. People have round and flat butts, long earlobes to no earlobes at all, they're tall and short, fat and thin. Wide variations exist in shapes and sizes of eyes, ears, noses, mouths, hair, cheekbones, chins, and hand sizes and shapes, lest we forget sizes and shapes of sexual organs. Minorities congregate so they won't be minorities anymore. Learning to tolerate one another is a constant effort. Now Siders, another minority, come along trying to integrate. Welcome to Planet Earth.

"One more thing. Look at the assortment of people here right here. Beneath the superficialities, we're all trying to figure it out and make it day to day, despite our differences and our backgrounds. Now, Siders, you're the ones who will be hired first and make the great changes because of your intelligence and your vision."

The first heavy drops of rain began to fall. Brahms played softly throughout the home speakers. The television was gone. At that moment the home shook. "Earthquake," Don said. Everybody looked at him for more information. "We don't have fault lines, per se, here in Nebraska. Our earth movement happens deep in the bedrock. It's typically low magnitude, say less than 4.0. Let me make a call."

Nobody sat down, waiting for Don, who pulled out his cell, dialed a number, spoke a few words, and hung up. He saw the concern in everyone's eyes. "Five point two. The earthquake is ascribed to activity of the New Madrid Seismic Zone centered in Missouri. This zone extends into numerous other states. Nebraska is not considered to be one of them. Aftershocks can last for weeks. That's light compared with what is occurring in other regions around the world.

"With the Richter scale, each whole number represents a ten-fold increase in strength over the previous whole number. A quake with a magnitude of 6.0 has 10 times the energy release of a 5.0 and one hundred times that of a 4.0. Also, the increase in water mass of the oceans puts more weight on the dozen or more primary and secondary tectonic plates. Another score or more tertiaries would follow suit.

Some people think the tectonic plates are beginning to shift for that reason. If that happens, coastal tsunamis would be the least of our worries. And yes, we can thank our Martian friend for that.

"I'm afraid the Mars Virus may have played a role in the actual eruptions of Olympus Mons on Mars. What does that have to do with us? In a word, Yellowstone.

It's one of the most seismically active areas in the United States. Located in the northwest corner of Wyoming in the Intermountain Seismic Belt, it's in a zone of earthquake activity that runs north-south, from Montana through Wyoming, Idaho, Utah, Nevada, and Arizona. It may blow."

"Oh, come on, Don. You can't be serious?" Jason snorted. "I'll go along with some of it, but that's a stretch."

Once Jason said that, Dustin's words to Jay in the lab years before popped into his mind. You think you fell off a cliff until you find out you're only on a ledge and the bottom is so far down you can't see it.

"I don't want to know." Jason said. "I'd rather check the current weather." The last time he had called the national weather service just after noon, four inches of precipitation had been forecast for the night. He pulled out his phone and punched the weather app, putting the phone on speaker.

This is NOAA weather radio WXL 68 broadcasting on a frequency of 162.5 megahertz out of Lincoln County. A severe thunderstorm is forecast to begin at 4:00 p.m. Central Standard Time and lasting until Sunday evening. Expect heavy amounts of rainfall which may exceed several inches in a short period of time. Microbursts are expected. Residents are advised to stay indoors at all times until further notice as winds may exceed 60 miles per hour with stronger gusts expected.

Doppler radar indicates a very large strong and slow-moving thunderstorm heading north to northeast from the townships of Geneva and Crete into Lincoln and is expected to impact Omaha within the next three to four hours. The communities of Crete, Wilber and Geneva are without power. A microburst struck the downtown area of Crete. The number of casualties is unknown at this time.

Be aware that with this storm there will be overflow of washes, rivers, streams and low lying areas.

Tornadoes are expected as part of this storm. If a storm shelter is present, its use is advised. If a tornado is heard, open all windows to the home. Emergency services and shelters have been established at Lincoln High School, UNL gymnasiums and all Sider schools in both Lincoln and Omaha.

Stay tuned to NOAA Weather Radio for updates.

Poor Crete didn't need any more problems, thought Don. First the Humans First fiasco, now this. For NOAA to say that tornadoes are expected suggests that a hook echo had been sighted, the comma-shaped portion of a severe storm following the southeast area of the northeast flow, the part that gives rise to tornadoes. The exceedingly low pressure in the center of the rapidly rotating mass of air could cause a building to explode from within, if two hundred mile per hour winds in its periphery didn't destroy it first.

The time on the phone read 6:00 p.m. "That report is two hours old. We should be getting an update soon. On the bright side, we've got a guest room with two beds." Jason declared, as though it were another day at the ranch.

Gottlieb complained, "Welcome to Nebraska."

June threw in, "Welcome to anywhere anymore. Do you want to know what I think is the truly ironic thing about this whole mess?" Without waiting for an answer, she said, "The world still doesn't know there is life beyond Earth and that the New Flu is caused by this life."

Deep within Jason's brain a compressed thought bubble began to float to the surface, expanding as it did so until in burst at the top. What's the worst that could happen? June had said the night she hatched the entire scheme. No big deal; just drill into a meteorite and remove a few micrograms of dust.

June faced Jay and said, facetiously, "Bet you always have nice balmy weather in England, Jay."

Jay shook his head. "Not quite. Let's see, Ireland was at sea level. It's completely gone. Scotland survived, being at a much higher elevation. Brighton and Liverpool and most of the coastal cities and washed out. The winters are worse than ever. Annually, we've got enough snow to rival the time when Mary Shelley wrote Frankenstein. "

Jay continued and appeared to be more open than

anyone could remember. "As you probably know, all of Western Europe is entering a mini-ice-age, while Eastern Europe and the Middle East bake in what promises to be a very long drought. "

Linda smiled at the Frankenstein analogy and looked at Don, who winked at her, then turned solemn, and said, "Pardon me for being morbid and maybe I'm not too bright, but the graphs I've put together suggests a final world human population of 10 million or less in another fifty years if things stay the way they are, which I doubt. There are always unknown factors which can decrease that number down to a hundred thousand or even down to thousands. I can tell you more about where survivors won't be living."

The maid began to place food on table starting with a tossed salad, portions of Jason's freshly caught deer and trout, along with mashed potatoes, gravy, and mixed steamed vegetables. Jason gave a broad sweep of his arm that ended at the table directing the guests to take a seat.

"But," Gottlieb emphasized, trying to remain upbeat and refusing to buy into the doom and gloom scenario, "one heck of a lot of people are being insulated from the cold by the availability of better clothing and better shelters. We've got lighter and faster airplanes, space flight, and colonies on the moon and on Mars. And we're just getting started."

"I'll bet the hydroponics on both worlds are doing nicely," added June, in her own effort to separate herself from her from Linda and Don's cast of darkness upon the dinner.

After a pause of several minutes in the conversation, while people began helping themselves to the food, Jay made a general statement in his direct manner. "Do you want to know how I knew you'd be here today? Dr. Gottlieb told me."

Linda wanted to ask him what areas of research he specialized in at Cambridge, but was reluctant to speak with the guest beyond what she had already said. She had kept the words in her heart for many years and felt relieved that she found the courage to release her feelings. He had burned her badly and she had no intention of renewing acquaintances with him. She had transitioned from an objective scientist trying to deal with the loss of two children at the start of the evening into a spiteful woman in a dark mood who sat in the presence of one of them who had returned uninvited.

June asked the question Linda had wanted to ask. Jay reached into one of the thigh pockets of his pants and pulled out a notebook. Jason was about to say something about reading at the table until he felt Linda squeeze his hand. She didn't have to converse with Jay to hear what he had to say.

Jay continued, "On the chemistry side, plastics. A number of years ago, before we first met, I read that certain bacteria had been discovered in a landfill. Reportedly, those bacteria possessed an enzyme capable of digesting plastic. I wanted to use it in the oceans. So I found a strain that produced a large amount of the enzyme, made it photosynthetic, which allowed the virus to speed its reproduction. It worked better than I thought. In the end, it's useless because nobody cares anymore. People have other worries. Dr. Gottlieb stayed in touch with me and had me work on this new city he's building. That's where I've been for the past year."

This mysterious Sider boy who came from nowhere, with whom they had developed a loving fondness, had turned on them. He was kidnapped to keep him quiet about the cultivation of the New Flu virus in RCR, and disappeared for 10 years. He became educated. Through it all, he understood what drove him and what he needed to become.

"Well presented, Doctor Whitcomb," proclaimed Gottlieb. "Now tell them the rest of it."

An aftershock shook the room. The earthquakes were becoming all too common and they had nothing to do with oil fracking. They would continue until pressures on the Earth were released and equilibrium had been achieved. When Jay thought about circumstances on a more personal level, he felt sick about the years he had wasted on plastics research; wasted on a dream that would never come true—chump change, some would call it in the light of the greater picture. As if the universe really cared about plastics. In fact, what did intelligence or fame matter among humans in the grand scheme of things? An intelligent Sider represented another piece of throwaway plastic. Perhaps life itself was just another throwaway in the eyes of the universe. And whole planets and star systems for that matter. For years he had been confused, angry, and vengeful. Then he became strong, proud and accomplished. Now he felt small and insignificant. Damn it, if he was going to freeze his ass off, he'd decided that he'd rather do it in Lincoln, rather than in Cambridge, England.

That is, until Gottlieb collared him upon his return and told him flatly, "Jay, I've been building an underground city. I need you to quickly learn how to become an engineer. Plain talk. To put the odds in the favor of man's survival, I tried to stay away from rivers, dams, large streams, oceans, and earthquake-prone areas. Put dams into the equation. That leaves very few areas of the county, one of which is at the base of the Superstition Mountains outside of Phoenix, Arizona."

Then Jay told them the rest of it. The time had come to hole up and prepare for the long haul. The following day, Jay and Gottlieb departed for the Arizona, where the city beneath the earth was ready for the installment of the hydroponics ring under the watchful eye of a Sider. If mankind could not survive on the surface, perhaps he had a chance beneath it.

Because the devil you knew was better than the one you didn't, it made sense to strip out the animal facility in the basement and turn it into a shelter replete with thousands of Meals Ready to Eat or MRE food packets, tools, and items necessary for long-term survival. They already had the freezers.

In addition, both buildings could be armor-plated with WG Corp. sheeting made from virus particles and turn the walkway between the institute and Jason's home into a tunnel. The entire compound was already heavily fenced and topped with razor-wire. There could easily obtain abundant generators, fuel supplies and holding tanks to fill with thousands of gallons of fresh water on the grounds. Outdoor water collecting devices had already been installed along with short-wave radios.

Holmes Lake across the street from them should not be a problem. It drained into a stream which led to a tributary and, in all likelihood, would remain frozen throughout most of the year for the foreseeable future.

During the time Jason was directing survival preparations for a worse-case scenario, Dustin approached him and the three others about him and his wife, Angie, moving in with them into their fortress. He offered, "Doc, you're going to need someone who understands electronics and security systems, operation of air handlers and air filtration, operation of shortwave radios and can repair vehicles. Tell you what— strip out the center counter from one of the labs and give us, say, lab Number Four, and we can make a deal. Besides, if you ever want to research anything, we can keep a lab open. And Angie can play a mean guitar."

All eyes turned to Jason. His held his arm around Linda's waist. It was his call. What was the downside? Food? Everybody needed to cut back on their consumption, anyway, and Dustin was about as conservative an eater as they came. They could use his skills. He had no dark side anybody knew about. "I don't see any issue, do any of you," Jason asked, ready to argue with any naysayers.

"You're in as far as we're concerned, Dustin," June said, as she looked at the others for approval. "But, if you get strange, we have the right to vote you out."

At that point, everyone wondered if her statement might apply to any of them. Dustin philosophized, "Is man better than a tree because he has intelligence? Both are equal in the eyes of the virus. Our own world is just another warm body. What does it mean to be black, or white or to be a Sider; or to be of good lineage?" Here he smiled at Jason and continued. "Will we never know how the pyramids of Egypt were constructed? What of the civilizations before the Chinese? Does anybody who ever lived and contributed toward good or evil have any relevance? Does Einstein or geological history or the history of art or of anything matter anymore?"

Jason listened to Dustin's monologue and understood its truth. He had to protect those around him with a clear head. "It's fair to say people will be concentrating on other things for a while. Besides, we'll have plenty of time to discuss those topics. We'll dig for answers as we always have. In a sense you're right. I suppose we can call the virus non-prejudicial in that it attacks life and non-life equally. You're in, Dustin. You and Angie. Tell her to bring a couple of guitars and plenty of replacement strings. Matter of fact, I've got a few smaller musical instruments and a number of board games stored for our amusement, if it comes down to it."

"Amusement?" asked Linda, stretching out the word, as a religious leader might stretch the word God over two seconds using two different tones. She pulled back and glared at her husband, but not angrily; understandingly.

Don ignored Linda's gibe and returned to the scientist in him. "I'll amend that to say we're not holed up because DNA got attacked. We're holed up because the planet itself got attacked as part of the grand scheme. No different than galaxies colliding. The only thing intellect may be good for is survival."

For Jason Randolph, life had been a mouse-teaser for the viral cat. He thought about the two circles he had once drawn of the planet, one he had labeled Blue and the other Green. Had he known their planet would have begun to appear with a glow from satellites in a few years hence, as if it were a self-contained flask of virus in solution, he would have added a third circle and labeled it Red.

For his part, Wilbur Gottlieb had not been idle in preparation for what was to come. What began as doodles became a multi- billion dollar enterprise— the construction of an underground city outside of Phoenix near the Superstition Mountains. If mankind could not survive on the surface, perhaps it had a chance beneath it.

EPILOGUE

Numerous climatic factors led to an increase in pressure on tectonic plates. This pressure triggered world-wide earthquakes, tsunamis, and the wholesale loss of cities and hamlets, leading to volcanic eruptions on a global scale. One of those affected was the Yellowstone super-volcano.

In addition to the many millions of tons of carbon dioxide that had been vented annually from the inactive Yellowstone site, it now released 100 times that quantity in a single burst. This amounted to perhaps a billion times more carbon dioxide released than could be attributed to the history of mankind's actions alone. The dense poisonous ash rained down like heavy hail for hundreds of miles around the blast site. The pyroclastic cloud, possibly the most powerful force of nature on Earth, was almost instantly formed. It gushed out from the eruption, leveling everything in its path. At hundreds of feet in height, the incredibly dense cloud consisted of hot sulfurous gases, ash, boulders, and blobs of molten lava that traveled at ground level at a speed approaching 500 miles per hour and reached a temperature exceeding 1000 degrees Fahrenheit, scorching and flattening everything it touched. Fireballs of ejected magma were hurled into nearby communities and into forests many miles distant from the blast site.

As the raining ash spread, it caused power grids to shut down and cities to go dark. Cellphone transmissions became impossible because of excess static electricity in the air and the destruction of cellphone towers.

Much more significant than the cloud that destroyed Pompeii, this dark roiling mass of destruction served as the immediate cause of death of over 100,000 in the kill zone and ten million people in the primary ash zone over a ten-state area. The high altitude jet stream captured ash and attendant sulfurous gases to spread them around the globe as water vapor in the air combined with the gases to form sulfuric acid, in some ways, similar to the atmosphere on Venus. The cities of Lincoln and Omaha found themselves beneath inches of fallout compared with many feet of ash that covered areas in closer proximity to the explosion. The roofs of buildings collapsed from the incredible weight of the heavy ash. The volcano erupted and belched for a period of weeks before lessening its activity.

A quarter-billion years ago, volcanic eruptions occurred with some frequency, in what is known today as Siberia, and caused the death of 96 percent of life on Earth. Life began anew.

Sixty-five million years ago, a rock fell from space. It measured 6-8 miles across and came in from the northeast on an oblique angle of 60 degrees, striking the Yucatan Peninsula off the southern tip of Mexico at a speed of 50,000 miles per hour. Seismic waves shook the planet with a quake that probably measured between 10- 11 creating an impact crater 20 miles deep and 60 miles across. The impact was so great, it may have contributed to the wobble of the planet. Less than an hour later, the wash of water carried sea life, vegetation, and land animals, as far northward as North Dakota, pushing water over the earth in the other directions. Perhaps a trillion tons of dust and soot were spread over the planet. The average temperature world-wide, in the dark period to follow, remained below zero for up to a dozen years; in all, destroying between 75–90 percent of all life, while the oceans grew cold.

In the modern era, another rock visited Earth. Leaving no impact crater, it weighed a little over four pounds and was measured in inches. The effects of this space rock took somewhat longer to be noticed, as it began to affect life first, with the planet to follow. In many regards, the results were more catastrophic than those caused by its larger cousin; yet, in another sense, they were the same when the sun stopped shining and a long nuclear winter made its entrance. After that, the thaw occurred more rapidly than any of the few survivors could have anticipated.

Watch for:

The City Beneath the Earth (Sequel to The Mars Virus)

by Mark R. Sneller

Constructed like a wheel, an underground city is built in the Desert Southwest to house six generations for well over a century in a post-apocalyptic world. The city's denizens find themselves in an isolated pocket of protection when an illness promises to decimate the entire population.

Sixteen year-old Jessica Galloway takes it upon herself to be the first of her people to voluntarily leave the comfortable clime of her city and go Topside into the blazing sun and blistering heat of Phoenix, Arizona, amid an unpredictable and catastrophic worldwide climate change. Her mission: Find a cure for the disease that has beset her people.

Jessica and her husband, James, must lead their superstitious citizens on a quest for independence from Topside. This means food, power, and water, all of which are nearly gone in the entire region. Her people must overcome fire, flood, wind, total darkness, and, worst of all, must interact with the surface population—even engage in warfare—in order to bring to fruition their desires for independence.

About the Author

Mark Sneller, PhD, is a former professor of microbiology and medical mycology. He lives in Tucson, Arizona, where he operates Aero Allergen Research, a company specializing in indoor air quality and the identification of mold in contaminated buildings. He is the author of several health-related books, as well as the Jeffrey Shenero series of adventure novels.